THE CUCKOO LINE AFFAIR

by Andrew Garve

"…an agreeable and ingenious piece of work."
—*The New Yorker*

"I hope there are some who share my fondness for the classic, pure-British detective story, as it flourished twenty-odd years ago, and particularly for the works of Freeman Wills Crofts, with their elaborate minutiae of time-tables and tide schedules. For such enthusiasts, long on a starvation diet, will find their solidest meal in some time in Andrew Garve's *The Cuckoo Line Affair*."
—*The New York Times*

Other titles by Andrew Garve available in
Perennial Library:

A Hero for Leanda
Murder Through the Looking Glass
No Tears for Hilda
The Ashes of Loda
The Far Sands
The Riddle of Samson

The
CUCKOO LINE
AFFAIR

BY ANDREW GARVE

PERENNIAL LIBRARY
Harper & Row, Publishers
New York, Hagerstown, San Francisco, London

A hardcover edition of this book was originally published by Harper &
Row, Publishers.

First PERENNIAL LIBRARY edition published 1978

ISBN: 0-06-080451-3

78   79   80   81   82   10   9   8   7   6   5   4   3   2   1

THE CUCKOO LINE AFFAIR

1

EDWARD LATIMER looked an odd figure as he pottered down his garden path on that lovely Saturday afternoon in June. He was a tall, spindly man of sixty with a slight stoop. All his clothes had a downward sag, as though there were not enough flesh on his bony frame to support them. From his sloping shoulders hung a black alpaca jacket, the pockets weighted down with pliers and screws and other oddments. Three inches of sock gaped between the turn-ups of his trousers and his shoes. On his head he wore a schoolgirl's panama hat which he had bought for sixpence at a jumble sale. He had been advised to wear a hat in the garden after a bad attack of sunstroke the previous summer, and this was the hat he had personally chosen.

As he stopped to level out a molehill with the rake he was carrying, the bushes beside his boundary fence suddenly parted and a small face appeared in the gap. Its expression was woebegone, and down each grubby cheek was a channel where tears had recently coursed.

"Hello, Mr. Latimer," the child said, and sniffed.

"Hello, Carol Anne," said Edward. He saw that one of the little girl's knees was bandaged with a handkerchief. "Well, and what have you been doing to yourself?"

"I fell off my swing." The five-year-old clambered through the wire to show off the damage. Under her arm was a doll which, with its rosy cheeks, china blue eyes and flaxen hair, was almost a miniature of herself.

"Dear me!" Edward inspected the knee. "Well, you know, I don't think that's much to cry about, do you? How about a sweetie?—do you think that would help to make it better?"

"Yes, it would."

Edward fumbled in one of his pockets and produced a wrapped bull's-eye from among the screws. "You'll have to be more careful with your swing in future, won't you?"

"I was being more careful in future," said Carol Anne. She put the bull's-eye into her mouth and switched it from cheek to cheek until it was comfortably lodged. Then she fixed a hypnotic gaze on Edward. "Mummy says I can play," she announced.

"I've got to go and meet a train," Edward said. "I can't play for long."

"You can play for a little, though," she persisted.

"Well, a very little. Now let me see . . ." He looked around the garden for inspiration. "I know—suppose we make a swing for your dolly?"

"Oh, yes, let's. Charlotte would love that." Carol Anne fell in happily behind him as he led the way down to the shed to look for raw materials. "Where will we make the swing?"

"In the wood. We'll find a tree with a nice low bough."

They pushed through the undergrowth and stopped in a mossy clearing. In a few moments Edward had suspended a small piece of plywood on two long strings and had tied the doll's hands to the strings so that it couldn't fall off. He gave the swing a gentle push.

"It's lovely," said Carol Anne, capering. "Let me."

Edward seated himself on a log in the dappled shade and removed his hat. At once, his appearance was transformed. Instead of looking bizarre, he looked impressive, almost noble. He was quite bald, except for a tonsure of thin gray hair, but he had a high benevolent forehead and a beautifully shaped head. His greeny-brown eyes twinkled with quiet humor behind his horn-rimmed glasses.

Carol Anne, her short blue frock swinging with the vehemence of her movements, scolded and instructed her doll in complete absorption. Edward scraped away some dead leaves for the friendly robin that always followed him about when he had a rake in his hand. His face wore an expression of deep contentment.

Presently he realized that Carol Anne had stopped chattering and was doing something to the string. A moment later the doll pitched forward and fell to the ground.

"Charlotte's hurt herself," said Carol Anne with satisfaction.

Edward took his cue and gave what he believed to be a whimper.

"She *is* a crybaby," said Carol Anne delightedly. "She's not really hurt, is she?"

"Of course she's not—just a little cut on the knee. Look, I'll wrap my handkerchief round it."

"Then it won't bleed, will it?" There was the sound of a bull's-eye being rapidly dispatched. "Wouldn't she feel better if she had a sweetie?"

As Edward smilingly fumbled among the screws again there was a call from the direction of the house. "That's Trudie," he said, giving Carol Anne her sweet. "I expect it's time for me to go."

The little girl put her hand in his and they walked up the path together. "We can give my dolly another swing tomorrow, can't we?"

"We'll see," said Edward, holding the wire for her to get under. " 'By, 'by." He waved, shouldered the rake, and slowly made his way to the cottage.

His daughter Gertrude was sitting in a deck chair on the lawn, reading a novel. She was a plump spinster of thirty with a shiny red face and straight bobbed hair. For the past ten years, since the death of Mrs. Latimer, she had kept house for her father, and she seemed perfectly content to go on doing so.

She looked up as she heard his step. "You'll have to hurry, Daddy, you'll be late."

"They'll wait for me," said Edward, who never hurried. "Anyhow, the train's never punctual."

"You're not going out like that, are you?"

3

He looked down at his clothes in surprise. "Why not?—I'm quite presentable."

"You look a freak in that hat. You don't want to give Hugh's fiancée a bad first impression."

"It's not me she's marrying," Edward said. "Put the kettle on—we shan't be long."

He backed the car out cautiously. It was an old box-shaped car, the oldest for miles around, and Edward, who had an unmechanical mind, was a little afraid of it. It wasn't true, as Hugh sometimes asserted, that he made a practice of putting the handbrake on when he was going uphill in case the engine stalled and the car ran backward, but it was true that he was never quite sure whether he or the car were the master. However, he made up in care what he lacked in confidence. He had strong views about the toll of the roads, on which he had written many letters to the Press, and as a magistrate he liked to set a good example.

Steepleford station was a mile from Lavender Cottage and the route lay through the village. On the way, Edward was stopped by the local constable, who was bicycling to the house with papers for him to sign. Even so, he arrived just before the train drew in. He wandered into the ticket office to see if an expected parcel had arrived and was still grubbing among the packages when he heard the sounds of people alighting and a peculiar snatch of conversation outside.

"But it's so slipshod to say 'pale as the underbelly of a fish,'" came a girl's voice. "I've known fish with *black* bellies."

And then Hugh's voice, bantering as usual: "You've known some pretty queer fish!"

Edward chuckled and followed them out.

"Oh, hello, Dad, there you are." Edward's younger son was tall, like his father, but much more solidly built. He wore his thick brown hair rather long and loose and looked young for his twenty-seven years. His eyes were like Edward's, with a mischievous glint. "Come and meet Cynthia."

Edward shook hands, smiling down at the girl. She was

dark and slim, cool-looking in a pale linen frock and pleasantly self-possessed. A marked improvement, he decided, on most of the others Hugh had brought down.

"Did you have a tolerable journey?" he asked politely.

"Very tolerable, thank you. Hugh kept saying the train would break down, but nothing happened. I like your railway —it's got personality."

"We call it the Cuckoo Line," Edward said. "I'm afraid it has more personality than passengers. They do talk of closing down this single-track bit."

"They won't, though," said Hugh. "The customers may be few but they're classy. V.I.P.'s in every village. Director of the Bank of England, famous surgeon, film star—why, even the Attorney General has a weekend house along the line." He helped Cynthia into the front seat and climbed up into the back. "Okay, Dad, what are we waiting for? Want some help with the gear lever?"

"I think I can manage," said Edward with dignity.

"When Dad first learned to drive," Hugh said, leaning forward so that he could talk to Cynthia, "Quentin used to sit beside him and change gear for him whenever they came to a hill. It was quite a drill—'clutch down, clutch up, right!'—and away they went. Good teamwork! Dad's an expert now, though—he's known around here as the 'Steepleford Flier.'"

Edward smiled at Cynthia. "I hope you don't mind my hat?" he said.

"Why, no—it's most original."

"He used to wear a ribbon with it," put in Hugh, "but the headmistress of the high school made him take it off. . . . I say, Dad, look out!"

They had reached the village, and on the corner a strange figure in shorts and a beret had turned the front wheel of a bicycle across the path of the car. Edward came to a convulsive stop and pressed the hooter, which failed to work. He leaned out and called in a tone of gentle remonstrance, "Out of the way, sonny!" The figure turned, and proved to be an

5

elderly gentleman with a beard. Hugh collapsed in laughter. "Oh, Dad, you'll be the death of me."

Edward drove on imperturbably and in a few minutes they were safely back at the cottage. Trudie came forward to greet them. She gave Hugh an enveloping hug and then, impulsively, kissed Cynthia too. She had had one unhappy love affair years ago and had been slightly gushing ever since.

Hugh said, "Still slimming, Trudie?" He watched his large sister take Cynthia up to her room and then strolled on to the lawn with Edward.

"What do you think of her, Dad?" he asked eagerly.

Edward smiled. "Give me a chance."

"You'll like her, I know you will. She's absolutely marvelous."

"This is the Real Thing, is it? No more flitting from flower to flower?"

"Definitely not. We want to get married pretty well right away."

Edward nodded. "On general grounds, I think it's time you did."

There were sounds of animated voices from the house and a moment later Cynthia reappeared, with Trudie close behind her.

"What a wonderful view!" Cynthia exclaimed, gazing out over the long grassy slope that ended in marshes and a glint of water. "Is that the river Hugh talks about?"

"Yes, that's the Broadwater," said Edward. "It doesn't look much now, but it's quite a sheet when the tide's right in. . . . .Would you care to come down and see the garden, such as it is?"

"I'd love to."

"Then I suggest Hugh helps Trudie to get the tea."

"Oh, I say . . . ! You're not trying to cut me out, Dad, are you?"

"You're not interested in the garden. You never were."

Hugh grinned. "I had too much of it when I was young.

6

Don't you remember how you used to mobilize us? 'Now we'll all of us put in a good hard day today,' you used to say. Then before we knew where we were, Quentin and I were digging like navvies while you were having fun with a bonfire!"

"Tea!" repeated Edward. He took Cynthia's arm and escorted her down the path. "I'm afraid you won't find it the usual type of garden," he told her. "I tried to grow things at first but the place was always on top of me and the rabbits used to eat everything so I decided to let it go back to its natural state."

"It's lovely," said Cynthia. "Almost like a piece of parkland."

"*I* like it. I don't know anything more attractive than well-tended grass and wild flowers. The primroses on that bank are a picture in the spring, and the woods are a carpet of bluebells."

He steered her round a sunken patch in which spiky green bulrushes were growing strongly. "This is the water garden. I didn't make it, it just happened. Everyone says it's the place where next door's bath water collects, but the kingcups don't seem to mind. The water lilies are coming along nicely, too. Of course, you've missed the bulbs, you'll have to see them next year. . . . How do you like my compost heap?" He plunged a hand proudly into a great pile of grass clippings, pulled it out brown and sticky, and wiped it on his trousers.

"Why, it's quite hot," said Cynthia.

"Oh, yes, it has to be hot. Then it rots down, and when it's ready I spread it over the turf. . . . So you're not a country girl?"

"I'm afraid not," she said. "Do I sound terribly ignorant? I was born in London and I've lived there all my life."

"I expect you like it, then?"

"Very much."

"I can't say I do. I have to visit it every week or so, but it's always a penance. Hugh, now, prefers to live in the city—he thinks of the country merely as a playground. That's very natural in a young man—he likes to be at the center of things, of course, and I suppose he has to meet people if he wants to be an author."

"He *is* an author," Cynthia said.

"Oh, I know he's written two books, but I gather he wants to live by authorship. I wanted to do that myself when I was younger, but I didn't have the background or the training or —I suppose—the talent. Hugh has all three—I think he may do well."

"I'm sure he will."

Edward's gaze rested for a moment on the girl's attractive, intelligent face and a glow of happiness warmed him. "Well, don't let him give up his job too soon. I know he finds financial journalism dull, but a check at the end of each month is a good thing to have when you're just married." He smiled. "Hugh seems to think he *is* going to marry you—I hope it's your idea, too? He does sometimes exaggerate."

"This time he hasn't."

"Well, I'm glad—and I hope you'll both be very happy. He's told me quite a lot about you—the 'build-up,' he called it. . . . Will you go on with your job, do you think?"

"For a while, yes."

Edward nodded. "I know the man you work for—he and I got into Parliament in the same year. But he stayed there and I didn't. There wasn't much security of tenure for a Liberal, even in those days."

"You had bad luck. Hugh said you ought to have got in five years earlier but that you were late with your nomination papers or something."

"That's so, but it wasn't bad luck—it was carelessness. I got the hours wrong and turned up with my papers five minutes after closing time and the Returning Officer couldn't accept them. It was very disappointing at the time."

"What an understatement! It must have been a terrible blow."

"It was a bad letdown for my supporters—I've never quite

forgiven myself. . . . Someone sent me a postcard the next day addressed to 'The Late Liberal Candidate.'"

"Oh, how mean!"

Edward smiled. "It must have been irresistible."

A halloo from the house told them that tea was ready and they made their way back. By now Hugh and Trudie had been joined on the lawn by another figure.

"This is brother Quentin," said Hugh. "He's the respectable member of the family—a lawyer, so watch your step! He's promised to be my best man. Quent, this is Cynthia."

Quentin gave her a cordial handshake. He was nearly forty, broader and stockier than Hugh and more deliberate in his movements. By comparison with the rest of the family he looked immaculate in his silver-gray flannels and dark blazer.

"It's a big risk you're going to take," he told Cynthia. "Are you sure he can support you?"

"Atlas is my second name," said Hugh.

"Besides," said Cynthia, "we're going to sell a lot of books —one day."

"I'm told you help to write them."

Cynthia laughed and shook her head. "I dress the heroines in the clothes I can't afford myself—that's about all."

"Nonsense," said Hugh. "She's my critic and literary conscience. She reads the rough drafts with an expression halfway between incredulity and nausea and then tells me exactly where I've gone wrong."

"It sounds a full-time job," said Quentin. "By the way, Hugh, I noticed the *Gazette* had a review of that last one."

Hugh grimaced. "Not so hot, was it? 'Just possible on a *very* wet day!' Those chaps are certainly hard to please. If you plunge straight into the murder they say the story starts well but tails off. If you keep the fireworks until the end they say it's a slow beginning. If it starts well and finishes well they say it sags in the middle. Difficult!"

"Why not keep the tension up all the way through?"

"Then it's melodramatic," said Cynthia.

Trudie looked admiringly at her prospective sister-in-law. "Well, I just don't know how you do it. Are you working on a story now?"

"We've just finished one, but there's not enough verbiage—we've got to find another ten thousand words from somewhere."

"We could make all the characters stammer, of course," said Hugh.

Quentin's expression was faintly disapproving. "Well, I trust you won't both starve in a garret. Why don't you take your job seriously, Hugh, and make some money? Then you could afford this literary luxury."

"What *I* want to hear," said Trudie, who had by now absorbed every detail of Cynthia's appearance, "is how you two met."

"The usual way," said Hugh promptly. "She picked me up at a bus stop."

"Hugh!"

"Well, it wasn't romantic, anyway, Trudie—sorry to disappoint you. If you must know, it was at a National Savings Rally. I was reporting it and Cynthia's boss was one of the speakers and we were so deeply moved by his eloquence that we decided to save together. . . ." He passed a bowl of salad to Cynthia, inspecting it closely *en route*. "What, no dandelion leaves? Dad, you're slipping."

Edward absent-mindedly sugared his tea twice. "Dandelion leaves are very good for the blood," he said.

"Yes, but you have to have blood to do good to. Dad's practically herbivorous, Cynthia. Lives off the plants in the garden. Of course, he hasn't much choice with only Trudie to look after him."

"You horror!" said Trudie without heat.

"No, seriously, Cynthia," Hugh went on, "if you ever feel in need of a pick-me-up just pop down here and Dad'll be glad to fix you up with some herbal pills. He's a wizard at home-opathic remedies—you should get him to show you his collection of little bottles. . . . That reminds me, Dad, what's the stuff in the big saucepan in the kitchen?"

"It's not 'stuff,'" said Edward. "It's wild strawberry jam."

"It looks positively ferocious to me. I say, Quent, do you remember the tomato ketchup . . . ?"

Quentin's rather solemn face relaxed into a grin and Trudie smiled and Hugh went off into a peal of laughter.

"I trust you're all enjoying yourselves," said Edward blandly.

Hugh put a clutching hand on Cynthia's knee. "We came into the kitchen one day," he said, "and there was Dad in an apron standing over the stove in a cloud of blue smoke reciting some incantation and stirring a dark green concoction that smelled like rotted seaweed and when we asked him what it was he said it was . . . *ketchup!*"

"It was an old recipe," said Edward.

"It was too old," murmured Hugh, wiping his eyes.

Cynthia gave him an amused glance. This was Hugh in an unfamiliar light—he wasn't usually so frivolous.

"Father likes to experiment," said Quentin. "Remember the milk bar, Hugh . . . ?"

"Now *really* . . . !" Edward remonstrated.

Hugh took up the tale again. "It was after he lost his seat, Cynthia. He wanted to make some money so he rented a milk bar—in Skegness, of all places!—and he was going to put his political agent in as manager and I went up there one day and they were living in a caravan in the sandhills like Robinson Crusoe and man Friday and they were painting fifty-two high stools a bright orange . . ."

"Go on," urged Cynthia as he broke off with a guffaw.

"That's all! It was a wonderful summer and hundreds of thousands of people went to Skegness and they were all in such a hurry to get to the beach they dashed by and never even noticed the place."

"Well, it was very courageous to try," said Cynthia.

11

"Thank you, my dear," said Edward. "I'm glad there's going to be one member of my family who appreciates me."

Trudie was looking at her watch. "It's time for the news, Daddie."

Edward got to his feet. "If you'll excuse me," he said, and went indoors, groping in his pocket for a stub of pencil.

Trudie had also risen, heaving herself out of her deck chair with ungainly movements. "If you two would like to go off by yourselves," she said to Cynthia pointedly, "you can, you know. Quentin will help me with the washing up."

"There's no need to be coy," Hugh said, "but it's not a bad idea, all the same. What about having a look at the boat, Cynthia?"

"You ought to put on some old clothes first," Quentin warned her. "I only saw Hugh's boat once, but it looked like something that had crawled up out of the primeval slime."

"Ignore him," said Hugh. "He's a landlubber. I'm afraid there won't be enough water to sail, darling, but we can give her the once-over and take her out tomorrow. Can we borrow your car, Quent?"

"I suppose so, you spoiled young devil."

"We'll be back before dark. Okay, Cynthia, I'm ready when you are."

Fifteen minutes later they were standing beside the Broadwater and Cynthia was gazing with a slightly dubious fascination at a scene that was quite novel to her. All the water in the channel had ebbed away, and the "river" now consisted of a basin of shining mud that hissed and popped as though it were alive. Skirting the mud on both sides were broad stretches of gray-green saltings, cut by a tracery of rills and creeks. Beyond the saltings were the two grass-grown sea walls that kept the high tides within bounds. Boats of every size and description, many of them leaning at sharp angles, were dotted about in the mud, giving the place an untidy and somewhat derelict appearance. There were two small boatyards near the road, and beside one of them lay an old light vessel which the sailing enthusiasts of Steepleford used as a yacht club headquarters.

"That's *Water Baby*," said Hugh, pointing across the brown expanse to where, fifty yards away, a tubby little sixteen-footer sat almost upright in the mud.

Cynthia's face registered both pleasure and misgiving. "How do we get there?"

"Walk, I'm afraid. Let's go and find Frank and see if he can lend you some Wellingtons. He usually has some spares around."

They crossed a mosaic of hard cracked earth and approached a large houseboat which served as the workshop for the more modest of the two yards. As they picked their way through dinghies and old anchors and rusty bits of metal, Frank Hillyer appeared from an inner room with a file in his hand. He was a little older than Hugh; a lean, deeply bronzed man with blue eyes and a quiet, friendly manner. He and Hugh had been cronies for years.

A slow grin spread across his face as he shook hands with Cynthia and the glance he exchanged with Hugh was almost conspiratorial. "Come for your baptism? I think I can fix you up." He went inside to get the boots, and Cynthia caught a glimpse of a camp bed.

"Does he live in his workshop?" she asked Hugh.

"Not all the time, but he often spends whole nights here when the tides are high, tending ropes and seeing that everything's all right. It's a big responsibility running a one-man boatyard and he's got a lot of craft to look after. He's quite the busiest man on the Hard."

"The what?"

"The Hard, darling. That's what this place is called—Steepleford Hard."

Cynthia looked round at the sea of mud. "Of course—silly of me!"

She took off her shoes and pushed her feet into the Wellingtons that Frank had found for her. "All right," she said with the courage of ignorance, "I'm ready."

As they stumped toward the edge of the mud, someone hailed them from a big ketch that was held with ropes against the steep-to bank of the saltings. Hugh waved cheerily.

"That's *Flavia*," he told Cynthia. "One of the landmarks here. She's owned by a fat man named Briggs and a thin man named Storey. Frank calls them Fat Barnacle and Thin Barnacle."

"Why 'barnacle'?"

"They can't prise themselves away from this spot. They used to do pretty ambitious cruises but the war set them back and now they can't seem to get away. They come down regularly every weekend, summer after summer, working like slaves to prepare *Flavia* for sea, and every year she gets a bit shabbier and they get a bit older."

"What a shame!"

"Yes, it's rather pathetic in a way. She's too big for them, actually, and painting and scraping her is like working on the Forth Bridge—no sooner done than they have to start all over again. Mrs. Briggs gets very fed up—at least, she pretends to. I think she has fun really. Right, let's go. Take my hand."

He plunged into the sepia mud, drawing Cynthia after him. At once they were calf-deep. With each step the suction threatened to drag the boots from their feet. Once or twice Cynthia staggered in her efforts to extricate herself and would have fallen but for Hugh's tight grip.

"Are you sure it's safe?" she asked, glancing apprehensively at the distance they still had to cover.

Hugh reassured her. "You might go in over your knees on some of the soft banks but that's the worst that could happen. And not here, anyway."

"It would be horrible to get stuck."

"That can't happen in the Broadwater. Further up the coast there are a few dangerous places where you can be sucked right down. The river Pye's very bad—that's the third estuary northward from here. A man was lost there last winter—he was out shooting duck or something and the theory was that he rushed to retrieve a winged bird without watching his step. That's the fatal thing, to rush. All they found was his gun."

Cynthia plodded on rather grimly. "I can't promise I'll ever get to *enjoy* this part of sailing, Hugh."

He laughed. "Sorry—it is rather a tough initiation. We'll time things better tomorrow and use the dinghy."

"It smells so foul."

"You'll get to like it. After a weekend or two here you'll probably find ordinary air insipid."

"You are an ass," said Cynthia. She was relieved to find that the mud wasn't getting any deeper and after a final burst they reached *Water Baby*. There was a scratching of small green crabs against the hull as they shook off their boots and climbed aboard.

"Of course," said Hugh doubtfully, "she *is* a bit old—well, very old. I wouldn't have been able to afford her otherwise. Still, she sails quite well and the engine works sometimes and the cabin top only leaks when the rain's really heavy."

Cynthia was prowling about, opening lockers and trying the berths. "It's rather cozy," she said, gazing round the tiny cabin. "I like the brass lamps." She peered into the cluttered forepeak and pulled out a frying pan. "You don't mean you actually cook here?"

"I used to. Your turn now!"

She kissed him and they went up on to the cabin roof to smoke a cigarette. The sun was a red ball just above the saltings and the mud had a rosy glow. Everything was very peaceful. The only sound was that of a scraper on a neighboring boat.

Hugh puffed contentedly. "Well, darling, what did you think of Dad?"

Cynthia smiled. "I think he's amazingly patient."

"You mean all that teasing? Oh, he doesn't mind that—

15

after all, you only tease people you like. He's a bit eccentric, though, isn't he?"

"Eccentricity," said Cynthia, "is one of the hallmarks of strong characters and original minds."

"Where did you crib that from? There's something in it, though—Dad's certainly a strong character. That outward appearance of his is deceptive. He potters around like an old woman but he's alert and he doesn't miss a thing. He's tremendously active, you know—chairman of this and vice-president of that, sits on committees, helps at the Youth Club, visiting justice at the School of Delinquents—and that's only the start."

"What does he live on, Hugh? Has he a private income?"

"Not he—he hasn't a bean. Never has had. First of all, when he was young, he was an underpaid schoolmaster. Then he had that stab at Parliament and got in and was as happy as a sandboy, meeting people and helping them with their little problems and trying to put things right generally. He's a great reformer, you know, in his quiet way, and the kindest man alive—if everyone were like him the world wouldn't be a bad place to live in. Anyway, things didn't pan out as he'd hoped —he lost his seat and then he had to decide what to do. He was over forty, with no particular qualifications except intelligence and energy, and he had a pretty big family."

"So what did he do?"

"Why, he bought Lavender Cottage—that was a time when a few hundred pounds was real money, don't forget—and he became his own peculiar variety of free-lance journalist. I don't quite know how he managed it, but he'd got to know lots of important people while he was in the House and he gradually built up a connection doing paragraphs for diaries and gossip columns. He'd watch the news, and when somebody he knew or knew about wrote a book or took up spiritualism or bought an estate in Jamaica he'd weigh in with a few well-chosen words about some incident that everybody had forgotten. He still does it. That's why he goes dashing off to listen to the news bulletins."

16

"It sounds rather precarious."

"It is, but he's done it for twenty years and we haven't starved. Mind you, he never spends a penny on himself—doesn't smoke, doesn't drink, doesn't give a hoot about clothes, doesn't take holidays. He cuts things pretty well to the bone. And then he's developed several useful sidelines—he started to study the bird life in the marshes round here, and now he does regular nature notes for several papers and that helps. He's broadcast a bit, too, and he wrote up someone's 'Life'—you know, ghosted it. He never talks much about what he's doing—just rubs along, picking up a little here and there."

"Do you think he likes it?"

"Darling, he loves it. He's been absolutely free for twenty years, and if mother hadn't died so suddenly he'd have been the happiest man in the world. . . . It's funny, he's an odd old stick, but we all adore him. That's why I want you to."

"I think I'm going to be proud to know him," said Cynthia.

2 THE week that followed Cynthia's visit proved an exceptionally full one for Edward Latimer. On the Monday morning he had to go on official business to the county mental hospital; and in the afternoon he and Trudie kept a social engagement with the Chief Constable, Colonel Ainslie, and his wife. Tuesday was always set apart for writing, and the whole of Wednesday was taken up with the fortnightly Sessions at the local court. In addition, Edward had two evening committees. He had earmarked Thursday for a quiet day on the saltings with binoculars and notebook but—whether from overwork or heat—he woke that morning with one of his severe headaches and had to spend the day resting.

On the Friday he left home early to pay one of his periodic visits to London. For these expeditions he always dressed carefully in the black jacket and striped trousers which he had worn in the House of Commons nearly twenty years before. Apart from an aroma of mothballs and a faintly green hue they were, in his opinion, as good as they had ever been. He also wore a white starched collar and black boots. In this outfit he looked extremely respectable in a rather funereal way— according to Hugh it made him look like Seddon the Poisoner —but he still managed to convey an impression of oddity, heightened by the cheap little attaché case which he always carried.

Steepleford station was at its most rural that morning as he sauntered across the grass-grown track to the mossy up-platform. The "Directors' Train," the one fast up-train of the day, had gone; and Edward shared the platform with a sportive rabbit. The atmosphere of the place was somnolent. The

18

porter-signalman was humming quietly in his box and exchanging an occasional ting-ting with some colleague along the line. Edward waited patiently on an ancient wooden seat, watching Tom Leacock, the station master, unhurriedly maneuvering a crate of eggs across the rails. Tom was a slow, unambitious countryman with a rugged, honest face who for thirty years had divided his time between the station and his allotment. As usual, he stopped for a few moments to chat with Edward. Normally they talked about the weather, but today Tom wanted advice. His daughter, he explained, had just had her second baby and she didn't want to have it vaccinated yet because her first one had been ill afterward, and wasn't there some form you could fill up? Edward explained the procedure and said he'd sign the form any time and Tom's face cleared as though a great burden had rolled from his mind.

Presently there came a wheezy whistle and the little train panted laboriously into the station. Its three grimy non-corridor coaches looked of 1905 vintage, the only spot of color being the vivid "British Railways" medallion recently painted exactly in the center of each. It seemed surprising that anyone should have wanted to claim them. The compartment which Edward got into was bare and narrow, with broken window straps and a slashed seat. A cloud of dust rose from the faded upholstery as he sat down. Framed under the narrow luggage rack opposite him was a streaky photograph of Southend Pier in which all the men wore straw boaters. Edward felt rather at home with it.

As the train pulled out he took a bundle of newspapers from his case and started to go through them with a blue pencil, marking any items which seemed to offer scope for "paragraphs." Usually he was quite happy doing this, but today his head felt a little muzzy and his attention constantly wandered. He stopped to wave a passing greeting to Joe Saberton, the young signalman at Southgate Mill Box who ran the football club of which Edward was president; and at the junction he broke off again to exchange a few words with Bill Hopkin, the itinerant ticket-clipper on the Cuckoo Line. Bill, on the surface, was a morose and unsociable man—the sort who on a lovely spring day would be certain to growl, "We shall pay for this." Edward still remembered with amusement their first encounter, when he had been alone in a non-corridor compartment and Bill had swung aboard as they left a station with a stern "Tickets, please!" Having fulfilled himself by clipping the only available ticket, and having no means of exit, he had then sat down aloofly in the remotest corner and looked everywhere but at Edward, as though to make it plain that he wasn't going to let the peculiar conditions of his job force him into intimacy with passengers. However, time had broken down his taciturnity, and Edward now knew him as a shy but fundamentally friendly man and the popular leader of a local team of handbell ringers.

Once the junction was left behind the train shed most of its oddities and the rest of the journey passed quickly. From Liverpool Street station Edward took a bus to Fleet Street and made several calls on newspapers. Personal contact was essential for a free-lance, however well-established he might be. Besides, columnists sometimes made suggestions which Edward could follow up, and one contact could lead to another. Business, on these trips, could never be described as brisk, but everyone always seemed quite pleased to see Edward and to be ready to help if he could.

Having completed his rounds, he ate a frugal lunch of salad, cheese and cold milk at an A.B.C. and went on to the House of Commons to see if any of his old friends were about. It always gave him a little thrill of pleasure that the policeman at the entrance still knew him; saluted, indeed, as though he were still a Member. Somewhat nostalgically, but without useless regrets, Edward walked through the lobbies. Several Members recognized him and stopped to talk, and the afternoon flew by. He had a cup of tea on the Terrace and caught a bus back to Liverpool Street in time for the 5:55, which was the last train of the day if you lived on the Cuckoo Line.

He felt rather pleased with his day's work. He had picked up a bit of good-natured gossip about the chairman of a Royal Commission which should be worth fifteen shillings or perhaps a pound, and that would more than pay for his fare. He had also found a new opening for his nature notes, which was highly satisfactory. He took out a little black book and methodically recorded his increased financial expectations. Living on such narrow margins as he did, he had to keep careful accounts. One day, he knew, he might have to accept a little help from Quentin and Hugh, but he wanted to postpone that time as long as possible. Quentin, a confirmed bachelor, should be quite well off in the end, but his practice had gone down badly during the war and though he was working with characteristic Latimer drive to build it up again it would be some time before he had any spare cash. And Hugh certainly wouldn't be established for quite a while.

However, Edward decided, there was nothing to worry about for the present if only these trying headaches would stop. He could still earn enough for Trudie and himself. He sometimes wished that he had the means to make Trudie's life a little more exciting, but she seemed contented enough and showed no sign of wanting to go out into the world, either to earn or to spend. How different she was, he thought, in appearance and temperament, from either her mother or himself! A throwback to some lethargic forebear, perhaps. Genes could play unkind tricks on parents and children alike. He hoped that Hugh and Cynthia would manage things better.

His thought switched to pleasanter channels. In a year or two, with luck, he might have a granddaughter—a Carol Anne of his own, as lively as Hugh, as charming as Cynthia. A grandson, too, of course—perhaps more than one. As he walked slowly up the platform, his smooth head glistening a little in the warm sun, his imagination rapidly peopled the earth with young Latimers.

The 5:55 was already waiting in the station. Although it was the homegoing "Directors' Train" it was still shabby enough to make the bright medallions look out of place. However, it was a little less dirty inside, and it boasted a corridor. The front section was filling up rapidly with City men and weekenders, but there was still plenty of room in the three rear coaches, which were the Cuckoo Line part. Edward, after a brief inspection, made for the middle one of the three, which consisted of two third-class compartments at one end and six firsts. He had an idea that the Thirds in that coach might be a little wider than most, and he had long legs. He chose the compartment second from the end, a non-smoker, and settled down in a corner with his back to the engine. The only other occupants were a woman in country tweeds and a boy in a school cap.

As he took his seat a man looked in from the corridor, said, "Excuse me, I think I've left my paper," and stretched across to gather up a *Times* from the rack above Edward's head. Edward smiled and nodded, opened his *Evening Standard* and settled down to read.

Almost at once a bright object swished in front of his face. He looked up in surprise and saw that the boy was brandishing a gleaming new fencing foil.

"You really oughtn't to wave it, dear," said the woman, in a loud, overcultured, county-bred voice. "You might hurt somebody. Why not wait until you can take it into the paddock?"

The boy, who was about twelve, gave her a glance of silent contempt and lunged fiercely across the compartment. Edward stirred uneasily. He had no objection to small boys, but he had strong views about obedience. He wondered if the lad would be lunging and riposting all the way to the junction. He caught the eye of the woman, who smiled at him. "They do so love a new toy," she said.

"Yes," murmured Edward, a little grimly. He felt as though his head might start aching again at any moment.

He tried to settle to his paper, but found it impossible to

concentrate. The boy had now begun to take the foil to pieces, unscrewing bits of the handle. From time to time the button-end swung dangerously through the air.

"I shouldn't take it to pieces now, dear," said his mother. "Keep it until you get home."

The boy still said nothing and continued to take it to pieces. Edward weighed his disinclination to hurt the mother's feelings against the obvious desirability of seeking another compartment. He had almost made up his mind to move when his attention was momentarily distracted by the entrance of a young woman who sat down in the corner opposite him. The boy seemed to subside a little, and he decided to stay.

The lull proved only temporary, however. Soon the girl was glancing at Edward with a look of half-humorous appeal. He was on the point of making a protest when a ticket inspector entered, narrowly escaped having his eye gouged out, and told the boy he'd better put the foil in the rack. The boy stared at him balefully and made no move, but afterward he was comparatively still and at the second stop he and his mother got out.

As the door slammed behind them, Edward smiled at the girl. "That's a relief, I must say."

"Isn't it?" She was dark and rather good-looking in a sharp-featured way and very smart. "I was wondering how long we should have to put up with him."

"Are you going far?" asked Edward. He was always prepared to talk in trains and had a weakness for pretty girls.

"To Alfordness," she said. She had a pleasant, low-pitched voice and a friendly manner. "I don't have to change, do I?"

"No, you go right through. It's rather a weary journey, I'm afraid."

"At least the country looks nice," said the girl. She gazed out of the window for a moment or two, and then bent over her book.

Edward studied her for a while, thinking what a pity it was

that poor Trudie hadn't the gift of self-presentation that most women seemed to have. Then he, too, resumed his reading.

No one else got in. There was a long stop at the junction while the three carriages for the Cuckoo Line were uncoupled and provided with a clanking little engine that belched a lot of smoke. As they started off again the girl suddenly said, "Oh!" and clapped a hand over one eye, feeling for her handbag.

Edward looked at her in concern. "What is it, a smut?"

"It feels like a large cinder," she said, rubbing the eye with the palm of her hand.

"You'd better not rub it," said Edward, "you'll make it worse. May I have a look?"

The girl smiled gratefully and tilted her head back. Edward took a white handkerchief from his breast pocket and carefully drew down the lower lid. The eye was rather red and watering a little. "I don't see anything," he said, trying the upper lid.

"It's probably come out," said the girl, taking out her mirror. "It's very kind of you." She looked at herself. "What a sight! I'd better go and make some repairs." She got up and went out. As she brushed by him, he caught the fragrance of her perfume and it stirred memories in him. It almost made him wish he were young again.

He sat watching the pleasant Essex landscape drifting by the window, a look of contentment on his face. Presently he felt the train slow down as it approached Southgate Mill Box and the Cuckoo Line Branch. There was always a near-stop here, for Joe Saberton, standing beside the track, had to hand a special staff to the driver as he passed on to the single line. It involved a nice piece of timing, like the transfer in a relay race, and until he had got used to it Edward had found it pretty to watch. He could remember only one occasion on which the engine driver had missed the staff and been obliged to bring the train to a halt.

In a moment or two the girl came back. Her face was freshly made up but the eye still looked rather red.

"All right now?" asked Edward.

"I'm not sure—there still seems to be a pricking in the corner. Would you mind awfully having another look?"

Edward got up and she moved to the window and held her face up to the light so that he could see better. As he bent over her he was aware again of that pleasant perfume, of her body pressing against him and—Heavens!—of lips so near to his that they seemed to invite him.

The next moment they were in a close embrace.

3 Hugh ripped the sheet of paper from his typewriter with an exclamation of disgust and gazed gloomily round the small, sparsely furnished room which he rented in Chelsea.

"Having trouble, my love?" Cynthia looked up from the slice of manuscript on which she was working, her pencil poised.

"We ought to be pruning this damn thing," said Hugh, "not spinning it out. Some of this conversation's absolutely banal."

"It *is* a bit patchy," she agreed. "If we're going to add ten thousand words we really ought to have some more incidents."

"But the story's complete—it doesn't need more incidents." Hugh screwed up the spoiled sheet and tossed it into the fireplace. "I know one thing—I'll never sign another contract that calls for eighty thousand words. Surely there must be publishers who can read as well as count?"

"Why were they so insistent?"

"Oh, some incredible rubbish about borrowers at libraries taking a day and a half to read eighty thousand words, instead of a day, so the libraries have to order more copies! Imbeciles!"

Cynthia looked fondly at his disgruntled face. "Why not pack up for tonight, darling?—I think you've done enough. Anyway, it's time I went. Tomorrow's Saturday—we'll tackle it when we're fresh."

Hugh pushed the typewriter away and joined her on the settee. "I could be pretty fresh right now with a little encouragement."

"I dare say you could, but you're not to start anything—it's much too late." Suddenly the telephone rang and he had to get up to answer it. "There you are, you see—I'm watched over!"

Hugh lifted the receiver. "Hello! . . . Oh, it's you, Quent."

Quentin's voice, always rather crisp on the telephone, now had an almost peremptory note. "Hugh, can you come down here first thing tomorrow?—to the cottage?"

"Tomorrow! I suppose we *could*. Why, what's the trouble?" Hugh's face took on a look of concern. "I say, there's nothing wrong with Dad, is there?"

"Not exactly, but . . . Look, I can't possibly tell you anything over the phone. It'll have to wait until you get here."

"Oh, lord, do you have to be so mysterious? Okay, we'll be down."

"Just you, Hugh—better not bring Cynthia this time."

"Oh, now look, Quent . . ."

"I'm sorry, but you'll understand when you get here. I must ring off now—don't miss the train, it's very urgent." He hung up.

Hugh slowly replaced the receiver.

"What is it, darling?" asked Cynthia. "Trouble?"

"Could be. Quent wants me without you—says it's important. It's something to do with Dad, I'm certain of that. Will you mind terribly being left?"

"I expect I'll survive—I'll get on with the book and you can give me a ring in the evening. Don't worry about it tonight, darling—there's nothing you can do. Come and walk home with me."

"Yes, all right," he said, with a preoccupied frown. "I'd like to know what the devil it can be, though."

He was up early next morning and caught the first available train. There was no car to meet him at Steepleford station so he walked the mile to the house, his apprehension increasing with every step. Was it possible that Quentin had been trying to break bad news gently? As he turned in at the gate of Lavender Cottage Trudie rushed out of the house to meet him. At once his fears seemed to be confirmed, for she threw her arms round his neck and straightway burst into tears.

Hugh looked at her crumpled, red-eyed face in consternation. "For heaven's sake, Trudie, what is it?"

"Oh, Hugh," she gulped, "it's too terrible for anything. It's Daddie . . . he's . . . ." She broke down, unable to finish the sentence.

Hugh strode into the house, his face suddenly white, but on the threshold of the sitting room he was brought up sharp. At least there had been no physical disaster. Edward and Quentin were quietly facing each other on opposite sides of the hearth.

Edward looked up with the ghost of a smile. "Hello, Hugh —sorry to drag you down here like this." His voice sounded flat and tired and his thin hands trailed limply over the arms of his chair as though age had overtaken him.

"Christ!" said Hugh, "I thought you must be dead! What's the matter with Trudie? What's happened?"

"Something very unpleasant, Hugh," Quentin said. He looked almost a stranger, sitting there in his office clothes, his face stern with anxiety. Hugh realized that he must have come straight from work on the previous evening and spent the night at the cottage. "The fact is, Father's expecting a summons for assault."

"Assault!" After Hugh's vivid imaginings, the news seemed trivial, almost comical. "Not brawling on the Bench, surely?"

"This isn't funny, Hugh. It'll be a summons for assault against a young woman in a train."

Hugh stood stock still for a moment, unable to believe his ears. "You *can't* be serious!" He stared blankly at his father. "When? How?"

Edward said wearily, "You tell him, Quentin."

"Very well . . . This is what happened, Hugh. Father was coming back from town on the 5:55 yesterday evening and there was a young woman sitting opposite him in the compartment. There were some other people at first but they got out. This girl complained of something in her eye—a smut or

28

something—and Father tried to get it out for her. They were standing together by the window, and—well, the girl suddenly called out, 'Let me go, you beast!' or words to that effect, and screamed for help."

"Good lord!" said Hugh, shocked. "But you don't mean to say she got away with it? She must have been crazy."

"That's only the beginning, Hugh. A man sitting in the next compartment heard her call out, and he rushed in and found the girl and Father struggling together. He shouted something like 'What do you think you're doing?—let her go!' and grabbed Father's shoulder, pulling them apart. The girl began to cry. Then the train ran into Steepleford and there was a most unpleasant scene on the platform and in Tom Leacock's office. The girl accused Father of having violently assaulted her—and the man said he'd seen Father actually doing it."

Quentin paused, and the room seemed very still. Edward, sitting with one hand over his eyes, might almost have been asleep.

"There's still worse to come," Quentin went on in a precise, detached voice, as though he were giving evidence in a police court. "You know Joe Saberton, the signalman at Southgate Mill Box? Well, apparently he was standing halfway up the steps of his box as the train slowly gathered speed—the way he always does after he's handed that baton thing to the driver— and he saw everything. He rang through to the box on Steepleford platform before the train arrived and reported that he'd seen a girl being attacked. He thought she might have come to serious harm, because according to him her head was being forced back almost out of the window. When he got to the station a little later he repeated his story. And that's the whole thing, Hugh. Now you can see why we're expecting a summons."

"But—good God! . . ." Hugh was almost speechless with indignation. "It's too monstrous for words—nobody's going to believe that Dad would do a thing like that." He looked anxiously at his father. "What *did* happen, Dad?"

Edward stirred and sighed. "Well, Hugh, we were standing by the window, as Quentin says, and I was bending over the girl to see if the smut had come out of her eye and suddenly she—she flung her arms around me very tightly and embraced me. I—I was so completely taken by surprise that I didn't do anything for a moment—and then, of course, I tried to release myself. I know it sounds as though it should have been an easy thing to do, but she was a strong young woman and—well, we did have a bit of a struggle. I may even have lost my head a bit, but I certainly didn't do anything remotely like what Joe Saberton says. And then everything else happened just as you've heard."

"I see." Hugh looked as though he were beginning to understand. "What was the girl like, Dad? Tarty?"

"Not a bit. She was attractive, but not at all in a flashy way. I had thought her a very pleasant young woman, as a matter of fact, until this happened—it was the last thing in the world I'd have expected her to do."

"Well, she obviously had it in for you," said Hugh grimly. "Is anything known about her, Quent?"

"Her name's Helen Fairlie and she lives in Kensington. Father thinks she might be about twenty-seven or twenty-eight. That's all we know at the moment. . . ." He hesitated. "The point is, Hugh, it's not the girl herself we have to worry about, so much as the witnesses. Everybody knows that it's not uncommon for neurotic women to make allegations of this sort against men, and if it were simply the girl's word against Father's we might hope to get by. But with two independent witnesses . . ."

"Oh, to hell with that, Quent! They were mistaken, and that's all there is to it. After all, if you hear a cry for help in a train and rush to the scene and find a man and a girl struggling together, what's more natural than to take it for granted the man's the aggressor? Anybody would, particularly if the girl put on a good act afterward. . . . Who was this fellow in the next compartment, anyway?"

"His name's Walter Vulliamy and he's a company director. He lives a couple of stations farther down the line, he's about sixty, and he's a member of a well-to-do Essex family. An absolutely reputable citizen."

"So what? Being reputable doesn't mean that he can't make a mistake." Hugh was beginning to get annoyed.

"Of course it doesn't, but he'll take a lot of shaking. Father says he was extremely indignant on the girl's behalf and didn't mince his words at all. In any case, we're still left with Joe Saberton."

A picture of Saberton came into Hugh's mind—the sturdy build, the frank open face and friendly eyes of the one-time butcher's boy he had played football with in his youth. He looked serious.

"Yes, I can see that'll be tough—I wouldn't have thought he was the type to imagine things. Still, he must have done."

"The train was going very slowly," said Quentin. He seemed determined, Hugh thought savagely, to extract every possibility of gloomy foreboding from the situation. "Saberton had a clear view, and I gather he's absolutely emphatic about what he—what he thinks he saw. He says that not only was the girl's head being forced back but that he actually saw Father's hand at her throat."

"But that's fantastic!" cried Hugh.

Quentin seemed less certain. "Father says that when they were struggling together she held her own head back and that he doesn't *think* he put his hand on her throat."

"Oh, my God!" Hugh was only now beginning to realize the full seriousness of the situation. "What a mess!"

There was another uncomfortable silence. Edward was gazing unhelpfully at the hearth, his only sign of awareness the heightened color on each cheekbone.

"Well, it's no good glooming about it," said Hugh after a moment. "What are we going to do? It's up to you, Quent."

"Not entirely," said Quentin stiffly. "I've been talking to

Father about it—in fact we've been churning it over ever since last night. We don't quite see eye to eye."

"Oh?" Hugh looked quickly at his father and then back at Quentin.

"Father wants to go before the court with a plea of 'Not Guilty,' tell his story, and say that the girl was deliberately lying and that the witnesses are mistaken."

"What else can he do, for heaven's sake?"

"If he does that," Quentin said, "there can be only one result. He hasn't a chance against that evidence, and as a magistrate he must know that as well as I do. What do you think his own decision would be on the Bench if a nice-looking, well-spoken, outwardly respectable girl made such an accusation and there wasn't any known reason why she should lie about it, and a reputable independent witness bore out her story and another reputable independent witness swore he'd seen it happen with his own eyes?"

"Well, that's a fine fighting attitude, I must say!"

"Look, Hugh," said Quentin, on a note of exasperation, "I'm as sorry about all this as you are, and just as much involved, but I'm trying to put personal feelings aside and look at things as a lawyer. And as a lawyer, I can tell you that the outcome is a certainty. The Bench will be full of regrets, of course—they'll talk about 'this painful case' and 'a lifetime of honorable service' and all that sort of thing—but they won't believe Father. And if he tries to discredit the girl and says she's lying, without a jot of evidence to support him except his bare word —well, they'll consider that an aggravation. I tell you frankly, I think he'll get a prison sentence."

"*Prison!* It's not possible." Hugh stared at his brother in horror.

"This is a serious charge, Hugh. Assault in a train is a very different thing from—well, say snatching a kiss in the street. I gather the girl made it sound pretty bad—when we see the actual charge it may turn out to be even worse than we think.

Let's not deceive ourselves—the sentence could easily be three months, possibly six."

"But . . . God, it's unbelievable! There must be *some* way out of it."

"I think there may be," said Quentin slowly, "but that's where Father and I differ. I've been over the ground with him already, but unsuccessfully. Perhaps you'll be able to influence him. The thing is, Father says he has no recollection of making any move to assault the girl . . ."

"I didn't say that, Quentin," Edward interrupted. The spots on his cheekbones grew redder. "I said I had a clear recollection of *not* doing . . ."

"Yes, I know." Quentin brushed the interruption aside as though it were something he didn't want to hear. "But recollections can be faulty, especially when there's been a mix-up like that. You talked to the girl coming down on the train, Father, and you agree that you thought she was rather nice, rather attractive. She was standing there, close to you—I hate all this, but we've got to face it—she was probably enjoying your attention, leading you on a bit. Then—well, something happened. You think you remember exactly who did what, but you may be wrong . . ."

Hugh broke in. "I don't get it, Quent. What exactly are you suggesting?"

"Last summer," said Quentin in a tone of quiet reasonableness, "Father had a very bad attack of sunstroke. He had some fearful headaches—you remember? And he had two short blackouts—he couldn't recall afterward what had happened. Well, he was out in the sun a good deal last week, too, and he tells me that the headaches have returned. Who can say whether the trouble has quite cleared up, whatever it was? The fact is that on the evidence—I repeat, *on the evidence*— he did something which in a normal condition of health we know he would never have done. Now if he goes to court, says he has no recollection of assaulting the girl—which is true— tells them about the sunstroke and the blackouts, says he's putting himself under medical care again, and expresses regret at what happened—well, I think they'll bind him over, and that will be that."

"And he'll leave the court with no more than a stain on his character!" cried Hugh angrily. "*Dad*, of all people in the world. It's unthinkable!"

"Don't imagine I like it," said Quentin. "I'm only trying to make the best of a bad job. It's going to be ghastly whatever we do."

"But—good heavens, Quent, it's like some scoutmaster volunteering to undergo 'treatment' for six months. It's revolting."

"Is it worse than a prison sentence?"

There was a sigh from Edward's corner and he got slowly to his feet as though he could no longer bear the discussion. The placid, contented man of the week before had vanished. His face now had a baffled look, and when he spoke there was an unaccustomed constraint in his tone. For the first time in the lives of all three of them, barriers had been raised.

"I know you're suggesting what you think is the best course of action, Quentin," he said quietly. "I appreciate that. But I couldn't possibly do what you say. You see—I *do* remember—very clearly. That girl, for her own reasons, has made a false and wicked accusation against me. I've searched my memory, and I know that I did nothing of which I need feel ashamed. She assaulted me, she held me so that I was forced to struggle with her, and she called out because she wanted someone to be able to give evidence against me. Don't ask me why she did it—I don't know. I'm not questioning the good faith of the witnesses, but they're mistaken. That's the truth, and that's what I'm going to say. I can't do anything else." He turned, and went slowly out into the garden.

Hugh was the first to break the silence. "Poor old Dad!—he thinks he's alone in this. Quent, I feel like a louse."

Quentin got up and began pacing about the room. "It's the evidence, Hugh—there's not a loophole. I was awake half the night thinking about it. Everything fits—everything. The friendliness of the girl, which a man might take as encouragement; the exceptional opportunity, because of the eye; the way she called for help and the words she used, quite natural and convincing; the instant reaction of the man who rushed in, and his complete certainty. And then Saberton—that damning sentence about her head being pushed back. Father says she was strong, but it appears she's quite small. He wouldn't have needed to push her head nearly out of the window just to free himself from her. And Saberton wouldn't have said that if it hadn't been true. He's got nothing against Father—very much the reverse. And he didn't even realize it was Father until he got to the station—he was merely doing his job. When he did hear he was absolutely horrified."

Hugh gave a reluctant nod. "I must say when you put it like that I can't see a glimmer, either . . ." He sat for a while in dejected silence. Presently he said: "Do you honestly think the old man may be seriously ill without knowing it—or was that just lawyer's stuff?"

Quentin took a little time to answer. "Father's human," he said at last, "and he isn't too old to want to kiss a pretty girl. But if he had done it and it had resulted in this horrible mess, he'd have told us—I'm sure of that. He'd never lie to us. So that means he *must* be a sick man. I know he thinks he can remember clearly, but obviously he's wrong. My guess is that he assaulted her and used quite a bit of force, when she struggled, without having an inkling of what he was doing, and that his recollections are honest but completely cockeyed."

"It's so unlike him," Hugh said miserably. "I'd have sworn that any sort of violence was absolutely foreign to him—sick or whole. In all his life he's never lifted a finger against anyone or anything. Can a person's whole nature betray him like that, without warning?"

"I frankly don't know, Hugh. I wish he could be persuaded to see a psychiatrist."

"He never will, Quent—we might as well save our breath."

Quentin nodded gloomily. Edward could be extraordinarily

obstinate when his mind was made up. "All the same, we've got to try."

"And if he won't agree—what's the next step?"

"Well, if he's determined to stick to his story we'll just have to carry on in the usual way. I'll find a colleague to take the case, we'll see if we can discover anything about the girl that might help us, and when the time comes we'll try to get admissions from the witnesses that they might have been mistaken. There's nothing else we can do—but it's a thousand to one against us."

"You say the summons hasn't been served yet?"

"No, but it'll come at any moment. After she'd made her complaint the girl continued her journey by the same train, so the police may have had a bit of a job to get hold of her. Anyway, you know how slowly they move in these parts, and they won't risk making mistakes in a case like this."

"Would it be any good your seeing Ainslie?"

Quentin pondered. "It won't make the least difference, of course, but he might tell me what's happening. Bit embarrassing, but it's not much good being friends with the Chief Constable if you can't approach him in a crisis. Perhaps I'll give him a ring."

"I should," said Hugh. "It's better than just sitting and waiting." He gazed unhappily out of the window. "God, I'd never have believed a thing like this would happen in a million years."

4 THE afternoon passed slowly. Quentin had made an appointment with the Chief Constable and gone off immediately after lunch. Trudie was out shopping. Edward, after writing one or two letters and taking them to the post, had put on his old hat and gone down the garden again to scythe the grass in the orchard. Hugh kept catching glimpses of him among the trees as he stopped to sharpen his blade and chat to Carol Anne, who was busy raking up the dry hay for him. Since that emphatic little speech of his, he appeared to have pushed the whole matter from his mind. He had certainly been the most unruffled of the four at lunch. Quentin had been solemn, and Trudie overconsiderate, and Hugh much too talkative, but Edward had behaved as naturally as though nothing had happened at all. His calmness seemed almost incredible in the circumstances, and Hugh had found in it an additional cause for anxiety. A child, with no developed sense of responsibility, might show the same resilience.

Now that Hugh had had time to reflect a little, he found it more difficult than ever to pick holes in Quentin's attitude. The more he thought about the evidence, the more overwhelming it seemed. He had as little hope as Quentin that the witnesses would change their stories. It did occur to him to run over to Southgate Mill and have a talk with Joe Saberton, but after consideration he decided it would be quite useless. Joe's story was on record, and he would stick to it however much he hated doing so. Quentin was right—the only hope was to rescue Edward from himself. Somehow or other, for his own and everybody's sake, he'd *got* to be persuaded to submit to an examination. This was a case where he simply wasn't fit to make his own decision; his stubbornness would have to be overcome. Hugh sighed as he recalled the struggle they'd had to make him see a doctor during his illness the previous summer.

He was about to join the haymakers in the hope of taking his mind off things when Trudie came in from her shopping expedition. She put her basket down beside his chair and at once began to weep again.

"Oh, for Pete's sake!" exclaimed Hugh, wishing that complete abandonment to grief didn't make poor Trudie so confoundedly plain. "Do try to snap out of it—you'll flood the place out."

"I can't help it," she sniffed. "It's so awful. Everybody's talking about it."

"Well, what do you expect?"

"But it's so unfair. Mrs. Burden says practically everybody who came into her shop this morning was against Daddie. And some of them said horrible things."

"Which were all carefully repeated to you, I don't doubt." He suddenly saw how tough it was going to be for Trudie, and felt a pang of sympathy. "Never mind, old girl, they'll forget in time. Talk can't make the thing worse than it is."

"But they all liked him so much—everybody did. And he's done so much for them. You'd think there'd be some gratitude. . . . Mrs. Hawkins said he ought to be made an example of!" She began to sniff again.

"Be your age, Trudie," Hugh pleaded. "You've had a sheltered life, that's the trouble with you. Dad's a fallen idol, and that means most people will be ready to kick him around. It's the way things are."

"They might at least have waited to see what he had to say."

Hugh shrugged. "It must look pretty conclusive to them. They'll have heard Joe Saberton's story, and that's all they need. That's all anybody needs. If *we* can't explain it away, how can we expect them to?"

"But if Daddie's ill . . ."

"They don't know that—we don't even know it ourselves for certain. Not in a way that would convince a court, I mean. Have *you* noticed anything strange about him, Trudie, apart from the headaches?"

"Not really. He does rather overdo things, of course, but he's been quite happy and cheerful."

"Oh, well, there's no point in *our* chewing it over," Hugh said glumly. "It's a job for experts, and somehow we've got to make him see one. . . ."

Just then a car pulled up in the drive and a moment later Quentin appeared round the corner of the house. His stride was brisker and he had an air of cheerful self-confidence. "Hello, you two!" he said. "I've got news for you."

"Good news?" asked Trudie eagerly.

"Much better than I expected. Where's Father?"

"Down the garden—I'll get him." She went to the edge of the lawn and called "Daddie!" in an excited voice, beckoning when he looked up.

Hugh said, "What is it, Quent?"

"Believe it or not, they're not going to prosecute."

"Not going to . . . !"

"I'll tell you when Father comes—it's quite a story." Quentin dropped into a deck chair and felt for his pipe. "You know, I feel ten years younger."

Hugh grinned for the first time that day. "You don't look it, old boy—not with that paunch!"

Presently Edward came sauntering up the path, unhurried as ever, with Trudie urging him on. Once he stopped to pull up a weed. If Hugh had known his father less well he would have suspected him of posing.

"What's all the excitement about?" he asked, as he joined them.

"Father, they're not going to prosecute."

"Oh?" Edward sat down and tied his long legs into a comfortable knot. "That's very surprising."

"I could hardly believe my ears when Ainslie told me. It seems the girl has changed her story."

Edward's face lit up. "You mean she's admitted everything?"

"Not everything, but a great deal. We'd have heard earlier but, as I expected, it took the police a long time to get in touch with her. They talked to Joe Saberton last night and they also interviewed the other witness, Vulliamy, but the girl had gone on and they didn't hear a word from her. So this morning, as they took a pretty serious view of the case—Ainslie was quite frank about that—they had inquiries made in London to see if she'd returned to her flat, and she had. Apparently she got back first thing this morning, and she was seen by a Yard man."

"And what did she say?" asked Edward quietly.

"She said she'd thought it over and she didn't want to make any charge. She said that the man—that's you, Father—had been very kind to her on the way down, and she'd liked the look of him very much, and she thought perhaps she had led him on and even encouraged him, and that one way and another she was ready to take fifty per cent of the responsibility. She said that the man had seized hold of her rather violently and she'd been upset and that's why she had made such a fuss at the station, but now that she'd had time for reflection she realized that he hadn't meant to do her any harm and she didn't want to make things bad for him. She said she thought she'd exaggerated the force he'd used, and it wasn't quite true that he'd pushed her head back—it had probably looked like it from the outside, but she was just leaning back herself to get away from him. In short, she was rather ashamed of her part in the affair and certainly didn't want any further action to be taken."

"Well, I'll be damned!" exclaimed Hugh.

"It's all very unexpected," said Quentin, "but I must say it's a tremendous relief."

"I think it's absolutely disgraceful," said Trudie indignantly. "What a frightful girl she must be!"

"She certainly sounds a hysterical type," Quentin agreed. "She behaved extremely badly all the way through—extremely badly. At the same time, I suppose it isn't every woman who would eat her words like that—it must have been quite a humiliating interview with the police officer. We must give credit where credit is due."

"Rot!" said Hugh. "She sounds an absolute bitch to me. If she admits half the responsibility, we can be damn sure she was entirely to blame. I suppose she thought she'd enjoy being the center of interest in a nice sexy case and then got cold feet about going through with it. It's obvious the whole thing was her doing from start to finish and we ought never to have doubted it." He caught Edward's glance and his face grew hot. "Dad, I'm sorry. Quent, we ought to be shot."

Quentin looked uncomfortable. He also was inclined to believe now that the girl had been wholly responsible. He wasn't prepared to blame himself for conclusions reached in different circumstances, but it was impossible not to feel some sense of disloyalty.

Edward said: "What about the police, Quentin? You mean they're dropping the case too?"

"Why, yes. As long as the girl admits fifty per cent of the responsibility they've no case to bring. Ainslie's tremendously relieved at the way things have worked out—he was most distressed by the whole business and he was only too eager to drop everything the moment he felt justified in doing so. Of course, young Saberton still sticks to his story, but since the girl herself doesn't go all the way with him there's no ground for a prosecution there. Vulliamy must have been equally misled. No, as far as the police are concerned I'm assured we've heard the last of the affair."

"I see," said Edward thoughtfully. "Well, in that case, of course, I shall have to take action myself."

They all stared at him.

"What action?" asked Quentin sharply.

"Why, for defamation of character. I've never believed in

41

litigation if it can possibly be avoided, but in these circumstances I've no option. This young woman has made charges against me which have been spread all over the district. And she hasn't withdrawn them. She's merely said it was partly her fault, which still means it was partly my fault. In any case, she only told a police officer—her retraction isn't going to be generally known, as the charges were. I've got to make her take it all back, and publicly. Her story is a pack of lies from beginning to end and I'm determined to make her admit it."

There was a moment's uneasy silence. Then Quentin said in a disturbed voice, "I know exactly how you feel about it, Father—we all feel the same—but honestly I think you'd be well advised to let the matter drop."

"Count me out of this for the moment, Quent," Hugh said. "I'm not at all sure—the whole position's completely changed now."

"You must see, Quentin," Edward went on, "that I've absolutely no choice in the matter. I was prepared to wait until a case was brought against me and then speak out in court, but if there's to be no prosecution I must find another way. I can't simply do nothing—what do you suppose will happen to us here if I don't clear the thing up beyond any shadow of doubt? You know what living in the country is like. I'm not trying to win your sympathy—I know I've got that—but the fact is that as things are my life here is finished. If I'd done what everyone believes I've done, no doubt that would be my proper punishment, but I'm certainly not going to allow a lying and unscrupulous woman to destroy me without raising a finger in my own defense." He sat back in his chair, the picture of quiet obstinacy.

"I'm with you all the way," said Hugh. "Let's make a fight of it."

"It seems I'm cast for the unpopular role in this affair," Quentin said bitterly. "The cautious lawyer—an unheroic figure. Perhaps it would be as well, Father, if you got another opinion—after all, I haven't exactly shone in this business so far. . . ."

"I'm not blaming you for that," Edward said, "but I confess your attitude now does surprise me."

"Look, Father," said Quentin earnestly, "I can fully understand how you feel about the girl and perhaps in my relief at the turn of events this afternoon I had rather overlooked the consequences to you if you let things slide. The question now is, are they going to be better or worse if you don't?"

"Surely they're bound to be better," Hugh said. "The girl made damaging statements publicly which she now admits weren't entirely true. I think the case should be a cinch."

Quentin looked at him coldly. "The next time you're writing a story, Hugh, perhaps you'll let me advise you?"

"Don't be an ass, Quent. Where am I wrong, then?"

"I'll tell you. The girl's talk with the police officer was informal—she wouldn't make any statement and nothing was taken down. All we have is knowledge of a verbal retraction of which there's no exact record, and that would be absolutely useless in a case against her. She can still go back on it if she wants to. It's the evidence she gives in court that will count."

"You mean if we sue her she'll repeat her first story? That's monstrous."

"What else could she do?—her only defense would be to prove her statements. We'd be forcing her into it. *And* she'd get away with it—she's still got those witnesses, remember."

"Well, has she or hasn't she? She seems to be having it both ways."

"She *can* have it both ways—if she wants them, they're ready to speak up for her; if she doesn't, they were mistaken. She's in a wonderful position. Even if by some miracle it came out that she'd been prepared to accept partial responsibility, she'd be able to explain it away as a generous impulse and win the jury's sympathy. If we took action, we should simply be inviting the verdict we've so narrowly escaped. It would be absolute madness. If the very best happened and some of the responsibility could be pinned on her, Father would still leave the court branded as a man who had actively and even violently participated in a most unsavory scene. There's not a hope that any shred of reputation would be saved."

There was a little silence while they all digested that. Then Hugh said: "What you're really telling us, Quent, is that there's no hope anyway—that Dad's *had* it, in fact."

"On the evidence . . ." began Quentin.

"Oh, for God's sake, I wish you'd stop saying that."

"It's what's going to count," Quentin said angrily. "We're not going to get anywhere by being impulsive. You think I'm being defeatist, but all I'm doing is to urge the lesser evil. If Father accepts the situation as it is—bad though it is—the gossip will at least be localized. Nothing's appeared in print, and it's not likely now that anything will. He can move to a new district and carry on. I'm afraid he'll have to give up some of his activities, but for his health's sake it's probably about time he did that, anyway. That's what I call the lesser evil. But if he sues the girl, there'll be publicity all over the country. It's the perfect story for the Sunday newspapers—an ex-M.P. and J.P. in a train assault on a pretty girl!—they'll really go to town on it. By the time they've squeezed all the nastiness they can out of the case, it will be impossible for Father to live with dignity anywhere. And the name of Latimer will be just a word that people snigger over."

"Easy, Quent!"

"It's true, and you know it. It's happened often enough to people before. And in one way or another we'll all be affected. It'll be horrible for Trudie, horrible for your Cynthia, and—quite frankly—it'll be a body blow for me. There are plenty of lawyers, and in a small town like Ramsford people shy away from scandal as though it were the plague. If I thought it would help to get Father out of this mess I'd be happy to let the practice go to the devil, but I'm damned if I see any point in sacrificing it when the only possible result is bound to be complete disaster all round."

"At least," said Hugh, "we'd go down with flags flying."

"Romantic twaddle! We'd go down with flags covered with mud."

Edward, the silent and unhappy auditor, sat with his head in his hands. He could see now that his impulse to take action had been a little hasty. His thoughts at that moment were less of Trudie and of Quentin's practice than of the two young people who were planning to get married and whose life together would start under such wretched auspices. Presently he gave a deep sigh.

"There's a lot in what you say, Quentin, of course, and I dare say most people would think you were right. Personally, I'm not sure. I'm not sure that injustice should ever be accepted, whatever the consequences. I think it should be fought, and if I were the only person concerned in this affair I wouldn't hesitate. . . . All the same, I do see that the decision isn't wholly mine to take. Heaven knows the last thing I want to do it to involve you all in a lot of sordid publicity. . . ." He broke off, as though his mind were still not made up. "I can't help wondering," he said after a while, "if there may not be some other way—some middle course. Surely this girl can't be as base and conscienceless as she seems—there may be some way of appealing to her better nature and getting her to admit the whole truth. I wonder—suppose I saw her and had a talk with her . . ."

Quentin nearly jumped out of his chair. "For heaven's sake, Father, don't do anything like that. If you start following her about she'll be accusing you of assaulting her again before we know where we are. You keep clear of her."

"I think somebody ought to go after her, all the same," Hugh said. "I'm doubtful about the better nature, but we might find out something useful. She may have a very bad record."

"All right," said Quentin, "but if there are any inquiries to be made, let's make them in the orthodox way. I doubt if it will do any good myself, but it's for Father to judge." He looked at Edward.

"I'd like to think the whole thing over before we do anything at all," said Edward. "I'll sleep on it and let you know what I decide. . . . Now let's try to forget it all for a bit, shall we?"

5 ON THE surface, life at Lavender Cottage returned almost to normal during the next day or two. If Edward hadn't in fact succeeded in "forgetting it all," at least he gave every appearance of having suspended thought on the subject and he said no more about taking action against the girl. He continued to listen to the news and write his "paragraphs" and deal with his correspondence as though nothing had changed. He pottered quietly in the garden as usual. Once or twice Trudie found him leaning motionless on his rake, staring at the ground with blank eyes, but he had always been a bit of a dreamer. He was his gentle and considerate self with her. He looked tired sometimes, and she suspected that he wasn't sleeping very well, but he brushed aside her suggestion that he should get something from Dr. Scott. All he needed, he said, was a bit of a tonic. He spent a morning gathering herbs from the hedgerows and boiling them up into a vile-smelling brew which he quaffed in large quantities with apparent pleasure. It was so characteristic of him that Trudie found it reassuring.

The family kept in close touch. Quentin rang up each morning from his office in Ramsford to see how Edward was getting on. Neither he nor his father made any further reference to the train incident. Hugh wrote from London that he'd told Cynthia the whole story and that she'd taken it in her stride and sent Edward her warmest love—a message which was more obviously effective in cheering him up than the herbal tea. Otherwise, nothing much happened. Trudie couldn't help noticing that when she went out the nods of people she knew seemed tinged with embarrassment and that they no longer stopped to talk to her, but she hoped that the awkwardness would pass. She had got over the first shock and was too busy watching over her father to worry much about herself and her feelings.

Then, on Wednesday morning, came the first rumblings of trouble. A letter arrived from the secretary of the Youth Club saying that "in all the circumstances" it might perhaps be better if they asked someone else to preside at the annual meeting due to take place in a week or two. Edward read it through unemotionally and then passed it to Trudie without comment.

"Well, it's their loss," she said after a pause, her lips quivering a little.

Edward broke a piece of toast. "I'm afraid we must be prepared for more like that. . . . Ah, well, it'll give me extra time for writing." He sat pondering for a while. Then he went to the bureau and sent off a brief note to the chairman of the local Bench saying that he would not be available for his rota on the following Wednesday and that he was considering his position. Proud defiance was all very well, but there was no point in inviting humiliation. Besides, it would be rather unkind to Smedley, the chairman, who was a good fellow and would hate to have to take the first step.

The evening post brought two more letters, one rather terse and official, one apologetic and circumlocutory. The gist of both was the same. It had been decided after all not to press Edward to open the new Recreation Ground extension; it had been decided that it would be better if this year he did not serve on the Hospital Fete committee. Edward replied in each case that he quite understood, but as he wrote his face wore a look of sadness. The fact that he'd foreseen these things didn't make the reality any less painful. Life seemed to be shutting him out; he wondered, in a passing moment of weakness, whether there would be anything left soon to make it worth while at all.

On the following morning a much worse blow fell. He received an anonymous letter—an illiterate scrawl, packed with venom. Its contents indicated that gossip, far from dying down, was assuming new and more horrible forms. This time he kept the letter from Trudie, but he couldn't insulate her from the talk. About eleven she returned white-faced from her shopping expedition, primed by Mrs. Burden.

"Daddie!" she exclaimed, flopping into a chair, "we'll simply have to do something—they're saying terrible things about you. They're . . . they're . . ."—she could hardly get it out—"they're saying the girl's clothes were torn—it's all over the village. How *can* they be so beastly?" And once again she burst into tears.

Edward put an arm around her shoulders with tender solicitude. "I knew what they were saying—I got an unsigned letter this morning putting it all very plainly. Trudie, my dear, I'm sorry. It isn't right that you should have to suffer like this on my account."

"It's not your fault," she sobbed. "It's those horrible people and their beastly minds. Oh, I *hate* this place."

"It's probably only one or two who are really responsible," said Edward. "The trouble is that as long as we do nothing and say nothing, the rumors are bound to flourish. People are taking silence as a confession of guilt—quite naturally."

"Then we *must* do something. It's wicked that they should be allowed to say such things."

Edward sighed. "There's only one way to stop them, and that's to bring it all out into the open. I imagine the police could very soon find out who wrote that letter, but then we'd be involved in a prosecution and that's what Quentin won't hear of."

"But when he knows about this . . ."

"It doesn't alter the problem, Trudie—we're exactly where we were when we all discussed the matter last Saturday. Now I've got a suggestion to make. Suppose you go away for a little while—I'm sure your Aunt Muriel would be delighted to have you."

She raised a shocked face. "What, and leave you alone? Daddie, how can you?"

"I'll be all right, you know I will. I've often looked after myself. I simply can't have you facing this sort of thing day after day. Quite truthfully, I should be much happier if you were away from it all."

Trudie's tears flowed again. "You're such an old silly. You know I wouldn't dream of it—if you can stick it, I can. It's only that I hate to hear such awful things about *you*. . . . Daddie, I just can't bear it."

Edward's hands clenched. His hope that he might be able to ride the storm was beginning to fade. "Well, don't cry, Trudie —I'll have to try and think of something."

"Couldn't we *both* go away? That's what Quentin thought we'd have to do and it does seem the only way."

"What, and leave the gossips in possession? My dear, I can't slink off like a criminal."

"I know that's how you feel, and I do admire you for it, but if you can't speak out you're not really doing any good by staying. You're only thinking and thinking, and getting more and more unhappy."

"I'm all right," said Edward in a flat voice.

"You're not, Daddie, and it's no use pretending you are. You look so tired and you've hardly eaten anything since yesterday morning and you're terribly on edge. I thought at first it was going to be all right, but since those letters began to come you've been quite different. If you go on like this you'll be really ill. You need a change—something to take your mind off it all. Couldn't we go just for a little while, perhaps . . . ?"

"If we run away, we run away. The result will be the same whether we go for a month or for good."

"Then I honestly think we ought to go for good—we'll only be torturing ourselves by staying. Would it cost a lot of money to move . . . ?"

"It would, but that's not really the problem. We could borrow on this house—it's worth much more than when I bought it and the garden's an attraction. . . ." He broke off, gazing down over the trees he had planted, the grass he had tended, the little summer house he had built in the wood, the bank where the primroses flourished. Half a lifetime of labor and love had gone into those few acres.

"There are other gardens, darling," said Trudie, following the direction of his gaze. "I know it'll be a terrible wrench for you, but—well, you can't pretend you're enjoying it much now, can you? And anyway, there's no need to make a final decision at this moment. Why couldn't we travel a little—just for a few weeks? You know you've always promised yourself you would, one day. And by the time we came back—well, everything might have blown over. Or if not I'm sure we could find a pretty place somewhere else. . . ."

Edward got up. "I'll think about it, Trudie. I can't promise more than that. I'm a bit old for tearing up all my roots."

He went into the little room he used as a study and dropped into his worn leather armchair with feelings near to despair. Perhaps it was because he was so tired, but the philosophical calm which had sustained him throughout his life seemed to have deserted him. He was horrified at the way *anger*, an emotion that was almost foreign to him in his personal relations, kept on rising in his mind. For the girl who had brought all this upon him he felt something near to hatred. It was as though the evil she had done him were corroding his own gentle nature.

He thrust her from his thoughts and made an effort to face his problem squarely. His position was worse, far worse, than even he had imagined it. Common sense, he knew, required that he should leave this place. The homely, affectionate common sense of Trudie, to whom he had a duty that outweighed any sentimental attachment to a bit of ground. The cold, logical common sense of Quentin, that made "sticking it out" look like a piece of quixotry. Anyway, Trudie was probably right—he wasn't doing any good to himself or anyone else by stubbornly staying on. It was just an obstinate pride that was keeping him there. Yet suppose he went—what would be achieved in his present state of mind? Relief for Trudie—that was all. He couldn't imagine himself settling down to work again with this bitterness gnawing at him, this sense of intolerable injustice. Would he ever know a moment's peace if he allowed himself to be ejected from his home and his interests without a syllable of protest? That was really what he couldn't stomach—the ignominy of flight. What a way to end his days!

He got up restlessly and his steps turned automatically to the garden. The hay in the orchard needed forking over but he hadn't the heart to do anything about it just now. He sat down on the bank and looked out over the Broadwater. He would miss that view. He would miss the river too, and in more than a sentimental way, if he left the district, for it was one of the main sources of his livelihood. What would he do about that?

Suddenly there was a stir in the shrubbery, and the pink-and-white face of Carol Anne peeped through. "Hello, Mr. Latimer."

"Hello, Carol Anne," he said with an attempt at a smile. "Why, I haven't seen you for a long while."

She looked at him rather wistfully. "I can't play with you."

"Never mind, dear—I don't much feel like playing myself."

"Mummy says I mustn't play with you."

Edward winced as though he had been struck. At that moment a voice from the neighboring house called "Carol Anne!" It was her Nanny. "Carol Anne, come here at once!" The little girl scampered off. As she emerged from the bushes Edward heard the voice again, sharp and scolding. "You're a naughty, disobedient girl—you know Mummy told you not to go down there." There was the sound of a smack, followed by a howl.

Edward stood listening for a moment, a lonely, drooping figure, and then he turned and walked uncertainly back to the house. Trudie, watchful at the open window, caught sight of his strained face and hurried out to meet him. "What is it, Daddie? What's happened?"

He groaned. "I'm a pariah, Trudie. Even the children have to be protected from me."

"Oh, *no!* You can't mean . . . ?"

"It's hardly believable, is it? But it's true. In the eyes of this community I'm a nasty old man who can't be trusted. Oh, *God,* to think that that woman has been responsible for all this!" His face was harder than she had ever seen it.

"Well, that settles it," she said fiercely. "We *will* go away. Daddy, even you must see now . . ."

"All right, Trudie. . . ." He sounded too weary to argue any more. "We'll go—we'll go and we'll never come back. It's no use—my hands are tied. I think I'll ring up Quentin right away and tell him."

That evening they talked a little about plans. Trudie still thought it would be a good idea to take a holiday before they did anything else and suggested a place in Sweden where an old school friend of hers had had a delightful fortnight the previous year. She was plainly excited at the thought of getting away and Edward tried hard to respond to her mood. He made a suggestion or two but tiredness prevented his giving the matter serious thought and at about ten he went off to bed.

When Trudie, a late riser, came down next morning she was surprised to find that Edward had already had his breakfast and was pouring coffee into a vacuum flask preparatory to going out. He had lost his brooding look and seemed in much better spirits. "I thought of having a day on the saltings," he said. "You don't mind, do you?"

"Why, of course not, Daddie, if you feel up to it." She gave him an anxious inspection. "It's going to be terrifically hot again—you're sure it won't tire you too much?"

"It'll do me good," he said with confidence.

"All right, darling, but don't be too late back or I shall worry about you. I ought to go into Ramsford myself, as a matter of fact, but I'll be back for tea."

She saw him off in the car and then went about her own affairs with a lighter heart. She felt sure now that everything was going to work out all right. She caught a bus into the local town, collected a bunch of travel folders, lunched off coffee and cakes, did a little shopping, and returned in the afternoon feeling quite limp from the heat.

It was nearly five when Edward got back, and one glance at him told Trudie that she ought not to have let him go. He was obviously ill. He looked pale and dazed and complained of a raging headache, which wasn't surprising since he had lost his hat. He was so incoherent about his day's outing that Trudie feared he was on the verge of a total breakdown. She helped him into bed and sent for the doctor.

Dr. Scott, a youngish man who had attended Edward the previous summer, arrived promptly. When he had joined Trudie downstairs after a brief examination of the patient, he was reassuring.

"You needn't worry," he said, "there's nothing serious the matter with him. A touch of the old trouble—he shouldn't have been bareheaded in the sun, of course. But what he's really suffering from, I'm afraid, is reaction and nervous exhaustion."

Trudie nodded. "We were thinking of taking a holiday. Would that be a good idea?"

"Best thing you can do, provided it's not too strenuous. But first he needs a complete rest. Keep him in bed for a few days—" Scott grinned—"if you can!" He still remembered Edward as one of the less amenable of his patients.

Trudie rang up Hugh and told him it would be better if he and Cynthia postponed the weekend visit they'd planned, and she also told Quentin what had happened. Then she turned herself into a sick nurse. For two days Edward's headaches persisted, with a slight temperature. He seemed unable to get any satisfying sleep, in spite of the sedative the doctor had prescribed. Trudie could hear him talking and muttering as he lay dozing upstairs. It was about the girl, Helen Fairlie, that he mostly talked, and in a way that Trudie would have thought impossible for him.

By Sunday, however, he was much better and insisted on getting up in spite of Trudie's protests. In the afternoon Quentin came over to see him.

Trudie intercepted her brother in the drive and gave him a situation report. "He's all right now," she confided, "but I was really worried to start with—he looked absolutely ghastly. He's had a terrible week, Quentin—you can't imagine what it's been like. Thank goodness we're going, that's all."

Quentin nodded gravely. "It was the only solution all along, but he wasn't in the mood to listen. He had to find it out for himself, poor old boy. Anyway, I've got a bit of news—let's go in and see the invalid."

Edward was in the sitting room, and he wasn't behaving much like an invalid. He looked quite fit again and was busily sorting his papers, with a litter of files and folders all round him.

"Hello, Father," said Quentin, dropping his hand lightly on Edward's shoulder in greeting. "Well, I must say you don't look so bad. What's all this—getting ready for the move so soon?"

"As a matter of fact," said Edward, "I was thinking that after Trudie and I have had our holiday and settled down somewhere I might be able to get on with the book at last."

"The book? Oh—'Wild Life in the Essex Marshes.' Yes, why not?—you must have a tremendous amount of material. By the way, Father, I've heard of a house."

"Oh?"

"It's on the outskirts of Woodbridge, in Suffolk. It's about the same size as this one, with a very pretty garden, and it'll be vacant in about a month. It belongs to a client of mine."

"Woodbridge? Why, that's on a river, isn't it?"

"Yes, the Deben. It's not exactly the sort of country you're used to but I'm told it's quite unspoilt and you'll certainly be able to go on with your nature notes. It's reasonably accessible to town by rail, and . . ." He broke off, hesitating.

Edward smiled. "And not too near Steepleford?"

"Well, that is a point, isn't it? Anyway, it sounds most attractive and I think it might be just the thing."

"What about the price?"

"That's going to be about right, too. When you've sold this cottage I should say you might even be a little bit in pocket. Woodbridge is a lively little town, and very charming—Hugh and Cynthia will love going down there. If you like, we can run over there next weekend, or you can take Trudie up alone. Cheer up, Father, everything's going to be all right."

At that moment a car drew up on the grass verge opposite the house and two men walked up the drive.

6

QUENTIN went to the door.

"Good afternoon, sir," said the shorter of the two, a man of about fifty with graying hair and deep wrinkles round his eyes. "Can you tell me if Mr. Edward Latimer is at home?"

"He is, yes." Quentin looked sharply at the two men, but their faces were impassive.

"I'm Inspector Holt, of the county C.I.D. Would it be convenient for me to have a word with him?"

"He's not too well, I'm afraid," said Quentin, frowning. "What's the trouble, Inspector?—not that train business, surely? I thought that was all settled."

"No, sir, it's not exactly that." Holt was evidently quite familiar with the train business. "Something arising out of it. I'll try to be as brief as possible."

"Oh, very well." Quentin held the door open grudgingly. "Come in, won't you?" He led the way into the sitting room. The inspector followed him, carrying a little bag, and the sergeant brought up the rear.

Edward gave an exclamation of surprise when he saw who his visitors were. "Why, hello, Inspector!—what brings you here?" A quick flush rose to his cheekbones. "Not official business, is it? I'm not really functioning, you know."

"I understand, sir." Holt gave an embarrassed little cough. "Very unpleasant affair—I was most sorry to hear about it. Er —this is Sergeant Farrow."

Edward nodded. "I think we've met in court, Sergeant. Won't you both sit down?"

They sat, looking a trifle uncomfortable. Then Holt said: "Sorry to butt in like this on a Sunday afternoon, Mr. Latimer,

57

but I'm afraid I had no option. It's to do with the young woman who was in the train with you that day."

"Oh, yes?" said Edward, with lively interest.

"She's been murdered."

There was a moment of absolute stillness in the room. Then there came a gasp of horror from Trudie, an incredulous "Good God!" from Quentin.

Edward stared at the inspector. "What happened?"

"She was strangled, sir."

"Where?"

"Not so very far from here. You know Cowfleet village, up the river? Well, about two miles from the village there's an old hulk of a barge lying in the saltings beside a small creek. The girl was found about a hundred yards farther along. There was a yacht race up the river yesterday, and one of the chaps happened to notice the body."

"I see," said Edward slowly. "Have you—have you any idea when she was killed?"

"Two or three days ago, they tell me."

"Do the police know who was responsible?"

"No, sir, not so far."

Edward sank back into his chair with a frown. "What an extraordinary thing!"

"Why exactly have you come to tell *us* this, Inspector?" asked Quentin.

Holt looked still more uncomfortable. In his thirty-odd years in the Force he had been called upon to handle only two murder cases and both of them had been straightforward. Neither had involved questioning a Justice of the Peace whom he had known and respected for a long time. He gave another little cough.

"The fact is, Mr. Latimer," he said, addressing Edward, "we found something in the girl's handbag which rather puzzled us and we thought we'd better ask you about it." He felt for his wallet and produced a piece of paper roughly torn across. Edward took it, and Quentin looked at it over his shoulder. It was the top third of a sheet of Edward's own notepaper, with the address and telephone number embossed. In the upper left-hand corner there was a crudely penciled sketch map of the Cowfleet district with a number of places blocked in in capitals. All the text of the letter had been removed by the diagonal tear except the three words "Dear Miss Fairlie"—in Edward's hand.

"Father—you wrote to her!" Quentin sounded outraged. "And you never told me!"

It was Edward's turn to look ill at ease. "I'd already sent it off, Quentin, when we had that discussion about whether I should get in touch with her, and as you were so emphatically against the idea there didn't seem to be much point in telling you that I'd written to her that day. You'd obviously have disapproved and I couldn't get the letter back."

Quentin made a clicking noise with his tongue. "What did you write about, for Heaven's sake?"

"I told her that my life would be ruined if she persisted in her accusations against me and I appealed to her to tell the truth. That's all."

"*When* do you say you wrote the letter, Mr. Latimer?" asked Holt, fingering the paper. "As you see, the date has been torn off."

"It was a week ago yesterday, Inspector. I caught the after-noon post."

"Did you write to her just once, or more than once?"

"Only once. This is the letter—the remains of it."

"What was the point of the sketch map, sir?"

"I know nothing at all about that—I didn't draw it." Edward had suddenly become very tense. "I suppose you're thinking that this is part of a letter in which I arranged to meet Miss Fairlie, and that I drew the map to show her the way?"

"Father!" Quentin cried. "What on earth are you saying?"

Edward put a restraining hand on his arm. "Quentin, you don't know how deeply involved I am in this. . . . The fact is, Inspector, the boot's on the other foot. I *was* going to meet

Miss Fairlie last week, but it was she who suggested the place and I suppose she drew this sketch map for herself on my old letter."

Quentin stared at his father in consternation. "You were going to meet her . . . !"

"I *went* to meet her," said Edward.

There was an iron silence. Then Holt said slowly: "I very much want to get at the truth of this matter, Mr. Latimer, but in view of what you say I'm not sure I oughtn't to tell you that you're not obliged . . ."

"That's all right, Inspector, I know the rules. I've nothing whatever to hide."

"Father, listen to me!" Quentin's tone was urgent. "Don't say anything more now—please! Be guided by me."

"It's no good, Quentin—it's my duty to tell the inspector everything I know, and I intend to do so. I've been gagged too long. You must let me be the judge from now on." Edward turned to Holt, pale but resolute. "This is what happened, Inspector. Last Friday morning I received a letter from Helen Fairlie. It said that she wanted to see me alone about a very important matter, and that the only day she could manage was that very day. She named the hour and the place. It was to be at two o'clock in the afternoon, and we were to meet at a deserted spot on the river above Cowfleet. She drew a sketch map for me on *her* letter—very similar, as a matter of fact, to the one you have there. The meeting place was to be beside that old barge you mentioned, underneath the sea wall."

Once again the room seemed very still. Holt failed to meet Edward's steady gaze. "Rather a strange place for her to choose, wasn't it, sir?"

"That's what I thought, but she obviously knew the district well."

"*Why* didn't you tell me?" said Quentin. "You ought never to have gone."

"There wasn't time to discuss it, Quentin—I had to make a quick decision. In any case I knew you'd only try to dissuade me, and I wanted to go. I *had* to go. She said in her letter that I'd be glad to hear what she had to tell me, and I thought— I hoped—that her conscience was troubling her and that she was going to confess everything. I thought I should be much more likely to hear the truth if I met her alone." He looked appealingly at Quentin. "I expect you think it was naïve of me, but it seemed my only chance."

Holt broke in before Quentin could speak. "May I see the letter, Mr. Latimer?"

"Of course—I'll get it for you." Edward rose and left the room. Quentin walked to the window and stood staring out across the garden. Trudie sat huddled in her chair, wide-eyed and frightened.

Edward was back in a few minutes, but without the letter. "That's strange," he said, "it should have been in my alpaca jacket. You didn't take it out, Trudie, did you?"

"No, Daddie, I haven't seen it. I didn't even know you'd had a letter."

Holt's lips tightened. "Didn't you say anything to your daughter, Mr. Latimer, about this meeting?"

"No—no, as a matter of fact I didn't. You see . . ."

Quentin swung round decisively, all his professional instincts in revolt. "Father, this can't go on—it's all *wrong*. For God's sake, think what you're doing. Inspector, my father's ill —he's been ill for a long time. I don't think he's fit to be questioned just now."

"I'm perfectly fit," Edward insisted. "I know all this seems very unorthodox to you, Quentin, but I'm simply not interested in anything but the truth. If only I could lay my hands on that letter . . . !"

"Would the postman be likely to remember bringing it?" asked Holt bluntly.

Edward flushed. "I hardly think so, Inspector—there were five or six letters that morning. But I can assure you it came."

"Well, we've obviously got to find it," said Quentin. "When did you last see it, Father?"

Edward's brows drew together in an effort to concentrate. "Let me see—I know I had it with me on Friday because I remember taking it out of the envelope on the sea wall to look at the sketch map. I don't think I've seen it since. . . . I suppose I might have dropped it somewhere."

"Trudie," said Quentin, "go upstairs and search everywhere. Look in all Father's clothes."

"Perhaps," Holt murmured, with an inquiring glance at Edward, "Sergeant Farrow could go too, Mr. Latimer? You wouldn't have any objection if he took a look round the place, would you?"

Quentin seemed about to protest again, but Edward waved his hand. "If you think it will help you, Inspector, the place is at your disposal."

"Well, now," said Holt more briskly, as Trudie left with the sergeant, "perhaps you'd care to tell me, sir, exactly what happened that afternoon?"

"I'll tell you all I can," said Edward. "I took the car and drove to Cowfleet village. I left it there and walked across the marshes to the sea wall and along the top of the wall toward the head of the river. After about twenty minutes I spotted the barge. It was just two o'clock when I got there, but there was no sign of the girl. In fact, there wasn't a soul in sight—in that country, you know, you can see for miles. I stood there for a moment beside the barge, feeling very disappointed, and then . . ." He hesitated, and as though in recollection his hand went to his head.

"Yes?" Holt prompted.

"It was at that moment that I suddenly became ill, Inspector. I don't know what caused it but I suppose it must have been the heat—that's what Dr. Scott thinks, anyhow. It's happened before, once or twice. I had a kind of blackout. I must have fallen, because the next thing I knew I was on the ground. I felt quite dazed and I had a splitting headache. I—I looked around for my hat, but it wasn't there—I think it must have got into the river, somehow, and been carried away on the tide. After that, I—well, I just came home."

Holt's manner had hardened during this recital. "You mean you didn't see Miss Fairlie at all?" he said in a detached, official voice.

"Not a sign of her."

"When you got back, sir, did you try to get in touch with her, to find out why she hadn't turned up?"

Quentin broke in angrily. "Really, Inspector, this examination is quite out of order—Father, the whole thing's preposterous. Why won't you listen to me?"

Edward brushed the interruption aside with a weary gesture. "No, Inspector, I didn't do anything—I was much too ill. I've been confined to bed—I only got up this morning. I was intending to ring her up tomorrow if I didn't hear from her."

"I see." Holt ignored Quentin's glowering looks—he had made too much progress to be put off now. "Mr. Latimer, how long did this—this blackout—last?"

"I can't tell you exactly, Inspector. Five or ten minutes, perhaps."

"And you've no recollection at all of anything happening during those five or ten minutes?"

"None whatever."

"You've no recollection of going *beyond* the barge?"

"None. And I'm quite sure I didn't. If I had I shouldn't have come round where I'd fallen, should I?"

Holt made no answer to that. Instead, he stepped across to his bag and opened it. From its capacious depths he drew a straw-colored object, mud-stained and battered.

"Would this be the hat you lost, Mr. Latimer?"

Edward took it and straightened it out. "Why, yes," he said, "this is my hat. Where did you find it?"

"We found it in a rill about twenty feet from the body," said Holt.

Edward stared at him, aghast. Slowly a look of doubt, of desperate anxiety, began to creep over his face. "Oh, gracious

63

heavens!" he murmured. He turned to Quentin as though seeking reassurance, and saw only a reflection of his own fears. "It—surely it must have blown there, Inspector?"

"Was it a windy day, sir?"

Edward shook his head. "It was very hot," he said, "and very still. Oh, if I could only *remember!*" He pressed his hands to his temples. "Inspector, I swear I've told you the whole truth as I remember it. Every word I've said is true and there's nothing I can add. To the very best of my knowledge and belief, I had no contact with Miss Fairlie that day."

The door opened and Trudie came in, with the sergeant close behind her.

"Did you find it?" asked Quentin sharply.

"No," she said, "I've looked everywhere. I suppose there's just a chance it might be in here, but I think I'd have seen it." She went across to the bureau and began to rummage.

Sergeant Farrow approached the inspector. He was holding what looked like a crumpled handkerchief. "I found this in the used-linen basket," he said in a confidential undertone.

Holt took the handkerchief and opened it out. It was a large white square—a man's handkerchief. Across it was a scarlet smear.

"Is this yours, Mr. Latimer?"

"Yes, I think so," said Edward faintly. He sounded very near to breaking point.

"Miss Latimer," said Holt, "have you by any chance been using one of your father's handkerchiefs?"

She gave an almost imperceptible headshake, her eyes on the scarlet smear.

"Do you use lipstick of this color?"

"I don't use it at all," said Trudie.

"Has anyone who might use lipstick visited the house since the basket was last emptied?"

Trudie looked at Quentin and hesitated. It was Edward who said, "No one, Inspector."

Holt put the handkerchief in his bag, with the hat. Then he

turned to Edward, his face grave. "I'm very sorry, Mr. Latimer, but I'm afraid I shall have to ask you to come along to the station with me."

"Yes—yes, of course." Edward got up unsteadily. "I understand. I'm ready, Inspector."

Trudie flew to him. "Oh, Daddie, don't look so awful. What is it? What's been happening?"

Quentin said: "For God's sake, Trudie, let's not have a scene. Go and put a few things in a case for Father." He laid a gentle hand on Edward's shoulder. "Don't worry, Father, you'll be all right. I'll get on to Dr. Scott."

7 AT RAMSFORD police station three hours later, after making and signing a long statement incorporating all he had told Inspector Holt, Edward was formally charged with the murder of Helen Fairlie. Quentin stayed to have a few words with Dr. Scott and Colonel Ainslie, who had both come straight down to the station on hearing what had happened. Then, heavy with responsibility, he hurried back to Lavender Cottage and broke the news to Trudie. He had feared that his return might touch off an explosion of hysteria but in the face of real calamity his sister had pulled herself together and already she seemed to have prepared herself for the worst. She sat dry-eyed and tense while he ran through the sequence of events which had ended in the inevitable arrest.

"It's a terrible thing to have to say, Trudie," he finished solemnly, "but I'm afraid we've got to accept the fact that Father is, or has been, completely out of his mind and that at a time when he wasn't responsible for his actions he did kill this poor girl."

"I suppose you're right," Trudie said after a long pause. "I'm still trying to make myself believe it—it's all happened with such frightful suddenness. . . . Oh, Quentin, *why* did I let him go out that day?"

"You can't possibly blame yourself for that," said Quentin. "If anyone's to blame in this affair, I am—I ought to have insisted on calling in a specialist immediately after the train incident, and I would have done so if I hadn't been disarmed by that partial retraction of the girl's. We had a clear warning, and it was inexcusable slackness on my part to disregard it."

"Oh, I don't know," said Trudie. "It isn't as though there'd been anything else to go on—except for that one incident and the headaches he's seemed perfectly all right. How was he at the police station, Quentin?—what did he say?"

"He didn't say much at all, apart from going over his story again. He was quite calm—too calm, I suppose, to be healthy. He seemed more bewildered than anything, poor old boy. He kept looking at his hands as though they were strangers to him."

"Oh, Quentin!"

"I think everybody felt sorry for him. It must be pretty grim to know you've done something horrible and not be able to remember a single thing about it. He made a terrific mental effort to fill the gap, it was painful to watch, but there's no doubt that those few minutes are a complete blank and in the end he had to give it up. He realizes now that he's got to let others sort it all out. 'Whatever you say I'll fall in with,' is his attitude. He does appreciate at last, I think, that he's very ill."

"What are they doing about him?"

"Well, tonight he's being kept at Ramsford under observation. Tomorrow he'll come up before the magistrates and be remanded to prison and then they'll give him a thorough examination."

"Is there anything we can do for him?"

"Not at the moment—he's got everything he needs. Just before they took him away he gave me a wry sort of smile and said, 'There's one thing about having been a prison visitor, I do know the ropes.'"

"Oh, poor darling! Quentin, what will happen to him in the end?"

"I expect he'll be sent to Broadmoor. I wouldn't worry about that now, though, Trudie—one thing at a time!"

"Isn't that a criminal lunatic asylum?"

"That's what they used to call it, but it's actually much more like a good mental hospital. They don't necessarily keep people there indefinitely—once they've diagnosed Father's trouble they may be able to do something for him. We mustn't lose hope." He got up with a sigh. "I suppose I'd better ring Hugh."

He was on the telephone for nearly half an hour. When at last he hung up he looked pale and shaken, and he accepted gratefully the cup of tea that Trudie had made.

"I'm afraid that's just about knocked Hugh flat," he said miserably.

"When will you see him?"

"As soon as I can get away tomorrow. There'll be a lot to do—I think we'd better try to get some sleep now. I'm going to take a couple of Father's tablets and I'd advise you to do the same. Good night, Trudie." He kissed his sister with unaccustomed tenderness and went up to bed.

Edward's appearance in court on the following morning lasted only a few minutes and immediately afterward Quentin drove to Chelsea. Hugh looked as though he were just coming out of the world's worst hangover, and it was plain he hadn't slept a wink.

"Quent," he said, gripping his brother's hand and searching his face, "this is the most unbelievably ghastly thing I ever heard. I feel as though I'm living through a bad dream."

"I know," said Quentin. "It's the sort of thing that only happens to other people, isn't it? It's going to take some getting used to."

"It's incredible. How do you explain it, Quent? What do you think happened?"

"Well," said Quentin, sitting down, "I'm afraid that's only too clear. The view I took at the time of the train incident was obviously sound. Father's been ill for some time without our realizing it, and the trouble came to a head with his assault on the girl. There can be no question now that he did attack her. But he had no recollection of the incident, so he wrote off and asked her to meet him in the hope that he could get her to change her story."

"But why did she agree?"

"Because she was sorry for him, I suppose. I'm afraid we've misjudged her badly. Meanwhile he was going through his own private hell in the village and the thing was preying on his mind. He felt persecuted and he blamed the girl—very bitterly, Trudie says. I don't suppose for a moment he had any intention of harming her when he suggested the meeting, but seeing her again after all he'd gone through must have been too much for him. Or perhaps the interview didn't go the way he'd hoped, and that provoked him. At any rate, he had a brainstorm or whatever you like to call it, and he throttled her without knowing what he was doing. That's my reconstruction, anyway."

"But you said something about him coming round in the same place where he blacked out, and nowhere near the girl."

"That's what he says, and he may have done, but it makes no difference. There's a gap from the time he got to the barge until the moment he came round there. In between, anything could have happened—he could have strolled off with the girl, killed her, and come back to the barge. He doesn't know what he did."

"Yes, I see. But Quent, *could* he have throttled her? I wouldn't have thought he had the strength."

"Apparently he has. His wrists are thin but they're sinewy—the result of all that gardening, I suppose. Besides, a man has more than his ordinary strength when he's in a manic frenzy. . . ."

"A manic frenzy . . . ?" Hugh seemed to savor the phrase. "You know, Quent, to me this whole thing has an air of complete unreality. I'd as soon believe that an infant-in-arms could slug its mother. A manic frenzy! What, *Dad?*"

"It's no good thinking of him as we know him, Hugh—surely you can see that? Insanity can change people out of all recognition."

"But Dad never showed any signs . . ."

"Not to us, but that's probably because we didn't know what to look for. If he'd been examined by an expert . . ."

"*Why* should he become insane—suddenly, shockingly, without warning? All from a touch of the sun? I don't believe it."

"Well, there must have been a cause. I've been wondering if that bomb in 1941 could have been the start of it all."

"He wasn't hurt," said Hugh, "only a bit shaken."

"I know, but he was fearfully upset by the horror of it—don't you remember, all those kids? He didn't smile for weeks afterward. I should think the impact of an experience like that on a sensitive mind could easily cause trouble."

"That's ten years ago—it's taken a hell of a long while to develop."

"These things do take time. Or again, there may be a constitutional weakness. After all, Aunt Harriet died in a mental home."

"That doesn't mean a thing—something of the kind happens in almost every family. And she certainly wasn't insane—she was just a nuisance."

"Still, let's face it—the tendency is there. I suppose I can consider myself fairly well balanced, but Trudie's unusually excitable and Father's whole life has been decidedly abnormal."

"I wouldn't say that. It's been eccentric, that's all."

"Very well, eccentric. But who's to say just where the borderline comes between eccentricity and real psychosis?"

Hugh gave an exclamation of impatience. "*I* certainly wouldn't attempt to. And if you want my frank opinion, Quent, I don't believe *you* know what you're talking about, either. Psychosis! These things don't happen out of the blue. The fact is that until a week ago Dad had never done a single thing that even remotely suggested he might suddenly break out into maniacal lunacy—and I must say I find it a bit grim sitting here trying to organize proof of his insanity."

"You'll find it a lot grimmer if we can't," said Quentin.

Hugh stared at him for a moment; then subsided into his chair. "Oh, God, yes, I suppose so. What a choice! Honestly, though, Quent, do you think it'll be possible to convince a jury that he's mad?"

"I haven't a doubt of it. For a man with a record like Father's, that assault in the train was a crazy action if ever anything was, and what has happened since is conclusive. No one is going to believe that a man of his character would suddenly lose every trace of moral sense if he were in his right mind. Besides, all the evidence shows that he wasn't—the dazed condition in which he came back that day, his illness, his obvious failure to realize what was hanging over him. A *sane* man would have been appalled by his danger."

"I see that," said Hugh, "but not everything fits so well. Some of his actions seem crazy, but others don't. You say he probably had no intention of harming the girl when he first wrote to her, but in that case why make the assignation in such a fantastically lonely place as the saltings? I know he wanted to keep the meeting a secret from us, but he didn't have to go to those extremes. A sudden brainstorm on seeing the girl is one thing, but getting her to a convenient spot for a brainstorm is quite another. There's a feeling of—well, skillful planning, in a way."

It was Quentin who stared now. "Great heavens, Hugh, you're not suggesting he was *responsible* for what he did?"

Hugh had a trapped look. "All I'm saying, Quent, is that to me the insanity theory doesn't seem watertight. Take this story of his about getting a letter from the girl, for instance— putting the responsibility for the appointment on her. If it weren't Dad who was concerned, wouldn't that strike you as a rather rational piece of invention by someone who was anxious to show there'd been no premeditation?"

"A man can be insane," said Quentin, "and still plan carefully and excuse himself skillfully."

"*And* have a sudden brainstorm?"

"I don't know that the two things are incompatible. Anyway, was there so very much skill after all? Look at the way Father left his hat lying there! It was an incredible piece of carelessness—not much planning about that! In fact it was just what you'd expect from a man who simply didn't know what he was doing. Look at the lipstick! The police say the girl's mouth was smeared during the struggle, presumably by Father's hands, and they assume he wiped them on his handkerchief afterward and then forgot all about it. No one in possession of his senses would be as casual as that after he'd committed a murder, but a man coming out of a frenzy might well not give it a thought. . . . Still, the fact is, Hugh, we're both hopelessly out of our depth—let's leave it to the psychiatrists. They'll probably have a complete explanation of the whole thing."

Hugh still looked skeptical but there was clearly no point in pursuing the subject. "What's the drill, then?"

"I suggest I ring up Arthur Howeson and ask him if he can go down and examine Father. He's supposed to be a first-class man, and he has a way of making juries understand what he's talking about. Of course, the prison authorities will do a routine check themselves, but we must obviously have our own man, too."

"All right, Quent. How about the defense—are you going to handle that?"

"No, I don't feel competent—I'm more at home with wills and conveyances. There's a man I know named Braddock who'd probably act for us—he's an experienced criminal lawyer and he's also a good friend of mine, so he won't mind my butting in and making suggestions."

Hugh nodded. "Okay—that's your pigeon."

He lit a cigarette and smoked in brooding silence while Quentin got on the telephone and, after explaining the urgency, succeeded in making an appointment to see Howeson at three that afternoon.

"Right," said Quentin, glancing at his watch. "I think I may just catch Braddock before lunch. I'll bring you news about four—you'll be here, will you?"

"I'll be here. I've arranged to take a few days off, so let me know if there's anything I can do. So long, Quent." Hugh turned moodily back into the room and picked up the morning paper. The story of Edward's arrest was prominently headlined on the front page, with some biographical detail and a photograph that must have been taken at least twenty years before. As Hugh gazed at it, a look of anguish crossed his face.

Presently he flung the paper down and went out to meet Cynthia for lunch. It was a melancholy meal. Both of them had had their say on the telephone early that morning and there was little to add. The tragedy was still too fresh in their minds for either calm discussion or easy avoidance. They parted with a hand squeeze, Cynthia to the House and Hugh back to the flat.

It was nearly five when Quentin returned. He seemed a little brighter. "Well, it's all fixed," he said. "I've been over the case with Braddock and he's going to act for us."

"What does he think about it?"

"He seems fairly satisfied. He doesn't like insanity defenses but he agrees that there shouldn't be much difficulty in this case. He was all in favor of getting Howeson to examine Father right away."

"Have you fixed that too?"

"Yes, it's all settled. Howeson seemed very interested—he put off a couple of appointments for tomorrow and he's going down first thing. He's made all arrangements with the prison authorities and he's going to see Dr. Scott on the way down. He's young, but he has a quiet assurance which I rather liked. I feel he's a man on whose judgment we can rely."

"Good. What did he say?"

"Very little, as a matter of fact. He asked me a few questions—family history, that sort of thing. I told him about Aunt Harriet and I mentioned the bomb. He didn't comment at all —just made a few notes. I briefed him as fully as I could—told him about the headaches and blackouts last summer. I think he's got a pretty complete picture. He was very intrigued about the train affair. . . . Anyhow, I've arranged to see him again at nine o'clock tomorrow night and hear his preliminary report, I'll come straight here afterward."

"Right. I say, Quent, this is going to cost a packet of money, isn't it? I'm afraid I've only got about fifty quid—you're welcome to that."

"I can raise something," said Quentin, "but not nearly enough. We'll need a Queen's Counsel—the best we can get. I'll have to talk to Father again about selling the house."

"I suppose that is the only way. Anyhow, it doesn't look as though he's going to need it now, poor old boy. What are the chances of seeing him?—will they let me go down?"

"I expect so—better wait a day or two, though, until we've got the defense under way."

"I tried to write to him this morning. Damned difficult to know what to say . . . ! What's happening about Trudie?"

"I'm moving my things over to Lavender Cottage for the time being—she obviously can't be left alone there, and she doesn't want to go away. She's bearing up well. By the way, I meant to ask you—how's Cynthia taken it?"

"She's pretty shattered, but she's rallying round. She doesn't believe it, you know."

"Doesn't believe what?"

"Doesn't believe anything. She says Dad couldn't have done it."

Quentin gave a rueful smile. "It's an odd thing how women have no respect for evidence."

8 By MUTUAL consent Hugh and Cynthia were making a determined effort to concentrate on a wireless program the following evening when, just before half past ten, a car drew up under the window. Hugh snapped off the radio with a sigh of relief. "That's sure to be Quent," he said, and went to let him in.

Quentin looked somehow diminished, Cynthia thought with a stab of apprehension, and his face was gray with fatigue. He dropped heavily into a chair after a perfunctory greeting. "Hugh," he said in a flat voice, "I'm afraid you've got to prepare yourself for a great shock."

They stared at him, bracing themselves for news of some fresh cataclysm.

"Howeson says that Father is absolutely sane and normal."

The anticlimax was so sharp that Hugh had an almost irresistible impulse to laugh out loud. It was on the tip of his tongue to say "How frightful!" but he controlled himself and said gravely, "What happened, Quent?"

"Well, Howeson went down to Essex this morning, as we'd arranged. He had a long talk with Scott and got all the background he needed about Father's physical health. Then he had a consultation with the two prison doctors—one of them's a psychiatrist, too, by the way—and afterward he examined Father alone. Apparently it's a very long and complicated business—I had no idea. They had two sessions, with all sorts of tests and masses of questions. I confess I didn't quite follow all the technical stuff, but there's no doubt that Howeson made a most probing and exhaustive examination. And that's his verdict—that far from there being any trace of insanity, there's

75

every indication of perfect mental health. He said that in different circumstances he would have hesitated to give a final opinion until he'd had Father under observation a little longer, but that in this case there was nothing to warrant delay. He said he'd rarely met a man who seemed so well-adjusted and—what was his phrase?—so well-integrated."

"That sounds pretty conclusive. Did the others agree with him?"

"Completely. They might have been speaking with one voice. Of course, I didn't let it go at that. I asked Howeson how he explained the blackouts. He said that as far as that trouble last summer was concerned they were probably just ordinary fainting fits brought on by overstrain and too much exposure to the sun, and that the headaches were a normal feature of mild sunstroke. He'd gone into all that very carefully with Scott, and they were both quite satisfied about it."

"What about the blackout on the saltings? Was that the same thing?"

"Well, Howeson was a bit cautious about that. You see, they only had Father's word for it that he *did* have a blackout there. Howeson was inclined to believe that he may have had some sort of attack, because of the after-effects that Scott described, but he maintains that whatever happened was purely physical and not the result of any abnormal mental condition. Incidentally he says that in any case he rather doubts whether a faint of that sort would have lasted anything like ten minutes. What he's absolutely sure about—what they're all sure about—is that there's nothing whatever in Father's record or present mental state to support the view that he could have strangled a woman without knowing the nature and quality of his action."

Hugh gave a brief nod and refrained from reminding his brother that he himself had never really doubted Edward's sanity. "Did Howeson make any comment on the case?" he asked.

"Not very much. He said that once he'd established the fact

76

that Father was mentally sound it was outside his professional province to speculate about what might have happened. He seemed a bit puzzled, though. He said that after talking to Father he'd carried away an ineffaceable impression of a man entirely at peace with his conscience—a man who honestly believed he was telling the truth. I told him that wasn't going to help us much in face of the evidence, and he had to agree. Still, it was nice of him to say it. . . ." Quentin gave a long sigh and stared down at his shoes. "Well, there we are, Hugh. You realize that the insanity defense is finished?"

"Yes, of course. So what happens now?"

"I wish to God I knew. Perhaps Braddock will have some ideas when I see him tomorrow. I'm afraid things look very black for us, Hugh—very black indeed. That's why I was so desperately anxious to establish the insanity defense—because the alternative was too terrible to contemplate. As things are, it's almost certain that Father will be convicted of willful murder."

There was a blank silence. Then Hugh said: "You know, Quent, I simply can't make my mind accept that possibility."

"On the evidence as we know it, you've got to."

"Then there must be something wrong with the evidence. Do *you* believe that Dad would kill anyone, in his right mind?"

"It isn't what I believe that will count—it's the facts. . . ."

"Oh, to hell with the facts! Insanity's one thing, Quent, but no evidence in the world is going to convince me that Dad was so consumed with hatred when he saw that woman that he *knowingly* took her by the throat and strangled her. It's just not possible. Think for a minute. Dad has never hurt a living soul. He's gentle, he's tolerant, he's easily the most civilized person either you or I have ever had anything to do with. To say he did this thing makes nonsense of his whole life, and I for one will never believe it. *Never*. Not this side of Kingdom Come."

Cynthia, who had been listening with the respectful silence

of a privileged observer, slid her hand over Hugh's and seemed to offer encouragement.

"Emotion's all very well, Hugh," said Quentin, stung by the implied reproach, "but Braddock and I between us have got to produce a defense. It's not enough to have faith in someone you and I know and believe in—we've got to convince twelve men and women who don't know Father. And look at the case we've got to answer—just *look* at it. First, there's motive—Father had the best of reasons for hating this girl, for he believed she had wrecked his life. Then there's opportunity—he admits having been in the neighborhood at the time and he says himself that nobody else was. He *says* he didn't go beyond the barge, but his hat was found beside the body. He *says* he didn't see the girl, but her lipstick was on his handkerchief. He *says* it was she who suggested the meeting, but he can't produce a shred of proof and what evidence there is points to the fact that he engineered it. He can't even give a satisfactory account of his own movements. Add to that the fact that he kept the meeting a secret from everyone both before and after it took place and you've got just about as cast-iron a case as ever went before a jury. And what can we say in reply? Only that Father was a good man and that it wasn't in his nature to be violent. And that's not going to be very convincing when the prosecution can prove that he had already assaulted the girl in a train. I tell you, Hugh, as things stand now we haven't a hope."

Hugh looked at him coldly. "You sound like Counsel for the Prosecution yourself," he said.

"If I were, I'd have fewer worries, I can tell you that."

"But Quentin . . ." Cynthia said with some hesitation, "surely the fact that no one actually saw what happened helps, doesn't it? I mean, the evidence is almost all circumstantial, isn't it?"

"Circumstantial evidence can be as damning as any other sort if there's no other possible explanation that fits all the facts. Murder doesn't usually have witnesses, you know."

Quentin looked at her almost angrily. "*I* can't think of any other explanation. Can you?"

"Not offhand," she admitted.

"Well, if you're going to help Hugh write his wretched thrillers, here's a chance for you to exercise your imagination." Quentin heaved himself out of his chair. "I really must go now—I shan't be home till the small hours and Trudie will be fussing. We'll continue this discussion tomorrow night, after I've consulted Braddock. Sorry, Cynthia, if I was a bit short with you—but frankly, I'm worried to death."

Hugh had been busy at the sideboard with a depleted bottle of gin. "One for the road, Quent? You look as though you need it."

"Thanks, Hugh." Quentin drained the glass gratefully. "I'll see you both tomorrow, then."

They sat in silence for a while after he had gone, wrapped in the gloom he'd left behind him. Then Cynthia stirred and said with a touch of defiance, "Anyhow, darling, I still think you were right—you know I've said all along that your father couldn't possibly have done it. Of course, I haven't seen very much of him, I admit, but sometimes an outsider gets a clearer impression than people closely concerned."

Hugh pressed her hand. "Angel! Quent's right, too, though. Faith isn't enough unless we can justify it. What else *could* have happened?"

"I can't imagine, darling, but it does seem to me we'll never answer the question if we begin by doubting our own judgment. *I* think we ought to begin by believing your father, and see where it leads us. Suppose that he *was* telling the truth in every respect? Suppose that he did receive the letter from the girl as he said, that he went to the place she mentioned and found no one there, that he had a blackout and after recovering from it went home—and that that is absolutely all he knows about it?"

Hugh's face wore a troubled frown. He wanted to believe—desperately. Quite apart from the horror of the actual murder, he could no more see his father in the role of a deliberate liar than Quentin had been able to do. All the same, he had to admit to himself that some of Edward's statements were terribly hard to accept. For one thing, that he had actually received that letter from Helen Fairlie on the fatal morning. Not just because he hadn't been able to produce it and because no one else had seen it, but because the whole thing sounded so wildly improbable. It was difficult enough to believe that the girl had intended to make fresh admissions—for what could she possibly have hoped to get out of it?—but even if she had, she surely wouldn't have suggested a meeting in a deserted place like the saltings? Unless she was a complete fool she'd have been scared out of her life at the idea of being alone in such a spot with a man she'd already done so much injury to. She'd have been much more likely to suggest meeting him in a teashop—the saltings *sounded* more like Edward's suggestion.

No, it wasn't easy to believe in the letter. Yet the girl had certainly been on the saltings—and what had brought her there? It was almost equally improbable that she would have accepted an invitation from Edward. . . . Anyway, the problem of the letter was only a minor one compared with some of the others.

"Look, Cynthia," he said, "it's all very well to say we should believe Dad, but how do you account for the hat and the lipstick?"

"Darling, I wouldn't account for them. I couldn't—on the facts as we know them. But that's the whole point—something must have happened that none of us knows anything about. Something absolutely fantastic. You see, darling, if your father didn't kill that girl—and I'm quite sure he didn't—then someone else did. That's obvious. And if your father didn't go near her, then he couldn't have left his hat twenty feet from the body or got his handkerchief smeared with lipstick. So the somebody else must have done those things, too."

"You mean it was a frame-up?" said Hugh incredulously.

"Well—what else could it have been?"

He nodded slowly. "If we're going to be absolutely logical that is the only conclusion, of course, but—good lord, Cynthia, why should anyone want to do a thing like that to Dad? I can't imagine there's a person in the world with a grudge like that against him."

"There needn't have been any grudge. The real murderer would naturally want to shift suspicion onto someone else if he could, simply to safeguard himself."

"But why pick on Dad, out of all the millions?"

"Darling, your father stands out a mile. After that train business, he must have seemed to have quite a good motive for killing Helen Fairlie. If some other man badly wanted to get rid of her for reasons of his own, and he knew about the train incident, your father would have been a wonderful cover."

"God, do you really think that's possible? A man would have to be a fiend to do that, in cold blood. A fiend *and* a genius—there'd be terrific difficulties from the practical point of view. For one thing, how could he have known that Dad would be on the saltings that day . . . ? Unless, of course . . ." Hugh broke off as an idea suddenly occurred to him. "I say, do you think this hypothetical man of yours could have persuaded Helen Fairlie to write that letter? Or perhaps even forced her to?"

"I'm wondering if he couldn't have arranged it more easily than that. Is there any actual proof that the letter your father got that morning *was* from Helen Fairlie? I know he thought so, but—well, does he know her handwriting?"

"I don't suppose he does, now you mention it—how could he? He only met her that once on the train. I say, that *is* an idea. If only we could find the letter and prove it was a forgery—that would just about put paid to the whole case." For a moment excitement gleamed in Hugh's eyes. Then he gave a sigh like a slowly deflating balloon. "No, that won't do. There's a snag, and I'm sure this Mr. X of yours would have been clever enough to see it. How could he know that Dad would lose the letter? And if Dad hadn't lost the letter—if he'd been able to produce it afterward—the police would have been able to compare it with other examples of Helen Fairlie's writing and they'd have discovered it was a forgery and the frame-up plan would have been exposed straight away. What's more, they'd have checked up on the paper and the ink and the handwriting and they might have been led to X—you know how smart they are with their scientific gadgets these days. He'd have foreseen all that—he'd never have taken the risk."

Cynthia suddenly laughed. "Darling, the map! We'd forgotten the map!" She looked at Hugh with dancing eyes. "It's all falling into place—honestly it is. Don't you see?—X deliberately chose a rendezvous that would be rather difficult to find without directions and he drew that little sketch map in the corner of the letter to make it practically certain your father would take it with him to the place. And X was there when he arrived, waiting to get it back from him. The letter wasn't lost at all—it was *retrieved!*"

"Christ!" said Hugh. Things were indeed becoming plain. A picture rose in his mind—a picture of lonely saltings and a black hulk; of Edward approaching the spot unsuspecting, his mind full of the girl; of X emerging from concealment and creeping up on Edward and striking him down; of the incriminating letter recovered and destroyed.

"So *that's* why Dad had a blackout. He was knocked unconscious."

"It does look like it, darling."

Hugh drew a sharp breath. "I hope we're not letting ourselves be carried away. Dad said himself there was no one in sight when he got there. Where could X have sprung from without attracting attention to himself?"

"Couldn't he have been waiting on the other side of the barge, perhaps—watching? Then as your father walked round to see if the girl was there he could have dodged round too and crept up behind him."

"Yes, that's a thought." Hugh's spirits were rising again. "And, Cynthia, this way we can explain almost everything—all the mechanical part of the frame-up. Once Dad was unconscious X could easily have smeared the handkerchief with lipstick he'd brought with him, and taken away the hat. And it fits in with Dad's story about coming round in the same place where he blacked out. Even the point Howeson raised about the length of the blackout is covered. Darling, you're wonderful!"

"There's just one thing—I wonder where X was when your father came round."

"Not behind the barge again, that's certain. I should think he cleared off a little way and took cover in one of the creeks —no difficulty about that. Cynthia, this is marvelous—I never dreamed we'd get as far. We've got the outlines of a theory, at least. . . . Still, it's going to take an awful lot of filling in. There are masses of things we still need to know—what X's motive was, and where he did the murder, and when, and what his movements were—and, of course, who he is. We're not going to cut much ice unless we can produce him, and as far as I can see the field's wide open. Where in heaven's name do we start looking?"

"Perhaps the police might help," suggested Cynthia.

"Not they! They're quite sure they've got the right man already, so why should they bother? It isn't as though we can offer them anything more than a theory."

"Then we shall just have to rely on ourselves. Let's think— what do we actually know about X?"

Hugh shrugged. "We know he's a man, an active man, and that he knew Helen Fairlie and had a reason for wanting to get rid of her. Full stop!"

"And that he knew about the train incident, darling, in spite of the fact that it wasn't reported. How far did the gossip spread, do you suppose?"

"I don't know that that helps. The girl might easily have told him about it herself—he could be a complete stranger to the district."

"Do you think so?—he seems to know an awful lot about the saltings."

"That's true. Still, it doesn't narrow the field very much."

"You know," said Cynthia thoughtfully, "I think the girl is the obvious starting point. She must have had friends and acquaintances who could talk about her, and perhaps some of them actually know X—now that we've got on to the frame-up idea it may all be much simpler than we think. Would it be a good idea if I took some time off tomorrow morning and tried to find out something about her and her boyfriends?"

"It sounds a first-class idea to me. I shouldn't think Quentin will have any objections—it isn't as though we've anything to lose. Hold on—I've got the girl's address somewhere." He produced a diary. "Here we are—11A Brandon Gardens, W.1. And she worked at Howarth's—in the lingerie department."

Cynthia smiled. "It's going to be a wonderful excuse to do some shopping—I shall send you my expense account." She got up. "Now I really must go, my love, or Mrs. Andrews will be sure I'm sleeping with you."

"You'll be careful tomorrow, won't you?" said Hugh anxiously. "Don't go doing anything rash—this X must be a pretty desperate type."

She laughed. "I ought to be safe enough in a shop—unless, of course, he's the floorwalker! Kiss me—and then I must fly."

9 CYNTHIA surveyed her wardrobe thoughtfully next morning. She was in some doubt how to present herself at the popular Oxford Street store where Helen Fairlie had worked. Would it help, she wondered, if she were to represent herself as a reporter, or even as a woman writer interested in crime? Or would that frighten off a shop assistant? Should she try to look intellectual and authoritative, or feminine and sympathetic? In the end she chose a rather elegant navy tussore suit and a small white straw hat, which she thought would serve for either role.

It was half-past ten when she pushed through the swing doors of the big store—late enough for her not to be conspicuous, but before the shopping crowds had become thick enough to take all the attention of the assistants. The June pavements were already uncomfortably hot and Cynthia felt as though she had swum into the cool shade of an aquarium as she made her way over acres of soft carpet to Howarth's lingerie department. It turned out to be quite a small one, and there appeared to be only two assistants. One, a tight-lipped middle-aged woman, was already serving; the other, a pretty unsophisticated-looking blonde in her middle twenties, was free. Cynthia applied all the charm she could to the selection and purchase of a set of nylon undies and maneuvered for an opening.

What would make this girl talk?—that was the question. It depended on so many things—on whether she had liked or disliked Helen Fairlie, whether she was by nature reticent or talkative, whether she'd already been questioned a lot. Superficially she seemed a friendly, simple sort of girl to whom

Helen Fairlie's tragic end would have come as a tremendous shock. Cynthia suddenly decided that the direct approach would be more likely to produce results than any suggestion of professional interest.

"You've had a rather frightful time here just lately, haven't you?" she remarked, as her parcel was being wrapped. "Wasn't this where Helen Fairlie worked?"

"Yes," said the girl, looking up. "Did you know her, then?"

"No, but I read about it all in the papers."

"It *has* been awful," said the girl with a shudder. "I still can't believe it. Poor old Helen!"

"As a matter of fact," Cynthia said in a low voice and with great earnestness, "I've reasons for being extremely interested in the affair, and I've just *got* to talk to somebody who knew Helen Fairlie. Would you be an angel and come and have lunch with me?"

The girl looked very surprised. "Isn't it all settled and done with?"

"No, not really. It appears to be, I know, but there's actually a lot more in it than most people think. Look, I know I mustn't take your time now, but if you *could* lunch with me I'd be so very grateful. And then I'll be able to tell you all about it."

Caution and curiosity struggled together in the girl's face. She had never before been invited to lunch by a customer, but there was something about Cynthia that she found very persuasive. Finally, with a doubtful look across at the older woman, she said, "Well, all right."

"That's so nice of you." Cynthia felt a surge of relief. "Shall we make it Lambert's, then, as it's near here? What time can you be there?—and what's your name, by the way?"

"Jasmine Blake," said the girl. "I'm first lunch. I'll meet you there just after twelve, if you like."

"Good." Cynthia gathered up her parcel, flashed a quick smile at the girl, and departed.

Jasmine Blake turned up promptly at Lambert's, her face bright with interest and expectancy, and under the influence of a gin-and-It and a leisurely atmosphere any shyness she might have felt soon vanished. The two of them were soon on excellent terms.

"The fact is, Miss Blake," Cynthia explained, as soon as they had ordered, "I'm engaged to the son of the man who has been arrested for the murder, and we think he's innocent—in fact, we know he is—and so we've set ourselves to find out who the real murderer is."

"Really!" said Jasmine. She looked very startled. "But—surely the police wouldn't arrest an innocent man? Wasn't there a lot of evidence?"

"There was, but we think there's been a clever plot—you know, what the Americans call a frame-up. We've found out a great many very suspicious things already." Mindful of the rigidity of the other girl's timetable, Cynthia merely toyed with her own food and plunged at once into her theory of the murder. Miss Blake ate and listened, her blue eyes large with amazement. By the time coffee was reached she was quite won over by Cynthia's logic and charm.

"So now you see," Cynthia concluded, "why I want to find out all I can about Helen Fairlie. . . . What was she like to look at, for instance? I don't know a thing about her except that she was small and good-looking."

"She wasn't as small as all that," said Jasmine. "She was about five feet four, I suppose, but she was very slim. She had dark hair, worn short and slightly wavy, and a lovely complexion, and she was always very smart."

"That sounds most attractive."

"Oh, she *was* attractive. At least, I thought so, though she wasn't by any means everybody's cup of tea. She could be very amusing and entertaining—really witty, you know—but often she wouldn't take the trouble. Not if she thought people weren't worth it. She was, well, not exactly hard . . ." Jasmine fumbled for the right word.

"Brittle, perhaps?"

"Yes, that's just it. Not very warm-hearted, really."

"How did men like her, do you know? Had she many men friends?"

"Well, I shouldn't be surprised if she had quite a lot, one way and another, but she didn't talk about them much and they certainly never seemed to last long. I think she was probably a bit too choosy. I don't blame a girl for not wanting to throw herself away and all that, but you can't afford to be too fussy, can you? Actually, I think she was probably too clever for most of them."

"Did you ever meet any of her friends?"

"No, I didn't, as a matter of fact. Helen was very cagey about her private affairs. Most of the girls talk about their boyfriends and meet them outside the shop and all that, but not Helen. Of course, men used to try and make dates with her in the shop sometimes. There was one only a few weeks ago—came in to buy cami-knicks or something for his girlfriend and tried to date Helen up there and then. I didn't see him because I was serving at the time but she told me about him afterward. I thought he had a nerve, but Helen only laughed. She said he looked interesting. She liked people with nerve—men especially, and anyway, she could always handle them. She was rather cynical about men, I suppose. There was another one, I remember, that she met in the shop, but that was quite a long time ago. He was much older—about sixty, and almost bald."

For a moment Cynthia was startled. "You don't know who he was, do you?"

"I haven't a clue. Somebody's grandfather, I should think—naughty old man."

"What was he like, do you remember? Tall or short, fat or thin?"

"Oh, he was on the short side, and plumpish. He came in two or three times and I believe Helen did see quite a bit of him. He was very well dressed and he gave her some rather nice things—the odd brooch, you know—but she dropped him after a while, or he dropped her. I used to tease her about her sugar daddies because she did seem to attract older men, but she took it in good part. She was very sure of herself."

"It looks as though she was a bit too sure, in the end," said Cynthia.

Momentarily, Jasmine Blake's flushed face became solemn. "Yes," she agreed. "But that was Helen all over—she never doubted she could deal with any situation. She was just the same in the shop—I used to envy her self-confidence. She never let herself get rattled by the customers, however difficult they were, and some of them *are* difficult, believe me."

"I'm sure they are." Cynthia smiled at Jasmine's serious expression. "It sounds to me as though Miss Fairlie must have been an asset in the shop."

"Oh, she was. Miss Niven never had anything but praise for her—that's our Super, I expect you saw her—and she's not easy to please. Everybody said Fairlie would do very well in the firm if she stayed, but between you and me I think she was on the lookout for something better."

"How long had she been at Howarth's?"

"Five or six years, and I think she'd had about enough of it. Promotions not very fast there, you know. She did talk about being an air hostess at one time but she was too old or something and then you need a nurse's training and I don't think she'd had any training really in anything. But that's the *kind* of job she'd have liked, I'm sure—where she could go about and meet people socially, you know, not just over the counter. I expect it sounds rather catty but I think what she really wanted was to marry a rich man—well, don't we all?—but they're not so easy to find, are they?"

"No, alas," Cynthia agreed. "But tell me, what did *you* feel about her—did you like her?"

Jasmine Blake stubbed out her cigarette. "Well, yes and no. She wasn't really my type, and yet I couldn't help admiring her, somehow. She was quite nice to work with, I'll say that for her, not petty and small-minded like some of the girls are. I think living in suburbs helps to make them like that—it's such a narrow life, but Helen was lucky, she had a flat of her own and did as she liked. She used to say I ought to do the same, but it's not so easy when you've got parents who fuss about you like mine do. I'd never hear the end of it if I suggested it, and anyway I couldn't afford it. . . . Still, we got on pretty well, Helen and I. She seemed to like me—goodness knows why. In fact she even wanted us to spend our holiday together this year."

"Then she certainly must have liked you," said Cynthia. "But could you have taken the time off together if you were in the same department?"

"Oh, I'm due to go off the lingerie any minute now. Helen knew that. Still, I don't suppose it would have come to anything. She wanted us to take a houseboat at first—did you ever hear anything so crazy?"

"A houseboat? Where?" Cynthia had become very alert.

"It hadn't been fixed. I must say I was staggered when she first suggested it, because she'd always been mad about hot expensive places like Cannes and Monte Carlo—not that she'd ever been, of course, but she was always reading travel folders and that kind of thing and a houseboat didn't seem at all her style. Not in this country, anyway. But she was very keen about it and I thought it might be amusing for a change so I said I'd go if she liked to make all the arrangements. She didn't mind that at all; she said there wasn't any point in both of us spending money on train fares and, being on her own, she had plenty of spare time. She went to look at quite a lot of houseboats that were advertised—in fact she was on her way to Alfordness to look at one the day she had that trouble on the train."

"Oh, was *that* what she was doing?"

"Yes, but it was a disappointment, like all the others. It was called *Sez-you* and it sounded awful. I don't think we would have done anything about a houseboat in the end anyway because she seemed to lose interest in the idea all of a sudden and she said it would be just as cheap and more fun to go to

Dieppe and we were working out fares and things when—when all this happened. I can still hardly believe it."

"Did she tell you about the train business at the time?"

"Yes. Funnily enough that was about the one occasion when she was rather forthcoming. She was quite worked up about it. She said she didn't really blame the man because she *had* led him up the garden a bit. Of course it never occurred to me that she might have been responsible for the whole thing but after what you've told me I wouldn't put it past her. Anyway, she said she wasn't going to do anything more about it and it all petered out but somehow I couldn't help feeling it was still on her mind. I did wonder as a matter of fact if she'd fallen for the man and when I heard that she—that her body had been found not far from his home and that he'd been arrested I thought I'd been right and that that was why she'd arranged to meet him. But of course if what you say is true . . ." Jasmine Blake wrinkled her brows and tried to look sympathetic.

"Did she say anything to anyone about having plans for that day?"

"No, she didn't, and I did wonder about that afterward because of course she ought to have been working that Friday and she just didn't turn up. As I say she never talked about her affairs much but it wasn't like her to slip off like that without a word to Miss Niven."

"Didn't anyone make inquiries about her?"

"Oh, yes, Miss Niven rang up her flat on Friday morning but there wasn't any reply so of course there wasn't anything we could do. We never dreamed of anything awful happening, naturally, and when the police came and told us about her body being found—well, we were absolutely thunderstruck."

"It must have been horrible. . . . So when did you actually see her last?"

"On the Thursday, when we left the shop at six o'clock."

"Did she seem quite—well, quite normal, then?"

"Oh, yes, she was all right—except as I say she'd been a bit upset ever since the train affair. Irritable, you know, and short-tempered with the customers, and that wasn't like her."

Cynthia gave a thoughtful nod. "Did you ever go to her flat?"

"Yes, I went once or twice, when we began to get friendly."

"What sort of place was it? I'm sorry to keep firing questions at you like this, but you do see how important it is for me, don't you?"

"That's all right," said Jasmine, "I'm sure I'd do the same in your place. Well, now, Helen's flat . . . oh, it didn't amount to much really, though it's got quite a good address. It's one of those big houses in Ovingdean Square, divided into flats. Hers was just inside the front door—one big room with a tiny bathroom and a sort of kitchen in a cupboard. I told her I thought it would be jolly handy for a boyfriend because he'd be able to slip in and out without causing a lot of gossip. She smiled a bit at that, but she didn't let on a thing."

"She certainly sounds a bit of a mystery," said Cynthia. "How long had she lived there, do you know? And what about her people—her background? Did she ever say?"

"Never. I think her people must have been dead—she always gave the impression that she'd been on her own for years. I know she'd had that flat for a long time. You're quite right, though—she *was* rather mysterious. For one thing, she didn't seem to have many women friends. I know she went out quite a lot because in the shop she was always ready to talk about films and shows and things she'd seen. I suppose the answer is that there *were* men, but that she knew how to hold her tongue about them." Jasmine glanced at her watch. "I say, I'll have to get a move on."

"Well, thank you *very* much for coming, Miss Blake—I'm most grateful to you."

"Not at all—thanks for the lunch. I wish you luck—though I wouldn't want to have your job, I must say. Good-by."

"Good-by," said Cynthia. "Perhaps we'll meet again some time."

She paid the bill, and then caught a bus to Knightsbridge. She had an idea that if she called at the house where Helen Fairlie had lived and said she was looking for a flat she might have a chance to see the girl's room herself. The moment she entered Ovingdean Square, however, she realized that she was going to be unlucky. There was a police car outside the house, and as she approached it she saw that two men were at work in the front room. Obviously she would have to come back some other time. A few minutes later she was on her way to the House.

10 IT WAS after seven that evening when Cynthia reached Hugh's lodgings, having compressed a day's work into half a day. She had just finished telling him of her lunchtime conversation when Quentin arrived. He had had a long session with Braddock, and if anything his gloom had intensified.

Hugh rallied him. "Cheer up, Quent!—we've got news for you. A theory—and what a theory!" And there and then he started to go over the ground that he and Cynthia had covered in their discussion the night before.

At first Quentin listened with a frankly skeptical expression, as though it were just the sort of fantasy he would have expected his brother to weave. Once or twice he opened his mouth to expostulate at what seemed to him some inconclusive piece of argument. But as Hugh dealt one by one with the objections that were in his mind his interest increased and his face slowly took on an absorbed look.

For a while, after Hugh had finished, he sat back and thoughtfully puffed at his pipe. Then he delivered his verdict. "Well, it's ingenious—it's fascinating. And of course it does explain some of the improbabilities. It was always inconceivable to me that a woman who'd been assaulted in a train would have offered to meet the man alone in the most desolate spot in East Anglia. . . ."

Hugh couldn't help smiling. "You're still assuming she *was* assaulted. What an obstinate old devil you are, Quent!"

"Well, let's not go into that again—things are confusing enough already and it's quite immaterial. Anyway, I do congratulate you both. Not that it's anything but the purest surmise, of course—there's not a shred of evidence. And I still see some snags that you haven't dealt with. For instance . . . what was this X of yours proposing to do about the envelope that the letter came in? As it happens, Father took that along with him too, but X could hardly have banked on his doing so."

"Would the envelope have conveyed much by itself, anyway?" asked Cynthia.

Quentin looked at her for a moment; then suddenly he gave an exclamation. "By Jove, you may be right! I remember now that in his statement at the police station Father said that it was addressed in block capitals. At the time, everyone thought it was just another piece of invention."

"There you are, then," said Hugh, "one snag disposed of! If the envelope was an ordinary cheap thing without any special character and the handwriting wasn't identifiable, the police wouldn't have been any wiser if it *had* fallen into their hands —as far as they'd know it might have been the envelope from some other letter."

Quentin gave a slow nod of assent. "Well, if we're right about all this," he said, impressed enough by now to want to share the credit, "the torn remains of the other letter, the one in the girl's handbag, were presumably part of the frame-up too?"

"Why, of course," said Hugh. "I think this whole business of the letters is pretty clear now. Let's reconstruct. First of all Dad sends a letter to the girl telling her she's ruining his life and begging her to tell the truth. X, who is on close terms with the girl, sees it, and he realizes that he's only got to send a faked reply purporting to come from the girl and hinting at a change of heart in order to get Dad to any meeting place he likes to name. Perhaps it was that letter that gave him the idea of the frame-up in the first place. Anyway, he sends the reply and makes sure he'll be able to recover it, by drawing the sketch map. So Dad is deprived of all evidence to back his story. But that's not enough—X has got to provide an alternative and convincing reason for Dad's presence on the saltings —one that will implicate him. So he plants the remains of the first letter in the handbag, with another penciled sketch to make it appear that Dad had initiated the meeting—remember, block letters were used for that, too!—having first torn off everything that indicated when the letter was written and what it was really about. . . . Hell, we ought to have realized from the beginning that the way that letter was torn was something more than an accidental misfortune for Dad."

"It's easy to be wise when you know," said Quentin. He sat pondering for a while. "I wonder what Braddock will make of all this?—I'd like to plug up as many loopholes as possible before I put it to him. For instance, I've never actually been attacked and hit on the head myself, but I would have supposed it might leave marks."

"Nobody looked for marks," said Hugh. "I don't suppose Scott went over Dad's scalp with a magnifying glass just because he complained of a bad headache."

"But could X reckon on that? Wasn't it rather a risk for him?"

"I don't think so. I expect he used something soft and heavy like a small sandbag—he could easily have provided himself with that—and then with anything like luck there wouldn't have been any external marks at all."

Quentin seemed satisfied. "It's certainly true that Father behaved exactly like a man who'd been knocked out. Not bothering much about his hat afterward, going home in a dazed state with a rambling story—yes, that's all right." He frowned. "I'm still worried by the risks that X took, though. Suppose Father had caught a glimpse of him just before the blow was struck—suppose he'd heard a step or happened to turn round. Then he might have remembered afterward what X looked like."

"Yes," said Hugh thoughtfully, "the approach must have been a bit tricky, particularly as Dad was on the lookout for the girl. X must be pretty spry. There is one possibility, though

—perhaps X took precautions to hide his identity—covered his face or something. Then it wouldn't have mattered if he had been spotted for a second."

"It would have spoiled any frame-up plan," said Quentin. "It was surely essential to the plan that Father shouldn't know he'd been hit."

"Was it, though?" put in Cynthia. "Suppose he'd gone home with a story that he'd been attacked by a strange masked figure on the saltings, and the police had investigated and discovered the girl's body there—do you think they'd have believed in the masked man? I don't—I think they'd have said the whole story was an invention and arrested your father just the same. I can't believe X's frame-up was in much danger there."

"Well, you may be right," Quentin conceded. "I see another weakness in the plan, though. Suppose for some reason Father hadn't turned up at all—suppose he'd been away from home when the letter came, or too ill to go out?"

"Perhaps X would have tried again some other time," suggested Hugh. "Or if he already had a body on his hands perhaps he'd just have had to make the best of a bad job and dispose of it in a different way. Or perhaps, if he's a local man, he *knew* Dad was at Lavender Cottage—he could easily have found out at any pub. Anyway, let's say he took a sporting chance. I think it was a reasonable one."

Quentin nodded again. "All right. Well, the question now is, what steps can we take to consolidate this theory?"

"We've taken a few steps already," said Hugh with a grin. "Tell the gentleman what you found out today, Cynthia."

For the second time, Cynthia recounted her conversation with Jasmine Blake, while Quentin listened with close attention. At the end he looked rather sheepishly at Hugh.

"Perhaps after all it's a pity we *didn't* start making inquiries about Helen Fairlie immediately after the train incident, but once she'd dropped the charge it seemed the wisest course to let things alone."

"Never mind," said Hugh, "we're beginning to catch up with her now."

"It's certainly a very thought-provoking picture that Cynthia's got of her. Like almost everything else in this confounded case, though, it can be interpreted in two ways."

"How do you mean, Quent?"

"Well, on those facts—always assuming that Jasmine Blake was giving a fair picture of her—Helen Fairlie *could* have been a sort of adventuress *manquée,* a climber who didn't quite get there; and that would suit us perfectly, because that's just the sort of young woman who might get into serious trouble. She obviously had a lot of the qualities—self-confidence, cool nerve, a cynical detachment about men—that kind of thing. Expensive tastes without the means of satisfying them. Yes, I'd say it was quite possible to believe she was out for big game, and that one of them proved too big for her. But we don't really *know.* All that stuff about her men friends is extraordinarily vague—we can't actually put a name or a description to a single one of them. And a girl isn't necessarily an adventuress, after all, just because she likes jewelry and hankers after foreign travel and goes out occasionally with a customer."

"That's perfectly true, of course," Cynthia agreed, "but you'll allow me to have a hunch, won't you? And I tell you I'm sure she was mixed up in something pretty odd. I can't see a girl of that type suddenly developing a genuine passion for houseboats, any more than Jasmine Blake could. It simply doesn't ring true."

Quentin gave a little smile, the first for days. "You didn't ring true either, my dear Cynthia, when you came back covered in mud from head to foot after a day in Hugh's boat —but you did it just the same. People do develop odd interests, you know. You have your reason, and I dare say Helen Fairlie had hers."

"Well, I'd very much like to know what hers was, that's all. It wasn't only her interest in the thing—it was the way she went about it all that seems so curious to me. I mean, if two girls plan to go on a holiday together they're usually both keen enough to share in the preliminaries—that's part of the fun, after all—but here was Jasmine Blake, obviously reluctant, not caring two hoots about the idea, and Helen Fairlie was going ahead alone as though her life depended on it. And what's even more strange is that all of a sudden she dropped the whole thing like a hot cake. I think it's all most suspicious."

"What do you suspect?" asked Quentin.

"I don't know—that's the trouble. But I'm sure all those journeys into muddiest Essex had some ulterior motive."

"Perhaps she never went near any houseboats," said Hugh. "It wouldn't be a bad idea when we go down there next time to make a few inquiries and see just how keen she was. Well, now, what's the next step? It seems to me it's time we had a few hard facts. When was this girl actually killed, Quent?—can we get a line on that?"

"All we know for certain," said Quentin, "is that she was alive in London at six o'clock on the Thursday when she left the shop, and that she was dead in the saltings on the Saturday afternoon when she was found."

"Doesn't the medical report help at all?" asked Cynthia. "In Hugh's stories it always pinpoints the time of death beautifully. We find it a great convenience!"

"Well, this report's different," said Quentin grimly. "It's full of qualifications and reservations and technical things about *rigor mortis* and the heaviness of the dew. . . . Anyhow, the consensus of opinion seems to be that death probably occurred between about midnight on Thursday and about three o'clock on Friday afternoon, which from the police point of view very conveniently covers the time when Father was supposed to be meeting her. But apparently no one would be prepared to swear to those limits."

Hugh's face had suddenly taken on a look of intense concentration. "You know," he said after a moment, "I think we can get closer than that ourselves. Surely, if it was X's intention to make it appear that Dad killed the girl at two o'clock on the Friday, she must already have been dead on the Friday morning—or if not dead, very much under his eye."

Cynthia looked surprised. "Why do you say that, darling?"

"Well, otherwise, don't you see, the whole frame-up plan might have been ruined. It wouldn't have been much good X going to all that trouble to get Dad to the saltings at two o'clock and fix the hat and the lipstick and so on if someone could pop up afterward and say the girl couldn't have been there at that time because she was riding on a bus or having a hair-do or something. X must have taken good care of her, not just for that particular time but for all the time it would have taken her to travel to the spot from wherever she was last seen publicly."

Quentin gave an approving grunt. "That's certainly a point I'd overlooked." For a moment he was lost in thought. "When you say 'under his eye,' Hugh, are you supposing she might have been alive and with him on the saltings that morning?"

"Not necessarily—I was just thinking aloud, really, trying to cover all the possibilities. As I see it, there are three. First, he could have taken her with him to the saltings and kept her under cover. . . ."

"I don't think that's a bit probable," Cynthia broke in. "After all, this wasn't a co-operative frame-up, was it?—she was the victim, not an accomplice. It would have been pretty awkward for him if someone had spotted them together, and anyhow I simply can't see that girl meekly hiding in a muddy creek while X dealt with your father."

"I must say I agree, Hugh."

"And now that I come to think of it I'm pretty sure she *was* dead on Friday morning, otherwise she'd almost certainly have got in touch with the shop. It's my belief X killed her on Thursday night."

"That's fair enough," said Hugh. "Let's say he did. Well, then, the second possibility is that he had the *body* with him on the saltings on Friday. The third is that he'd got it tucked safely away somewhere else until he was ready to plant it. I wonder which is right." He considered for a moment. "You know, if X killed her on Thursday night I don't see how he could possibly have got her body to the saltings by next day. She was in London at six, and he had to meet her, and get her to some quiet spot without arousing her suspicions, kill her, and then somehow get her to the barge, all before daylight. It would have been a hell of a program."

"It certainly would," said Quentin. "I suppose he has a car, whoever he is, but I frankly doubt if there'd have been enough darkness for him to do the whole operation in one night. In that case it looks as though your third possibility is the right one—she was hidden away somewhere else. . . . Incidentally, Hugh, don't you think the body must have been taken to the saltings by water? That barge place is all of two miles from the nearest road and even allowing for the fact that the girl was fairly slight I can't see X *carrying* her all that way across the marshes and along the sea wall. Especially in the dark. The fellow might have broken his neck."

"Pity he didn't!" said Hugh. "I think you've got something there, though—it would have been a stupendous operation. Well, let's think, now—water!" He frowned. "That might not have been exactly simple, either—transferring a dead body to a boat."

"Perhaps she wasn't dead at that point," Quentin suggested. "*I'm* thinking aloud now, but—well, suppose X owns a boat—like yours, for instance—and he persuaded the girl to go there with him on the Thursday night and killed her when he got her on board? It would have been a very good place to hide the body until he needed it."

Hugh looked at Cynthia. "What do you think, darling?"

"I think she'd have taken an awful lot of persuading, unless it was a luxury yacht! Especially just for one night, and with a working day ahead. What would have been the point? After all, if she wanted to see X she'd got her flat—why should she go rushing off to a muddy old boat? And if she had intended to, wouldn't she have said something about it at the shop, because she was bound to be late next day. I must say, it all sounds most unlikely to me."

"And to me," said Hugh. "In that case, I suppose X *must* have brought the body to the water and transferred it. Presumably from his car. Now where could he have done that?"

"Well, darling, try to put yourself in his place. I know it's most unlikely—at least I hope so—but if you'd had a body in a car and wanted to transfer it to a boat and take it to those saltings, what place would you have chosen?"

"It would depend on how much time I had," said Hugh thoughtfully. "It seems to me that X had very little spare time. On Thursday night he killed the girl, on Friday he was meeting Dad on the saltings, and on Saturday the body was discovered. That means he certainly wouldn't have had time to bring the boat any great distance—say, from another estuary. My guess is that the transfer was made somewhere on the Broadwater itself."

He crossed to his bookshelves, which were crammed with maps and nautical volumes, and returned with a chart of the Broadwater River which he opened out on the table and studied intently. Presently he gave a low whistle. "You know, if we're right he didn't have much choice."

"There's Steepleford Hard, of course," said Quentin, following Hugh's moving finger as it circumnavigated the outline of the river.

"I can't see him choosing that—not with a couple of boatyards and the Yacht Club there. You never know who may be around on a summer night. No, I'm sure he'd have chosen some place where a quiet bit of road passes very close to the water, and as far as I can see there are only two suitable spots." He indicated two places on the chart where minor roads skirted the heads of creeks leading into the main river. "Goldbury Creek and Stancott Creek. I wonder!" Hugh's eyes had taken on an active gleam. "Quent, I think it's worth having a look, honestly I do. We may be completely up the pole, of course, but we may not."

"Well," said Quentin seriously, "I'm inclined to agree with you. I'm afraid I shan't be available tomorrow—I shall have to go over all this stuff with Braddock—but I certainly think it would be well worth while for you to run down. You could take Father's car when you got to the cottage."

"I'd sooner go by water—then I could have a look at the scene of the crime on the way. Let's see, how are the tides?" Hugh picked up the evening paper and studied the weather column. "High water London Bridge, 11.15 A.M. Deduct two hours and ten minutes—say just after nine. H'm—it'll mean an early start. Suppose I come down with you tonight, Quent?"

"By all means."

Cynthia had been showing signs of increasing restlessness during these exchanges. "Hugh," she pleaded, "can't I come too? After all, a good part of it's my idea, you know. We could easily pick up my things."

"That would be wonderful, darling, but what about your boss?"

"I'll ring him up straight away and tell him it's a matter of life and death. He knows about all this trouble—he won't be a bit surprised."

She took up the telephone and dialed her employer, who was "paired" that evening and was giving a dinner party at his flat. In a moment she was pouring out her story. The two men exchanged amused glances over her technique—the tone of urgency that merged into coaxing appeal and was followed by a little display of charm as it became clear that she was going to have her way. At last she dropped the receiver and turned to Hugh with a triumphant expression. "It's all right— he's going to borrow a secretary. He says I can take several days if I want to."

"That's marvelous," said Hugh. "Right, I'll just throw some things into a bag." He disappeared into the bedroom.

"You know," Quentin called, "while you're down at Steepleford there's something else you might do."

"What's that, Quent?"

"Why, go along to Cowfleet village and station and see if any of the railway people or the tradesmen can remember seeing a girl around there on Friday afternoon who answered to Helen Fairlie's description."

Hugh appeared in the doorway, looking startled. "What's the idea?"

"Well, the prosecution's case is that she kept an appointment with Father on Friday afternoon, and if she *had* she'd presumably have gone by train or coach from London and walked through Cowfleet village. If we can show that no one saw her —well, it won't prove she *wasn't* there, of course, but it'll raise a useful doubt and help to whittle down the prosecution case."

"I get it. All right, we'll fit that in somehow. What was she wearing, by the way?"

"When she was found she was wearing a yellow frock, and she had a silk scarf round her head. It wouldn't have been easy to miss her."

"What sort of shoes?" asked Cynthia.

Quentin consulted a paper on which he had a lot of notes. "Smart black ones. Rather high heels."

"There you are, then—of course she didn't walk there. That's definitely a point for us."

Hugh emerged from the inner room. "What did Braddock say today, Quent?"

"Not much. He was shaken by Howeson's report—his jaw dropped a mile when I told him. We had a gloomy session, I can tell you. Tomorrow should be very different."

"When are you going to see Dad?"

"Now that all this fresh stuff has come up, I hope tomorrow afternoon. It'll cheer him up to know we're all solidly with him."

Hugh nodded. "Well, give him our love and tell him we're

104

chasing the ball. By the way, don't forget to ask him what *exactly* happened just before his blackout. It's rather important the way he approached the barge."

"Yes, I see that."

"When does he come up before the magistrates?"

"On Monday, I expect." Quentin sounded much more philosophical now.

"What'll happen, Quent?"

"Oh, he's bound to be committed for trial, of course. We shall reserve our defense. As we haven't got one yet, we can't very well do anything else."

"Never mind," said Cynthia. "We've got a very healthy theory."

11 HUGH and Cynthia were up and away next morning long before the rest of the household had begun to stir. Both of them were conscious of a tingling excitement as they bumped their way in Edward's car toward Steepleford Hard. As Trudie had put it in one of her less felicitous phrases, everything seemed to hang on their discoveries that day. The next few hours could establish or destroy their carefully constructed theory.

It was a perfect morning on the saltings. The sun had already begun to penetrate the thin heat haze and the cracked earth was still warm from the previous day. Only the faintest of light airs stirred the dusty-looking sea grass. There was a gentle murmur of grasshoppers and bees, a slumberous summer sound. Out in the channel the tide had already been flowing for some hours and the river was more than half full. *Water Baby* and many of the boats around her were floating placidly, with little strain on their cables. The place no longer looked derelict and untidy, but serene and lovely. It seemed unbelievable that violence and murder could have taken place in this sort of setting.

There was no one about at that hour except Frank Hillyer, who was sandpapering a spar mounted on trestles outside his workshop. He was whistling happily to himself, his shirtsleeves rolled up, his blue jersey discarded, his battered yachting cap stuck on his head at a jaunty angle. He looked up in surprise at the sound of voices, and when he saw who it was his welcoming grin was tinged with embarrassment. He hadn't seen Hugh since before the train affair.

"Hello," he said, abandoning the spar and coming forward to meet them. "You're out early."

"Yes, we're going to take the dinghy up the river."

Frank surveyed the slowly filling channel. "You should have a pleasant morning." He hesitated, evidently feeling the need to make some reference to the tragedy. "I was sorry to hear about the trouble you're in, Hugh."

"Thanks, Frank—it's pretty bloody but I expect we'll get over it. . . . Mind if I have a squint at your tide tables?"

"Help yourself," said Frank. "High water's at nine thirty if that's what you're after." He turned to Cynthia, smiling at her efforts to put her Wellingtons on without sitting down. "You're beginning to look quite the sailor."

She clutched his arm for support and got the second boot on. "I'm not at all sure that's a compliment," she said, stamping around a little. Old slacks, an open-necked cotton blouse, and a beret gave her a well-equipped appearance, but she felt far from glamorous. "Have you been down here long, Frank?"

"Since four o'clock. These summer mornings are too good to waste."

"Yes, I'm just beginning to understand the attraction of the place. It's so incredibly peaceful."

In a few moments Hugh appeared from the workshop with his oars under his arm. He gazed thoughtfully down the bank of mud to the line of brown bubbles that marked the edge of the sluggish stream. "Not much run in the tide, Frank."

"No, we're at the bottom of neaps today. It'll start making tomorrow."

"Making what?" asked Cynthia.

Hugh smiled. "Don't pay any attention, darling—he's only trying to impress you! Nautical terms, you know." He strode over to the little seven-foot dinghy and laid the oars across the thwarts. "Come and help me shove her down the mud. See you later, Frank."

He seized the painter and plunged into the ooze, dragging the tiny boat toward the water. Cynthia staggered along be-

107

hind it, making a rather unconvincing show of pushing. Once Hugh called, "Easy, now!" as they negotiated the protruding fluke of someone's anchor. He was still very particular about the dinghy, which was almost new and had cost him more than he could afford. It was a mass-produced job, one of many scores turned out by a local yard practically on a conveyor belt, but though it had no frills it was excellent value for the money and the type was one of the most popular on the coast.

Cynthia pushed a lock of hair out of her eyes, leaving a streak of mud across her forehead. There were mud splashes on her brown arms, and a careless step had sent mud cascading down the inside of one of her boots. She no longer felt any alarm about what might happen, but she was quite glad when the dinghy at last took the water and she was able to clamber aboard.

Once they were launched, life suddenly became clean and tranquil again. The surface of the water winked and sparkled in the sunlight. Overhead, in the wide, pale sky a lark trilled. The air was soft and caressing. With the tide in their favor, and Hugh plying his oars with vigor, the dinghy was soon shooting upstream at surprising speed.

Cynthia lay back in the sternsheets, watching Hugh. She liked watching him in all his moods, for the expression of his lively green eyes was quick-changing and his eager face was an open window for his thoughts. Looking at him now, as he gazed past her at the receding Hard, she wondered if that determined compression of the mouth, that slightly preoccupied gravity which he had shown in the past few days, would outlast the crisis he was living through. She half hoped it would. Maturity sat well on him, and this tragedy had certainly matured him.

He suddenly realized that she was studying him. "Penny for them!" he said.

"I was just thinking you were rather sweet, darling."

"I can't imagine why—I feel like a bear. . . . I'm afraid all this isn't being much fun for you, Cynthia."

"It isn't exactly fun for anybody."

"No, but—hell, you shouldn't have been dragged into it. Everything ought to be gay for you, and instead it's just being grim."

"Don't worry, darling, we'll make up for it afterward. I'm glad I can share it all with you."

"It certainly helps to have you. Sometimes I think you've more faith than I have."

"In your father?" She looked surprised. "I wouldn't have said you showed any lack of faith."

"I meant in our ability to clear him."

"Oh, I see. Well, you must admit we've made tremendous progress."

"I know, but I'll be a lot happier when we've got a bit of solid proof. Just one hard fact would do—something we can touch, something we can photograph, something we can take into court. I get cold feet sometimes. Last night I had a beastly dream . . ."

"Don't tell me!" Cynthia was silent for a while, watching the bubbles streaming by. "I'm sure it'll all come right in the end."

Hugh grunted. "The odds against us still seem pretty heavy. Quent thinks the Attorney General will be briefed for the prosecution as the case has caused such a stir. Have you come across him at the House?"

"Ferraby? I've seen him from a distance, that's all. He's very good-looking."

"I don't suppose he'll look so good when he's cross-examining. Quent says he's deadly—all quiet charm and merciless logic."

"Well, that's his job, of course. He always seems human enough in the lobby—I should think he has a nice sense of humor."

"From our point of view, a bullying type might be better. . . . Ah, well, if we have a bit of luck, perhaps it won't come to that."

"If it does, who will defend your father?"

"Quent thinks we shall be able to get Colfax—in fact, it's practically decided. *He's* pretty good, too—the newspapers will have a whale of a time. Poor old Dad!" Hugh gazed around at the smiling landscape. "Imagine him stuck in prison on a day like this!"

His thoughts seemed to spur him to greater efforts, and the boat raced by the low banks. Once or twice he flicked a glance over his shoulder, making mental notes of the tributary creeks that branched off to left and right. It would have been easy to take the wrong channel, for they were low down between the mudbanks and nothing was visible but the tufts of coarse grass at the margins of the mud. But this river was a familiar highway to Hugh at all states of the tide and he rowed steadily on.

Presently Cynthia said: "I believe I can see the barge. Isn't that it?"

Hugh turned to look, and nodded. "That's the spot. Let's go in and have a look." He let the dinghy drift upstream until it had reached a point about fifty yards beyond the hulk. Then he swung it sharply in until it grounded, and dropped the little anchor in the mud. Though the tide would soon be high, the water was still some distance from the edge of the saltings.

Cynthia stared at the fringe of virgin mud between the dinghy and the grass. "I say, Hugh, if our Mr. X brought a body here in a boat, wouldn't there be footmarks? There's not a sign that anybody's been about."

For a moment Hugh looked anxious. Then his face cleared. "No, that's all right. There were spring tides last week."

"Does that explain it?"

"Why, yes. The water would have risen to within a few inches of the saltings, you see, so if X had come in at high water or thereabouts he'd have been able to step straight out of his boat on to the grass without leaving any marks at all."

"Oh!" Cynthia seemed willing to take that on trust. "I'm

afraid I'm not very clever about tides—all I know is that they come in and go out."

"Nonsense!—you know more than that. You know that the height of high water changes each day—that's why there are all those different lines of seaweed on the shore at the seaside. What happens is that for about a week, the high-water mark gets lower and lower down the beach each day until neaps, which is where we are now, and then it comes up a little higher each day for another week until the highest point, which is springs."

"Yes, I see . . ." Cynthia was still gazing at the bank. "But Hugh, even if X did come here on a very high tide wouldn't he have had to anchor his boat somewhere—I mean, he couldn't just have left it to float away, could he? And wouldn't that have made a mark?—*our* anchor has."

"I should think he probably ran into one of the rills, and then he wouldn't have needed to anchor. Still, we'll have a look. Want to come ashore?"

"I'll force myself," said Cynthia. Once more she committed herself to the ooze, following in Hugh's tracks. The mud was even more gluey here, and at every step their boots came out with horrible sucking noises. From the glistening surface came a faint sizzle of escaping air. Cynthia bent to examine a large grayish-white patch in the dark slime and recoiled with an exclamation of disgust as she saw that it was made up of thousands of wriggling sea lice.

Once ashore, they had no difficulty in finding the place where Helen Fairlie's body had rested, for the police had marked the spot with small stakes and had not troubled to remove them. Cynthia gazed down at the little plot, so like the site of a grave, and shivered. Following the track of a real murderer was a very different thing, she decided, from working out clues for stories in the security of a cozy sitting room. If they were right about X and his movements, there must have been a nightmarish scene here. To this place, so lovely now and yet so sinister, a man without compassion or con-

111

science had brought the corpse of a girl, with black marks round her throat that he had made, and dumped her like a sack, and gone away leaving another man to take the blame. It was horrible in its calculated cynicism. For the first time since they had begun their investigation, X ceased to be a mere symbol in a mental exercise and began to assume a shape, a physical reality.

Hugh was concerning himself with more practical matters. He had begun to go carefully over the ground, looking for any marks that might bear out their theory. But the surface of the saltings was hard and sunbaked, and had taken no impressions.

"Probably hasn't been covered since the big March tides," he said, squatting back on his haunches, "and it's over a fortnight since we had any rain to speak of. . . . I suppose that must be where the hat was found." He pointed to another stake a few feet away beside a rill. "It's all pretty bare, isn't it?"

They walked along the edge of the saltings, jumping the smaller inlets and scrambling through the mud of the wider ones. Nowhere could they see the slightest trace of anchor or boat or dinghy. If X had really been here, he had chosen his time perfectly and completely covered his tracks. The same was true at the barge itself. The grass beside it was a little trampled, but again there was nothing that told any story. One flattened patch *might* have been the place where Edward had fallen, for it was near the end of the hulk and just where he might have been struck down, but one needed imagination to see the depression. There was nothing conclusive. All that was clear was that such an attack would have been feasible. Anyone approaching the barge from the Steepleford side could have seen neither over it nor through it. A skulking figure could easily have dodged round to deliver his blow.

They climbed to the top of the sea wall and looked down over the lacing of rills and creeks that the tides had carved.

112

Even from that vantage point, they decided, the rounded bows of the barge would have provided good concealment.

On the landward side of the wall, marshy meadows stretched away for miles without any sign of habitation or life except for a few grazing cattle. The fields were cut by deep dikes and drains, and linked for the most part by narrow planks. The scene was as desolate as any that Cynthia had ever imagined, and it was repeated on the other side of the river.

"What a place!" she said. "I can see now how right Quentin was when he said that X wouldn't have been able to bring the body here overland."

Hugh nodded. "Yes, it was water or nothing. Let's hope to God we can prove it, that's all."

They struggled back to the dinghy and continued upstream. By now the tide was growing slack and Hugh had to pull harder to keep up the pace. Fifteen minutes' rowing brought them in sight of Goldbury Creek. It was little more than a shallow bay, with banks that rapidly converged and came together in a *cul-de-sac* bounded by a sea wall that no longer needed to be high. Just beyond the earth mound they could see the telegraph posts of the road.

It took them very little time to satisfy themselves that no one had embarked a body at this spot. The road itself was narrow, hardly more than the breadth of a car, and there was no place to park. A thorn hedge shut it off from the river, and there were no gaps to facilitate the passage of a body. On the inside of the hedge, long grass grew rankly, strong and upright. No one had walked there in any recent time.

Gloomily, Hugh led the way back to the boat. "One chance gone," he said as they shoved off. "I'm beginning to be afraid, Cynthia."

She said nothing—she was afraid too. They'd built up their theory layer upon layer, with beautiful logic, but perhaps they'd missed a step somewhere. The strain on Hugh's face was like a physical ache to her.

113

Stancott Creek was only a few hundred yards higher up the river and in shape it was almost a replica of Goldbury. Hugh left the dinghy without a word and disappeared over the bank. He was gone only a few minutes, and when he returned Cynthia knew at once that he'd found nothing.

"Just the same as Goldbury," he said. "Same road, same hedge—and not a trace." He looked the picture of dejection.

"Are you absolutely *sure* there isn't anywhere else, darling?"

"Not that's practicable—at least, I don't think so. Chuck the chart across, will you?"

Cynthia fumbled under the stern seat and passed it to him.

"You see . . ." His finger, tracing the river's outline again, suddenly stopped. "Well, of course, there's Mawling Creek— but the road there is more than a quarter of a mile from the water."

"I should think he could have carried the body that distance if he's a strong man—and perhaps he deliberately chose the place that seemed less likely. Where *is* Mawling Creek?"

"We passed it about a mile down river—it's over there where the trees are. I suppose we might as well have a look."

He rowed slowly back the way they had come. He looked tired and Cynthia suggested she should take the oars but he shook his head and went on pulling. Despondency enveloped them again and they were silent until they turned into Mawling Creek. It looked very like the other two, except that the sea wall was a little higher. Nothing was visible from the boat except the tops of the distant elm trees that flanked the road. Hugh pushed the dinghy through the shoaling mud and water, using an oar as a pole, and once again he plowed his way to the bank while Cynthia sat and waited.

But this time there was a difference. As Hugh reached the top of the wall he suddenly let out a terrific shout. "Darling, come here!—come and look!"

Cynthia was out of the boat and up the sea wall in a jiffy, clutching Hugh's arm and following the direction of his pointing finger.

114

At the head of the creek, almost at the edge of the soft mud, there were two clear-cut marks about three feet apart—the unmistakable marks of a dinghy's forefoot where it had been driven hard ashore.

12 So WE were right!" said Hugh softly. "There *is* a Mr. X—and he did embark the body. Look, you can see where he crossed the sea wall. And there's a clear track all the way to the road."

Cynthia gave a jubilant nod. She could see that the grass on both sides of the wall had been flattened, just as it would have been if someone had scrambled over it with a heavy load. On the landward side there was a stretch of waste ground, full of docks and ragwort and thistle, and for five hundred yards the grass and weeds had been parted and beaten into a path by the passage of feet. The evidence couldn't have been plainer.

"And to think we might have missed it, darling, if you hadn't had another look at the chart!" She turned and stared down at the V-shaped incisions in the mud. "Why are there two marks? Not two boats, surely?"

"No, the same boat twice, I should think—the marks look pretty well identical to me. Interesting!"

Cynthia's gaze switched to the margin of hard caked mud between the dinghy marks and the sea wall. "There don't seem to be any footprints."

"No, he was lucky with his weather—and brilliant with his timing. Never mind, we haven't done so badly. Let's follow his trail to the road and see if we can find any signs of a car."

With a feeling that the chase had started in earnest now that theory and fact had converged, they dropped down into the field, following the track that X had made until it petered out under the trees. Beyond the trees there were some leafy bushes and beyond the bushes a ribbon of white deserted road, unhedged and unfenced. Almost immediately they found what they expected. A complicated pattern of depressions on the grass verge showed where a car had recently been driven off the road. Behind the bushes, in the leafy mold, there were several faint but unmistakable tire marks.

"Well, that seems to settle it," said Hugh. "You know, we are dolts!—we ought to have brought a camera."

"It would have been too much of a challenge to Providence, darling."

"Providence might have allowed us a tape measure, though! Still, we'll get somebody to take proper photographs tomorrow." He gazed in satisfaction at the wheel marks. "Aren't they a lovely sight?"

"The thing I can't understand," said Cynthia, "is how he could have been so confident. I agree he chose his spot carefully, and the car wouldn't have been visible and all that, but he has left quite a trail."

"I suppose he felt certain that the frame-up would work and that no one would think of looking further. For that matter, he's still 'X'—there's not a clue to his identity."

They took a last look round and then returned to the creek. Hugh produced cigarettes and they sat down on top of the sea wall, smoking and contemplating the dinghy marks.

"If only they could talk!" said Cynthia.

"Well, as a matter of fact, you know, they do . . . !"

"Then you'll have to translate for me—I don't know the language."

Hugh smiled. "I'm just trying to puzzle it out myself, but it's quite fascinating. See that line of dried scum?"

"The high-water mark?"

"That's right. Well, now, on our side of it the mud's quite dry, isn't it?—bone dry. And the other side is just slightly moist. So that's evidently the line made by the highest of last week's spring tides . . . . What are you grinning at?"

"I was just thinking, my love, how you once said we must never put anything about tides and timetables into our thrillers because they bored people so—and here we are in the thick of it! Sorry, do go on."

"Well, now look at the boat marks. They're almost up to the water line, aren't they, and they're quite short and clear-cut. That means the boat wasn't dragged at all, it came in afloat. And if it floated in as far as that, it *must* have come in on the top of the high tides. Do you follow?"

"I'm tagging along," said Cynthia, her face screwed up in an effort to concentrate.

"Right. But that's not all. . . ." Hugh's excitement was growing as the story of the marks became clearer to him. "You remember I was looking at Frank's tide tables just before we left the Hard. Well, the thing is this. There were three days last week when the tides were about at their highest—Wednesday, Thursday, and Friday. Thursday was actually the top of springs, with Wednesday and Friday just an inch or two lower and about the same as each other. But on both Tuesday and Saturday the heights were appreciably less—six or seven inches. So if X's dinghy had been brought in here on either of those days, the mark of the forefoot wouldn't be anywhere near where it is now—it would be at least four or five feet further out in the creek, because there wouldn't have been enough water to float it in."

Cynthia nodded. "I'm still with you."

"So it's Wednesday, Thursday, and Friday that we're interested in—and not the day tides, of course, the night ones, because we've already agreed that X wouldn't have done any moving about in daylight. Actually, the night tides were perfect for him—high water on Wednesday was about 1 A.M. Now the next thing. Those two marks couldn't have been made on the same night—the water level changes very quickly at springs and if the dinghy had come in twice one of the marks would be farther out than the other. So it came in on two different nights. But we're pretty sure that on Thursday night X killed the girl, and when he'd done that there would hardly have been enough left of the four or five hours of darkness for him to go and fetch a dinghy and bring it in here. So the conclusion seems to be that one of those marks was made on Wednesday night and the other on Friday night."

Cynthia gave him a rewarding look. "That really is rather bright of you, darling. I wonder why he brought the dinghy here on Wednesday, though?—there wasn't a body for him to collect then."

"No—and he would hardly have been spying out the ground at that late stage. . . . Look, let's put down what we know of his movements and see if it helps at all." Hugh produced an odd scrap of paper from his pocket and wrote:

Wed. night —X brings dinghy to Mawling Creek
Thurs. night—X kills girl
Fri. 2 P.M. —X knocks out Dad on saltings
Fri. night —X brings dinghy to Mawling Creek for second time

For a few moments they both studied the brief timetable. Then Hugh pointed thoughtfully to item three. "If X wasn't going to take any chance of being seen around the place, he must have waited on the saltings till nightfall after attacking Dad. But it didn't get dark till well after ten, and an hour or two later he was bringing the dinghy in here. It seems to me he couldn't possibly have done that unless he already had it with him at the saltings."

"Hidden away, you mean?"

"Yes, he could have tucked it into one of the rills, and I bet that's what he did. . . ." Hugh's face lit up. "Ah, now I begin to see. He knew when he was planning this thing that he had to get to the saltings before daylight on Friday, and he knew he'd have to take the dinghy with him in order to have it available for Friday night. But he also knew that on Thursday night he was going to be fully occupied with killing the girl and would therefore need to have the dinghy in a place where he could easily get at it—so he brought it here on Wednesday night and parked it in readiness. How's that?"

Cynthia nodded. "It seems to make sense."

"Good. Well, now we can go back to the beginning again. On Wednesday night he starts the operation by bringing his dinghy from wherever it was based to this creek. Then he clears off—we don't know how, but it's obvious from that criss-cross of tire marks on the grass verge that he brought the car here more than once, and my guess is that he'd already hidden it behind the bushes ready to take him home. Let's assume so. On Thursday he catches up on his lost sleep, and on Thursday night he kills the girl."

"I wonder where he did it—we never discussed that."

"Well, again it's bound to be guesswork, but I should think he probably brought her out into the country and strangled her in the car. . . . Anyhow, now he's got a body on his hands, and he's got to keep it somewhere until Friday night—we agree that he wouldn't have had time to plant it in the saltings on Thursday night."

"That was before we knew there was a dinghy waiting here," Cynthia pointed out.

"True." Hugh frowned. "But if he'd transported the body on Thursday night, there'd have been no earthly reason for him to bring the dinghy back here on Friday night—the operation would have been over. No, I'm pretty sure Friday was transportation night."

"Then where did he hide the body in the meantime?"

"I think it's pretty obvious he must have left it here in the car."

"Would that have been safe?"

"I don't see why not—he could have pushed it down into the back and covered it with a rug. If the car was behind the bushes and the doors were locked I don't think he ran much risk. Anyway, let's see what the revised schedule looks like on that basis." He added the new items, and the timetable now read as follows:

Tuesday	—X brings car to Mawling Creek and leaves it behind bushes
Wednesday	—X travels to "base" where dinghy is kept
Wed. night	—X brings dinghy to Mawling Creek and parks it
	—X leaves Mawling Creek by car, probably for London
Thurs. night	—X kills girl
	—X brings body to Mawling Creek by road and leaves it in car
	—X takes parked dinghy and goes to saltings before dawn
Fri. 2 P.M.	—X knocks out Dad on saltings
Fri. night	—X takes dinghy back to Mawling Creek and collects body
	—X plants body on saltings with hat, etc., and goes on with dinghy to his base

Cynthia smiled. "Creative imagination's a wonderful thing!"

Hugh gazed at the schedule with some pride. "At least, that's how it *could* have happened, it's practicable, and it takes in all the facts we know. After he'd planted the body I suppose he came back here at his leisure, probably on Saturday, and drove his car away. Gosh, though, what a plot!"

"There's one thing about it," said Cynthia, "if X really did do all that he must be a man with a lot of leisure. Allowing for getting his car into position and collecting it afterward, the whole thing must have used up nearly five days."

"Perhaps he was taking his annual holiday!" said Hugh grimly.

"What a macabre idea! Anyhow, I think we've made great strides, I really do, and you've been very clever. What's the next move?"

Hugh glanced at the creek. "Well, *our* next move is to get out of here as fast as we can or we'll be left high and dry.

Then we must try to find out where X's dinghy came from in the first place."

He poled out into the main stream. When they were in deeper water again, Cynthia said: "Where *could* it have come from?"

"From almost anywhere—that's the trouble. I suppose one possibility is that it was already secreted somewhere in the saltings and that X simply went to it after dark on the Wednesday night."

"You don't sound as though you think that very likely."

"I don't, as a matter of fact, because I don't think X would have wanted to do any more messing about on the saltings than was absolutely necessary. It can't be ruled out, but frankly I think he'd have given the place a wide berth until the actual start of the operation."

"Yes, that does seem sensible. What are the alternatives?"

"Well, most of the local dinghies are kept at the Hard, of course—it's by far the most convenient spot. He *might* have brought it straight from there on Wednesday night."

Cynthia looked dubious. "Wouldn't it have been rather a risk for a local man to take his dinghy away from there for four or five days—if he were planning to use it for a murder, I mean? Wouldn't he have been afraid that someone might remember it had been missing?"

"*I* certainly wouldn't have felt very comfortable about it, frame-up or no frame-up. We'll talk to Frank about it—he knows most things that go on at the Hard. The other possibility, of course, is that X brought the dinghy up from the mouth of the river, from a larger boat there. He could just about have done it in the time if he'd worked his tides skillfully."

"Isn't that much more likely?"

"I suppose it is. I can't help feeling that a man who normally kept a dinghy in the river would have hesitated to use it for a plot like this, whereas someone just looking into the broadwater for a day or two could have acted with much more assurance—as our X in fact seems to have done."

"Anyhow, that does exhaust all the possibilities, doesn't it?"

Hugh gave a wry smile. "It exhausts the probabilities. There's always the chance that the dinghy was brought overland on the top of a car!"

"Oh, for heaven's sake!"

They dropped the topic for the moment and Hugh concentrated on his rowing. By the time they drew level with the Hard again, just before noon, the channel was nearly dry. They dragged the dinghy up the mud slope and at once sought out Frank in his workshop. He looked up from a scraper he was sharpening as he heard their voices.

"So you didn't get stuck?" he said. Long experience had taught him that people usually got stuck on ebb tides, even experts.

"Look, Frank," said Hugh, "we want your help. Do you happen to know if anyone took a dinghy away from the Hard for three or four days last week? Wednesday to Saturday, say?"

Frank gave Hugh a long, shrewd stare. "I don't know of anyone," he said at last. He looked out of the window and across the Hard as though by a mere glance he expected to know whether any craft had been missing. "People don't usually go out in mid-week for more than an hour or two."

"That's why I thought you might have noticed. We think a dinghy went up to Mawling Creek on the flood last Wednesday night and stayed out."

"Wednesday?" He shook his head. "Not from here, it didn't. I was around all that night, helping to float *Flavia*."

"*Flavia!*" Hugh cast a surprised glance at the berth where the Briggs's boat had lain for so many years, and saw that it was empty. "Good lord, you don't mean to say she's actually got away at last?"

Frank grinned. "She's only gone down to the Ray. . . . Anyway, Hugh, there's your answer. There was no one about at all that night except the Barnacles and me."

"Was it a dark night?"

"It was a bit cloudy—but I'd have heard a dinghy leaving."

"Would you have noticed if one had come by on the flood from lower down the river?"

"Oh, I see. Well, no, probably not . . ." He looked at Hugh curiously, but refrained from asking questions. "Not if it had just drifted by, anyway."

"Thanks, Frank. Sorry to be so mysterious—I'll tell you all about it when I know a bit more myself. See you later."

They returned thoughtfully to the car. As they climbed in, Hugh said: "You know, darling, the more I think about it the more likely it seems to me that X *did* come from lower down. I think we ought to take a trip downriver tonight."

"*Tonight!* Aren't you tired?"

He laughed. "Time and tide and all that . . . Anyway, it'll be no great effort in *Water Baby*. We'll waste a whole day if we wait till the morning and there's so much to do."

"Where exactly do you suggest we go?"

"Only to the Ray. That's the anchorage at the mouth of the river—it's quite a pleasant place."

"You think it might have been X's base, do you?"

"It's about the likeliest place if he didn't use the Hard and we ought to check up right away if we're going to. There are always a few boats there at this time of the year and we might just get the information we need."

Cynthia nodded. "All right, darling—you know I'm game for anything."

"And we can fill in the afternoon by doing a few small jobs —we still haven't been over to Alfordbury to test the genuineness of Helen Fairlie's houseboat inquiries. Now, let's go and have a drink—I'm parched."

They had a snack and a well-earned rest in the garden of Hugh's favorite local pub. Then, much refreshed, they set off in the car toward the coast.

Alfordbury was the termination of the Cuckoo Line—a dull and insignificant hamlet beside the sea just north of the Broadwater estuary. Presumably the men who had planned the

124

branch had imagined that one day the place would become a thriving holiday resort and the line a carrier of lucrative summer traffic. If so, their hopes had been disappointed, for the few half-hearted attempts at development had come to nothing and today the village hardly boasted a whelk stall. It lay, bleak and windblown in its desolate marshes, an unmatured fruit on a dying stalk. What little life there was in the place was concentrated in a small creek that joined the Broadwater near its mouth. Here there was a considerable colony of houseboats—boats ancient and modern, bright and drab, barges and landing craft and converted lifeboats—all huddled together in tatty confusion and all approached across the saltings by an old and rickety wooden footbridge. It was along this bridge that Hugh and Cynthia were soon walking in search of the holiday residence *Sez-you*.

They found it without much difficulty, and though Cynthia was still inclined to doubt whether Helen Fairlie had in fact ever looked at it, it certainly bore out the description she had given to Jasmine Blake. It was a small and squalid box of a place, with dirty curtains and peeling paint and a contraption of rusty pipes for the conveyance of rain water. Judging by the number of children playing in the mud, it was temporarily accommodating quite a family. A slatternly blonde woman, hanging out clothes on a wire line, told them that the owner could be found in another houseboat along the creek, which on investigation turned out to be almost a replica of *Sez-you* except that it was called *Sez-me*.

The owner, a man named Tucker, was sitting in shirt sleeves and braces on an upturned box beside his boat, smoking a pipe. He seemed quite ready to talk and it soon appeared that in one respect, at least, Cynthia had been wrong. He remembered quite clearly the young woman she described, and he even remembered that her name had been Fairlie. She'd arrived on a Friday evening just before nine o'clock but she'd had her journey for nothing, because as a result of an advertisement he'd put in the local paper back in March, *Sez-*

you had already been booked up for the whole summer. She had been very disappointed, said Mr. Tucker, because she had seen the outside of *Sez-you* and thought it would have been "just the thing."

"Well," said Hugh, as he and Cynthia made their way back over the footbridge, "at least she came."

"She came, yes, but what a phony visit. 'Just the thing!'—did you ever hear such nonsense? Can you imagine those two girls spending a holiday in that dump?"

"Perhaps she was just being polite—or perhaps Tucker made that up. He'd hardly have told us if she thought it frightful."

"You know what I think, darling?—for some reason or other she wanted to establish that she'd been here. Otherwise she wouldn't have bothered to talk to Tucker—she'd have seen the place was hopeless long before she reached it. Anyway, why come all this way to see a houseboat that had been advertised all those months ago? Think of that long, dull train journey. . . ."

"Hardly *dull*, darling!"

"Dull enough for her to get bored and decide to brighten it up a bit, and certainly long—and she arrived here so late that she must have had to stay the night in the village and there isn't even a decent pub. It's my belief that she had some jolly good reason for putting up with all that, and it had nothing whatever to do with houseboats."

"I think you're probably right—but *what* reason?"

"I still can't imagine—but if only we knew who X was, the answer would probably be staring us in the face. Never mind —our visit hasn't been wasted. Now what do we do?"

"I suggest we go to Cowfleet," said Hugh. "Remember what Quent said about asking if anyone saw a girl answering to Helen Fairlie's description on that Friday afternoon? Now's our chance—we can just fit it in."

The run to Cowfleet was short, but the task of trying to prove a negative was long. However, they did succeed in establishing during the next hour or two that no railway official at Cowfleet station could recall having seen a girl like Helen Fairlie on the fatal Friday; and that she had not been noticed at the bus terminus, or been seen by the postman, the grocer's roundsman, the village policeman, or by any of a gang of navvies who had been opening up the road on that Friday and were now busy filling up the hole. By the time they returned to Lavender Cottage for tea the prosecution's case was —as Quentin had hoped—appreciably whittled.

While Cynthia told Trudie of their discoveries up the river, Hugh gathered together the sleeping bags, food and other supplies that they would need for a night in the Ray. Trudie was excited by their news, but when she heard that they were planning a night out together she looked rather uncomfortable.

"Do you think it's all right, dear?" she asked Hugh.

"Good lord, yes. Safe as houses."

"I don't mean that . . ." She hesitated. "After all, you *are* only engaged. . . ."

Hugh gave a guffaw. "My dear Trudie, we'll be dead to the world by the time we reach the Ray. We shan't have a thought in our heads except sleep."

Trudie blushed. "Well, I suppose it's all right . . ." she said dubiously, and went in to make the tea.

"Don't laugh, Hugh," said Cynthia. "I'm sure she means well."

"Oh, she means well. Heart of gold! It's a pity she's a bit dim, though."

They were still having tea when Quentin arrived from Ramsford. He had been visiting Edward and had come away rather subdued.

"How is the poor darling?" asked Cynthia.

"Oh, he's more cheerful, of course—that blackout was bothering him a good deal and he's greatly relieved to know he was merely knocked on the head. He thinks we must be on the right lines and what he told me about his movements just before the blackout certainly fits our theory."

"How's he looking, Quent?"

"A bit peaky. I must say I find him unbearably pathetic—he's so obviously making the best of things. He says he's finding prison life quite restful and getting on with his bird book and will we cut the lawn, because he doesn't want it to look like a field when he comes out. . . . It's a damned shame! Anyway, tell me *your* news—did you discover anything to-day?"

"I'll say we did." Hugh described in detail his trip with Cynthia and the deductions they'd made from the evidence.

Quentin took fresh heart from the recital. "Why, that's a real advance, Hugh—quite the best news yet. I agree you ought to get after the dinghy without delay, but what about the photographs?—it's most important we should get them. You won't be able to do anything about it if you're going to the Ray tonight."

"Could you see to it, Quent? I expect Swaythling would go over there with you and he's quite good."

Quentin put down his cup and nodded. "All right, I'll run down now and find out when he's likely to be free—he might even come with me this evening. See you tomorrow, if not before. Good luck at the Ray." He went off briskly.

Hugh and Cynthia spent a quiet hour or two at the cottage before setting out once more for Steepleford Hard. The river was filling up fast when they got there and this time they were able to row out to *Water Baby* in the dinghy. As Hugh lit the tiny navigation lamps and began to coax the engine into life, Cynthia felt a tremor of excitement. It would have been exhilarating just to be going out in their own boat at dusk—but this trip smacked of real adventure. Every moment, now, seemed to be bringing X a little nearer.

They were soon away and crawling past the low banks as they punched the last of the flood. The noise of the engine made conversation difficult in the cockpit but by now they were both beginning to feel the effects of the long, exhausting day and were quite content to sit without talking. Hugh was relaxed beside the tiller—with a full river there was no danger of running aground and though darkness was falling fast over the land the silver channel gleamed invitingly ahead, broad and empty. The was warm and still, the night scents delicious. After a while, Cynthia found herself dozing.

Just after half-past ten Hugh nudged her and pointed to some white riding lights ahead. "There's the Ray," he said. "See the line of boats? Some of them aren't lit but you can just make out the loom of the hulls." They crept closer, and presently Hugh turned *Water Baby* into the tide and anchored at the end of the line. He got out the lead and made sure they were in the deep channel and then he switched off the popping little engine with a grunt of satisfaction. By the time he had finished attending to the riding light, Cynthia was already asleep.

For a while Hugh lay awake, listening to the chuckle of the passing tide and thinking about X. It seemed strange to know so much about his activities and so little about the man himself. A crude picture of him formed in Hugh's mind—a picture of a tough, saturnine man with a thin cruel mouth and a hard, desperate look about him. An unsmiling monster—the sort of man from whom people would instinctively recoil in fear. A dangerous man to meet—a killer. It wouldn't do to take risks, Hugh thought, particularly with Cynthia. Better have Quent along for the final showdown.

He glanced across at Cynthia. He could see her face glowing palely in the darkness; her bare arm flung carelessly across her sleeping bag. The picture of X faded from his mind and he thought how wonderful it would be when this nightmare was all over and he and Cynthia could live their lives as they had planned. . . . A moment later, he too was asleep.

13 BRIGHT sunlight was streaming through the porthole above his head when Hugh stirred again.
He glanced at his watch and saw that it was nearly eight
o'clock. Cynthia was wide awake, with an open book beside
her, and she was smiling at him.

"Sluggard!" she said.

He sat up and stretched. "Morning, darling. Gosh, I certainly slept." He leaned across to kiss her and then stuck his
head out into the cockpit. "I say, it's a heavenly day."

"I know. I got up and watched the sun rise."

"Oh, you're too smug to live. Conscience troubling you?"

"No, we were swinging and I felt a bump so I went out to
see what it was."

He grinned. "What was it—a liner?"

"Just mud, I think. It was an extraordinary sight, Hugh—
there was hardly any water to be seen at all, and the mud was
terrifying. We were right down at the bottom of a narrow
channel and there was an almost vertical wall of it about eight
feet high and only a few yards away. I couldn't believe my
eyes at first—it was like being in a canyon."

Hugh nodded. "I've seen it like that—it's amazing how a fall
of eighteen or twenty feet in the tide can change the landscape. . . . Feel like a cup of tea?"

"I'd love one."

Hugh got the primus going and filled the kettle from the
freshwater can. Then he stood for a while in the warm sun-
shine looking out over the anchorage. Most of the boats were
small craft of twenty or thirty feet, but at the head of the

line there were tall masts which he recognized instantly as *Flavia's*.

Cynthia called out, "Are we going to swim?"

"The tide's a bit strong," said Hugh, glancing over the side. "I'll let you out on a rope, if you like."

"No, it doesn't matter—perhaps we'll have a chance later on."

Hugh sluiced himself while the water heated and then made tea. Afterward he left Cynthia to get the breakfast and rowed the dinghy slowly down the line of boats, making a note of their names. There were ten of them in addition to *Flavia* and he recognized all but two as belonging to people whom he knew at the Hard. There was Dr. Munro's *Penguin*, Sylvester's *Agnes*, Frampton's *White Wings* . . . thoughtfully he ran through the list. He couldn't see any of *those* people as Mr. X. At the moment the whole eight were deserted. Of the two that were strange to Hugh, one was occupied by an elderly man and a small girl who might have been his granddaughter, and the other by a young couple with a baby. Nothing very promising there, either. He answered their smiles and called a greeting as he rowed by. Finally he made a circuit of *Flavia*, but her occupants were still below deck.

By the time he got back to *Water Baby* there was a pleasant aroma of frying bacon in the cockpit. Breakfast always seemed to Hugh the pleasantest meal afloat, and both of them had sharp appetites. Afterward they sat lazing over cigarettes.

They had just finished the washing up when an engine sprang into life at the far end of the anchorage and a moment later *Flavia* came nosing out of line. For a moment Hugh was worried, thinking she might be off to sea for the day and that he'd missed his chance to talk to the Barnacles, but instead she began to move in toward the saltings.

"What's she trying to do?" asked Cynthia.

"It looks as though they're going to beach her," said Hugh. "We'll go over and talk to them when they've settled down."

"Is that Mr. Briggs with the boathook?"

131

"That's right."

"Why does he keep dashing about and poking it over the side?"

"He's taking soundings, darling. You see, when you beach a boat you have to choose a place where the water's pretty well the same depth all round—then when the tide goes down you're left in a nice comfortable berth. Otherwise you might ground on the edge of one of those high walls of mud you were talking about, and that wouldn't be funny. I've heard of boats actually tipping right over."

"What a horrible thought!"

Flavia was still feeling her way cautiously into shoal water. Judging by the sounds which reached *Water Baby*, there seemed to be a certain amount of dissension about the best spot to choose. Presently, however, she ceased to move and the engine cut out. Hugh allowed them a few minutes and then rowed Cynthia over in the dinghy. Mrs. Briggs, a homely gray-haired woman with glasses, had taken a camp stool onto the saltings and was already busy knitting. Mr. Briggs—Fat Barnacle—was lolling beside her on the grass, smoking a pipe. He had a chubby, contented look. His friend and companion, Mr. Storey, was long and lanky, and his expression was somewhat mournful.

"Ahoy, there!" called Hugh, and clambered out on to the bank.

There was an exchange of greetings. Hugh sensed a certain constraint in the air, very natural in the circumstances, but he decided to ignore it and none of the three referred to his domestic problem. He introduced Cynthia, and Thin Barnacle spread a newspaper on the grass for her to sit on.

"So you got away at last?" said Hugh.

"We did," said Mrs. Briggs, "and 'bout time too. I told 'em I was sick and tired of spending all my holidays up there on the saltings and if they couldn't get the boat moved I was through with it—" she fixed a severe eye on Mr. Briggs—"yes, *through* with it."

Hugh smiled at Fat Barnacle. "Well, I never thought I'd hear that engine again."

"She's all right, that engine," said Mr. Briggs. "Came down a treat, we did."

"Did she make much water?"

Thin Barnacle looked more melancholy than ever. "We only pumped half the perishin' river through her," he said.

"I expect she'll take up all right. What are you planning to do today?"

"Going to black varnish her bottom," said Mr. Briggs. "Starboard side. We did the port side yesterday."

Mrs. Briggs sniffed. "Two grown men, and it took 'em a whole day to do one side!"

"She's got such a big bottom," said Fat Barnacle.

"'Ark who's talking," said Mrs. Briggs. "The trouble is, you don't keep at it. If it isn't tea it's beer, and if it isn't beer it's foolish chatter. Just like a couple of old women, they are. Worse! 'Remember that time we went round the Isle of Wight, Alf?' 'And that time we got caught out off the Cork Light, Joe?' Living in the past, that's what they're doing, 'stead of getting on with it. Else the future. 'When we've got her properly fitted out, Alf, what say we take a nice trip to the West Indies? See the flying fish.' *Flying fish!*" Mrs. Briggs gave her husband a glance of affectionate disgust.

Hugh said: "When did you come down—Wednesday night?"

"Thursday," said Mr. Storey. "It took us all Wednesday night getting her out of that ruddy berth."

"I'm surprised she hadn't taken root," said Hugh. He hesitated for a moment, gazing across at the grounded boat, which was already taking a bit of a list. "I suppose you didn't see any dinghies out on Wednesday night, did you?"

"Dinghies?" said Mr. Storey. "No, we were too perishing busy. Why?"

"We're trying to trace a dinghy that was moving on the river that night. It seems there was one."

"I didn't see nothing," said Mr. Briggs.

"We wondered if it came up from here. Have any of these local boats been occupied while you've been here?"

Fat Barnacle shook his head. "Not a soul's been down from Steepleford, only us."

Hugh nodded. That simply confirmed what Frank had said —it looked as though the local boats could be ruled out.

"When you arrived here on Thursday, were there any other boats around that aren't here now?"

Storey looked at him shrewdly. "What's the idea, Hugh? You trying to do a bit of Sherlock Holmes stuff or something?"

"I'm trying, yes."

Mrs. Briggs's needles clicked noisily in the rather glum silence that followed. Then Fat Barnacle said: "Well, I wish you luck, chum." He sounded as though he were saying good-by to someone about to shoot Niagara in a barrel. "What was the name of the flashy cruiser, Alf?"

"*Night Jar*," said Mr. Storey. "Bloomin' silly name, if you ask me."

At the words "flashy cruiser" Hugh had become sharply alert. "Did you see who was aboard her?"

"There was no one aboard when we got here," said Mr. Storey. "The owner was a young chap about your age, but we didn't see anything of him until he came in in a sailing dinghy midday Saturday."

"Where did he come from?"

Mr. Storey shrugged and jerked his head toward the sea. "From out there, somewhere."

"What did he look like?"

"Just a young chap," said Fat Barnacle. "He was off in a jiffy, wasn't he, Alf?"

Mr. Storey nodded. "We were too far away to see much. She was a smart craft, I can tell you that, only a bit too flashy—on the spivvy side, I'd say."

Hugh's interest was growing. *Night Jar* sounded quite a hopeful line of inquiry. "Was she the only one?" he asked.

"There was another cruiser," said Mr. Briggs. "She was a

134

white streamlined job, too, but not so well kept. What was *her* name, now? *Swallow*—that's it."

"Joe wouldn't forget a name like that," said Mrs. Briggs.

"But we never saw who was aboard her, did we, Alf? She was lying here all shut up when we dropped anchor Thursday, and Sat'day morning when we woke she was gone. Kind o' ghost ship."

"And they were the only two?"

"You don't 'alf want something, don't you?" said Mr. Briggs. "What do you think this is—Southampton Water?"

Hugh laughed. "Well, I'm very grateful to you. You've given us something to work on, anyway."

"You're welcome," said Mr. Briggs. "Wish we could help you more."

Mrs. Briggs jerked her head toward *Flavia*, which by now was beginning to lean over at a sharp angle. "What about starting the scrubbing, Joe?"

Fat Barnacle winked at Cynthia and got lazily to his feet.

"Well, we'll leave you to it," said Hugh. "Hope you get her finished." He gave Cynthia a hand and they returned thoughtfully to the dinghy.

"It was rather lucky they were here, wasn't it?" said Cynthia. "What do you think about *Night Jar* and *Swallow*, darling? Do they sound possible?"

"They sound very possible—no one aboard on Thursday morning and both slipping off on Saturday—they fit into X's schedule perfectly. I'd be happier if we'd excluded all other possibilities—we can't be absolutely *certain* that the dinghy wasn't a local one. Still, no good worrying about that."

"Is it going to be easy to find out who owns them, do you think?"

"I don't know about easy, but we'll do it. They can't either of them have got very far and boats have to put into ports. We might even be able to trace them on the telephone."

"You mean ring coast guards and people?"

"Boatyards. Frank's got a directory—we'll pick it up on the

way back. Look, Cynthia, I suggest we beach the dinghy on the north shore and walk back to the Hard along the sea wall. It'll be hours before the tide serves and time may be precious. We can come back and collect the dinghy when we're free."

Cynthia nodded. She, too, was eager to get to work.

On the way back to *Water Baby* Hugh dropped in on the elderly man and the young couple, hoping to get more precise information about the owners of *Night Jar* and *Swallow*. They had all seen the two boats and were able to add something to the descriptions of them, but they were as unhelpful as the Barnacles about the occupants.

"Never mind, we'll find them," said Hugh confidently to Cynthia as they climbed back aboard *Water Baby*. A few moments sufficed to tidy up the cabin and make the vessel secure and shipshape, and then they rowed away to the north shore and began their walk home.

The day was warming up, and they found it heavy going through the long grass of the sea wall. Each step stirred up a cloud of fine dust that parched their throats. Hugh had forgotten, too, how the wall curved and twisted round the creeks and how much farther it was this way than by water. When at last they arrived back at the Hard they were footsore and weary.

Frank showed no surprise when Hugh asked for his directory. "Hot on the scent?" he asked.

"Just hot!" said Hugh. "I say, you don't know anything about two white cruisers called *Night Jar* and *Swallow*, do you?"

Frank thought for a moment and then shook his head. "I don't think they've ever been up here."

"Okay. I'll let you have this back later."

They drove quickly to Lavender Cottage and refreshed themselves with beer. Then, while Cynthia once again brought Trudie up to date with the news, Hugh went into the sitting room for a debauch of telephoning. His plan was to ring a couple of boatyards in each of the main East Coast rivers, starting from the Medway and working northward, and he was soon deep in his quest. All the people, he found, were very friendly and quite ready to discuss *Night Jar* and *Swallow* over the telephone. Some went out into the yards to make their own inquiries while Hugh held on. But it took a long while. The connections were slow, and some of those who might have helped were at lunch. Cynthia looked in once or twice, but judged from the expression on Hugh's face that he was better left alone.

He had had the receiver to his ear for nearly an hour when he got his first positive reaction. A boatbuilder at Leigh had often seen *Night Jar* and believed that its home port was Benfleet. Two calls to Benfleet were even more productive. The first produced the name and address of the owner—a George Salmson, who lived at Westcliffe. The second discovered a man who had actually been drinking with Mr. Salmson the previous evening and knew about his trip up the coast. *Night Jar's* owner had apparently been on a short fishing holiday.

Hugh restored the sticky receiver to its rest and went off to tell Cynthia. "He may easily be our man," he said with satisfaction. "A fishing holiday doesn't explain why he was away from his boat for so long—unless he was camping in his dinghy or something. Look, would you like to take over for a while—I'm going to have a cold shower. . . ."

Cynthia settled down with the directory. Hugh had his shower and then went out into the garden, thinking of Mr. Salmson. He could hear Cynthia talking—by the sound of her she seemed to be making good progress up the coast. He wondered about the next step. Somehow they'd got to find out exactly what Salmson had been up to and that presumably meant tackling him in person—getting him to explain his movements over five days. It was going to be a tricky approach. . . .

Suddenly there was an excited cry from the sitting room and the sound of a slamming door and then Cynthia came flying out into the garden.

"I've found out who owns *Swallow!*" she cried triumphantly. "Hugh, you'll never guess who it is—*never!*"

"You're dead right," said Hugh. "Tell!"

"It's a man named Vulliamy!"

14

Hugh stared for a moment. Then it registered. "Good lord!" he said softly. "The fellow on the train!"

"That's right, darling. It must be the same man, mustn't it? It's such an uncommon name."

"If it's someone else, it's an incredible coincidence. Gosh, I wish Quentin were here. Where did you find this out, Cynthia?"

"A place called Figgis's, on the river Creech."

"I know it—it's a big yard. But didn't they say anything about him?"

"The man I talked to was frightfully abrupt—he almost spat out the name and then hung up. What shall we do—ring him again?"

Hugh looked at his watch. "It's only twelve miles to the Creech—we could run over there in half an hour. I think we ought to make quite sure it's the same fellow before we go barging in on him—and anyway Vulliamy works in London, he wouldn't be home now. Come on, let's go to Figgis's."

Once more they piled into the ancient car and were soon bumping their way across the narrow peninsula that separated the Broadwater estuary from the Creech. Hugh sat tense behind the wheel, his hair blowing back, his eyes shining.

"Talk about the plot thickening!" he said. "If Vulliamy owns *Swallow* it's as certain as anything can be that Vulliamy is X, and that means he must have known the girl for a long time—known her well, too, or he wouldn't have had a motive for killing her. So what the hell was he doing in the next compartment and why didn't he give any sign of knowing her when he went in? Do you know, Cynthia, I believe those two must have been in cahoots! They could have planned that phony assault between them. She'd make the charge and he'd back it up. But why, *why*? What could they possibly get out of it?"

"Did Vulliamy know your father?"

"Not as far as I'm aware. I dare say he knew *of* him, but that's about all."

"Well, I'm completely baffled," said Cynthia. "Wasn't Vulliamy a rather elderly man—what I mean is, could he have done all that rushing about with the dinghy? What about carrying the girl's body across that field?"

"I should think an active man of sixty could have done that all right, but I don't know about all the rest—it must have been a grueling five days."

"Of course," said Cynthia, "he might have lent his boat to somebody else."

"That's true. Anyway, he was on the train, so he must be in the affair up to his neck. I say, didn't Helen Fairlie meet a bald, elderly man in the shop?"

"She met a good-looking young one, too, and there must be lots we don't know about."

"Let's stick to the one we've got. Suppose Vulliamy was all tangled up with her—respectable citizen in wildest Essex, sugar daddy in town. Got into bad company—blackmail—all that sort of thing. Girl winding him round her finger . . . !" He broke off, smiling. "Sorry, I'm afraid I'm drooling."

"It's none of it impossible," said Cynthia. "After all, we agreed the solution would be pretty fantastic."

Hugh nodded. "Anyway, it was Vulliamy's boat—he can't get away from that. And in many ways he's absolutely right for X. He's a local man, so he'd be likely to know something about the creeks and tides. He'd be in a position to work out that dinghy schedule. And he'd be the sort of chap who might very well pick on the saltings as a nice quiet rendezvous . . ." He broke off as he slowed for a turning. "I say, I wonder if those phony houseboat-hunting trips of Helen Fairlie's were really a cover for meetings with Vulliamy—I wonder if she was actually coming down here to see him each time, and giving herself an alibi, perhaps, for some other boyfriend in town . . . ? Anyway, we'll soon know a bit more—there's the Creech."

They dropped down to the straight, shining river which, unlike the Broadwater, never quite dried out, and a couple of inquiries brought them to Figgis's yard. It looked as large and prosperous as its reputation. There were three big sheds and three slipways and the place was humming with activity. On one of the slips a costly racing yacht had just been hauled out. At moorings in the river there were at least half a dozen smart and expensive-looking craft, as well as innumerable smaller ones dotted about in the saltings and at anchor. A very different place, Hugh reflected, from Frank's modest establishment.

He parked the car at a discreet distance from the main building and paused by a youth who was varnishing an oar in the sun. "Tell me," he said, "who's the boss here? Is there a Mr. Figgis?"

"Commander Figgis is in the office, sir."

"Thanks." They followed the direction of his pointing finger and went through a door marked "Figgis Yacht and Slipway Company Ltd." A pretty girl was typing in a small room.

"Is Commander Figgis about?" Hugh asked.

The girl looked up and smiled. "Have you an appointment, sir?"

"I'm afraid not. Is he busy?"

"He's got a client with him just at the moment. Would you mind waiting? I don't think he'll be very long."

Hugh nodded, and they made themselves as comfortable as possible on a narrow wooden bench. Through the thin partition wall came a booming voice and the sound of robust laughter. Commander Figgis seemed to be having a good time with his client. Hugh was just beginning to get a bit restive when the inner door opened and a small man came out, very dapper in a brass-buttoned reefer jacket and a dazzling yachting cap. He was followed by a very big man in loose expensive tweeds.

"All right, then, Sir William," the big man said, "she'll be ready by Saturday, you can be sure of that. 'By!" He stood for a moment watching his departing visitor. Then he turned to the bench. "Ah!—you two waiting for me?" His glance skimmed over Hugh and rested for a pleasurable moment upon Cynthia. "Come in, won't you? Have a pew." He placed a chair for Cynthia and dropped into his own seat behind an enormous mahogany desk, knocking out a massive pipe on a huge brass ashtray. Everything about him was rather overwhelming. He had big hands, thick muscular wrists, big fleshy ears and a strong, cleft chin. From his spotless white collar an old school tie hung carelessly.

"That was Sir William Endicott. Lovely little ship, his *Balandra*. Won the Fastnet twice. . . . Well, now, what can I do for you?"

Hugh felt that the very least that was expected of him was an immediate order for a new fifty-footer. He took a deep, fortifying breath. "My name's Latimer," he said. "This is my fiancée, Miss Howland . . . I believe you spoke to her on the phone a little while ago about the owner of a boat named *Swallow*."

The Commander's cordial smile disappeared as though it had been rung off on a ship's telegraph. He glanced pointedly at his watch. "Well?"

"We know a man named Vulliamy," said Hugh, "and we want to make sure he's the same man as the owner of the boat. We thought perhaps you could help us."

"Is Vulliamy a friend of yours?" asked Figgis curtly. His tone clearly indicated that an affirmative answer would terminate the interview there and then.

"By no means," said Hugh. "Very much the reverse, I imagine."

There was a slightly less frosty look in the Commander's glacier-blue eyes. "I see. Well, that's different."

"The Vulliamy we're after," said Hugh, "is a bald, elderly man, about sixty. Is that right?"

"Bald and elderly? Oh, no, you're right off your course. The owner of *Swallow's* a young fellow—not much older than you, I'd say. Sorry!" Figgis began to ease himself out of his chair.

A wave of almost unbearable disappointment swept over Hugh. So it *had* been a coincidence after all. . . .

Figgis, half-risen, suddenly paused. "It's an unusual name. What's your man's first name?"

Hugh frowned. "Walter," he said after a moment.

"Ah!" Figgis lowered himself back into the chair. "That's the uncle."

"The uncle?"

"Yes, Walter Vulliamy—lives over beyond Steepleford. The owner's his nephew Guy—Guy Vulliamy." The Commander mouthed the syllables as though they gave him physical pain. "Biggest scoundrel on the coast!"

Hugh made a rapid mental readjustment. "Commander Figgis," he said, leaning forward earnestly, "I know this is taking up your time and isn't selling any boats for you, but the fact is we'd be eternally grateful to you if you would tell us all you know about Guy Vulliamy. You see, we think . . ." He hesitated on the brink of accusation, the shadow of cautious Quentin upon him. "Well, he's caused a spot of trouble, and we're deeply involved."

Figgis's lips sagged in a grim smile. "A spot of trouble, eh? Ha!—that doesn't surprise me. Fellow's always making trouble. Well, what do you want to know?"

"In the first place, sir, what does he look like?"

The "sir" was tactful. Figgis was thawing visibly. "Oh, he's a good-looking fellow—tall, broad, black curly hair. . . . Black record, too, only the dashed thing doesn't show."

Hugh nodded. It was a rather different picture, he thought, from the one he'd had of X on *Water Baby*—the tough, saturnine desperado—but somehow more convincing. "What does he do for a living, Commander?"

"He *calls* himself a yacht broker, confound his impudence."

"Isn't he?"

"Only thing he ever broke was his word. What he knows about yachts would go in this ashtray. He's a landsman—lives in Knightsbridge. Want his address, or do you know it?"

"We'd like it, if it's not too much trouble."

"No trouble at all. Everything's right to hand, here—a place for everything and everything in its place, that's the sailor's motto. You know anything about ships?"

"I sail a three-tonner," said Hugh modestly.

"That's the spirit—we all have to start. Had a little half-decker myself for years. Well, now . . ." He picked up a file and riffled through some papers. "Here we are—13A, Park Mews, London, W.1. Not that you'll find him there—he spends most of his time up and down the coast when he's not at his place in the Stickle. Know the Stickle?"

"I've been there," said Hugh. It was the next river northward from the Creech.

"He has an interest in a small boatyard there. Shocking dump—positive death trap to walk around. He's got a damned cheek to call himself a broker—fellow's a complete fool with boats. Buys and sells, but he doesn't know what he's buying and doesn't know what he's selling."

"It doesn't sound very profitable," said Hugh.

"Hell's bells, that's not what he lives by. The blighter's a smuggler."

"A *smuggler!*"

Something in Hugh's tone seemed to amuse the Commander. "Oh, I don't blame anyone for running a few cigarettes and a bottle of brandy occasionally—bless you, I've had many a pleasant nip myself from an uncustomed bottle. Happens all the time—bound to with all this damned duty they charge. But this fellow's a bad type—city slicker. He's in the business up to his neck. You should read the papers."

"You mean he's been prosecuted?"

"Ipswich. Last October. There were two other fellows involved, brothers. Ex-R.A.F. chaps. They were caught smuggling three thousand watches and a thousand pairs of nylons. One got three years, one got twelve months."

"What happened to Vulliamy?"

"He was charged with aiding and abetting—he'd had a secret compartment built into their boat at his yard. Clear case, if ever there was one, but the scoundrel got away with it. Swore he hadn't known what it was for—told some yarn about understanding it was to keep ship's property in because of thieving from the shore. He was always a glib rogue. Anyway, the damned fools of jurymen gave him the benefit of the doubt and he was let off."

"I shouldn't think that would make him very popular with the other two."

"Oh, they probably fixed it between them—he can afford to make it worth their while when they come out. There's a dashed lot of money in that racket—you can tell that by the way Vulliamy goes on. Can't live the way he does on the profits of a tiny boatyard, believe me."

"Is it so easy to smuggle?" asked Cynthia.

"It's easy to bring the stuff in, m'dear, if that's what you mean. There aren't nearly enough coast guards, and those there are spend most of their time pedaling about on bicycles. Vulliamy's pals happened to be unlucky—ran smack into a revenue boat. In the ordinary way it's plain sailing—you simply take a boat out a few miles, rendezvous with a foreigner outside territorial limits, and run the stuff into a quiet creek at night. There are places round here where there isn't a habitation for ten miles. Can't go wrong if your organization's good. The problem is to get rid of the stuff, and that's where young Vulliamy comes into it, or I'm a Dutchman. Knows the people in town who'll take it without asking questions!"

Again Hugh was forced to readjust his ideas. The whole case had suddenly undergone a kaleidoscopic change. From being a quiet little three-cornered affair on the saltings—almost a personal matter between Helen Fairlie and Edward and X—it had begun to smack of the criminal underworld, of "fences" and shared loot and clandestine meetings in low "dives." And somehow it seemed more real. It wasn't difficult to imagine the girl against that background, enjoying the intrigue, living off the illegal proceeds, perhaps even helping in the work. Had those visits of hers to the remoter parts of Essex been connected in some way with smuggling? And Guy Vulliamy, the clever back-stage organizer, fitted easily into the picture, too. It seemed hard to believe now that they had suspected his uncle. Guy filled the bill so much better—he was a risk-taker, he knew the creeks intimately, and he was young and strong enough for the labor involved. But one thing puzzled Hugh.

"Why do you say, sir, that he knows nothing about boats? He seems to get around quite efficiently on his own, doesn't he? I know for a fact that he's been pretty active in *Swallow* this past week."

Figgis snorted. "Pure luck, my dear fellow. He's a marine motorist—drives about on the water when it's flat calm and doesn't realize the dangers. He'll come to grief one of these days, you'll see. Of course, he's picked up a bit of sailor's jargon by now, but aboard ship he's a menace—hardly knows port from starboard. First time I ever met him he ran his bowsprit clean through the porthole of a lovely little racing job I'd just had done up inside. Absolutely wrecked the cabin. And then had the effrontery to say it was my fault."

"You feel very strongly about him, Commander."

Figgis took his pipe from his mouth and looked grim. "I have reason to. Fact is I was completely taken in by him before I found out what sort of a scamp he was."

"What happened, sir?"

"Well, it was after he ran into my *Betsy Ann*. I was dashed annoyed about that at first but he climbed down when I showed him where he'd been wrong—accepted responsibility, offered his apologies like a gentleman. I thought I'd misjudged the fellow and we got on quite well for a time. Actually it was I who sold him *Swallow*—let him have her cheap. He told me he hadn't been long out of the Forces and was hoping to make a go of the boat business himself and like a dashed fool I swallowed his yarn hook, line, and sinker. Even did a couple of hundred pounds' worth of work on *Swallow* before he took her away. He looked good for the money—smart, well-dressed, good tone, persuasive—never occurred to me he couldn't raise the wind. But it took me nearly a year to get the cash."

Hugh smiled. "Perhaps he needed all his capital for the smuggling business."

"I wouldn't be surprised. Kept telling me he was coming into money—that's how I got to know about his uncle. Trustee, or something, for a will. Anyway, there seemed to be plenty of money in the family so I didn't worry too much but young Vulliamy kept on stalling and in the end I got tired of waiting and said I'd sue. Then he paid up quickly enough. But I knew by that time he was a thoroughly bad hat. Fellow ought to be keel-hauled." Figgis shot a sharp glance at Hugh. "What's he been up to with you? Same sort of thing?"

"Something much worse," said Hugh, "if we're right about him."

Figgis regarded him narrowly for a moment, then grunted. "Well, that's about all I can tell you. Don't know where he is now—he gives this river a pretty wide berth. But you'll find him—if he's not at his flat he'll be around the coast somewhere, you can be sure."

Hugh nodded and got to his feet rather reluctantly. Now that X had been identified he could have listened to gossip about him indefinitely. "Do you know anything about his private life, sir?—friends, haunts, that sort of thing?"

Figgis gave an emphatic headshake. "Nothing at all. He talked a lot but never gave much away. 'Fraid I can't help you there."

"You never saw or heard anything of his girlfriends?"

"No," said Figgis, "and after knowing him I wouldn't want to."

"Well, sir, it's been very decent of you to give us so much time—we're immensely grateful."

"Not at all, young fellow—hope you lay the scoundrel by the heels. And good sailing!" He beamed at Cynthia, nodded a dismissal to Hugh. "Jackie," he called through the open door, "get me Lord Clacton on the phone, will you? Show a leg!"

Hugh's gaze switched to the pretty girl. Cynthia took his arm. "Come along, darling, it's only a nautical term."

15

THE air at Lavender Cottage that evening was thick with plans and counterplans.

Hugh was all for finding Guy Vulliamy right away and having a showdown. "Surely, Quent, it's in the bag? All we've got to do is to insist on an account of his movements during those five days. If he can supply it, we can check. If he can't, it'll be as good as a confession of guilt. Anyway, I want to have a look at his dinghy and see if it could have made those marks in Mawling Creek."

"That part of it's all right, I agree," said Quentin, "but I'm doubtful about the showdown. We haven't enough proof yet to force his hand. If he's a wily type, and I should think he's bound to be, he'll refuse to say anything—and we're not in a position to make him."

"What's the alternative?"

"As I see it, we must try to establish a link between him and Helen Fairlie before we do anything else. We might perhaps be able to do that now, working from Vulliamy's end. I think I'll tell Braddock the latest news, and see what he says." He went in to telephone.

Twenty minutes later he returned with orders. "It's all arranged," he said. "Braddock's going to have inquiries made at Vulliamy's flat tomorrow. Meanwhile he agrees we ought to find out where Vulliamy is if we can—but no showdown."

"Right," said Hugh. "We'll get to work in the morning."

Considering the progress that had been made, the next twenty-four hours were disappointing. After an unproductive telephone call to the London flat, Hugh and Cynthia set to work next day to track down Vulliamy by the method they had used before. All through the day they took turns at the telephone, ringing boatyard after boatyard for information about *Swallow*. This time they found several people who knew both the boat and the owner, but no one who could say where they were. In the afternoon Hugh decided to extend the inquiries northward and southward, but still they found no trace. *Swallow* seemed not to have put in anywhere since her departure from the Broadwater.

Hugh became nervous. "A boat can't simply disappear," he said disgustedly at the end of a fruitless day. "Either she's lying low in some deserted creek or Vulliamy's taken her abroad. And if he's done that we're really up the spout."

Quentin, on his return, had an equally discouraging report to make. A private inquiry agent briefed by Braddock had been to Vulliamy's flat in the morning but had made no progress. The flat was a self-contained one in a discreet and impersonal block. The porter had succumbed to inducements but had been unable to say more than that Vulliamy had occasionally brought girlfriends home with him, though not recently, and not anyone who answered to Helen Fairlie's description. The agent would be continuing his inquiries among tradesmen, cleaners, and others, but it would take time to get results.

"Well, I don't like it," said Hugh. "If we're not very careful Vulliamy's going to slip through our fingers while we're messing about trying to get more evidence. I'm in favor of seeing Colonel Ainslie right away and putting all our cards on the table."

Quentin shook his head. "It's no good being precipitate, Hugh. We can't afford to disclose our defense while it's still incomplete, and I'm certain the police wouldn't act on the evidence we've got."

"Then where do we go from here?"

"Well," said Quentin slowly, "it'll probably be a difficult interview but it looks as though we'll have to try the uncle."

16 WALTER VULLIAMY was sitting alone in the drawing room of his unpretentious but comfortable Georgian house, awaiting the arrival of his self-invited visitors. He would have preferred to avoid this meeting, but he was a man who weighed every decision in the scales of his conscience and he had decided that a flat refusal —particularly as the request had been very courteously made —would be un-Christian and unneighborly.

The Latimer case had been a great shock to him. The idea that a respected magistrate, a man of status and dignity, a man of years and wisdom, could have involved himself in a sordid assault on a girl in a train had filled him with disgust. He had been unable to stop thinking of it—the scene in that compartment had even invaded his dreams and had become embellished in his subconscious with shameful accessory detail. Mr. Vulliamy, who on principle had always striven to subdue the flesh, felt contaminated. The subsequent strangling of the girl had appalled him, though on reflection he had felt no great surprise. A man whose passions were so out of control was clearly capable of anything. Insanity could be the only possible explanation. It was a very tragic business and he felt sorry for the family, but at the same time he had no wish to extend his sympathy to the Latimer sons in person. This could not fail to be a most repugnant interview.

He picked up his horn-rimmed glasses and turned again to the letter he was writing. It was addressed to the organizers of a village film show advertised for the following Sunday evening, and it pointed out politely but quite firmly that such a performance would be illegal and must be canceled. Mr.

151

Vulliamy, when not in London exporting and importing, spent much of his time tracking down breaches of the licensing and Sunday observance laws in the interests of public morality. "Yours very sincerely," he was writing solemnly, when footsteps on the path outside told him that the Latimers had arrived. He got up with a sigh, went to the open French windows and called, "This way, gentlemen, please."

Quentin introduced himself with a gravity appropriate to the occasion, and presented Hugh. Vulliamy gave each of them a formal handshake. While Quentin murmured some rather perfunctory apologies for the intrusion, Hugh studied Vulliamy with interest. He saw a tall, bald man with a prominent nose and a long, humorless upper lip. Eminently respectable, as Quentin had reported, but not, at first glance, a very attractive personality.

"Well, gentlemen," said Vulliamy, politely waving the apologies aside and his visitors into chairs. "I won't pretend that I was pleased to get your telephone call, but I presume you had good reasons for making it." He addressed Quentin as the elder and probably more responsible of the two. "How can I help you?"

"Mr. Vulliamy," began Quentin earnestly, "you know all about the trouble my father is in, I believe?"

Vulliamy solemnly inclined his head—the angle came naturally to him after twenty years as sidesman at the local Baptist chapel. "A very tragic business—very tragic indeed. You have all my sympathy."

"Thank you," said Quentin. "The point is, we believe him to be absolutely innocent."

Vulliamy was obviously embarrassed. "The quality of loyalty is a very fine one, Mr. Latimer," he said, after a slight hesitation. "I would be the last person to decry it."

"This is more than loyalty. My brother and I have some evidence that the girl Helen Fairlie was in fact murdered by another man, and that this man deliberately arranged things to implicate my father."

152

Astonishment and skepticism struggled in Vulliamy's face. "Do you seriously mean that?" he asked, staring at Quentin in blank amazement. "Why, that's extraordinary news! Have you told the police?"

"No," said Quentin.

"But, my dear sir . . . I should advise you to do so at once. Or at least to consult your counsel. They're the proper people to go to, you know. In fact I can't think why you've come to me at all."

"We are not in a position to go to the police, Mr. Vulliamy, because our evidence isn't complete—indeed, it's far from complete. But we believe that after you've heard the whole story *you* may find yourself in a position to fill in some of the blanks. Will you allow my brother to tell you what we know?"

Vulliamy gave Hugh a startled glance. "It seems I must, though for the life of me I can't conceive how I can be of any assistance to you." He sat back with an air of outrage. Quentin felt that Mr. Vulliamy senior was more accustomed to having an audience than to being one himself.

He and Hugh had discussed their tactics on the way up to the house and had agreed that their only hope of getting Vulliamy's co-operation—a slender one, at best—was to impress him with the weight of facts. Hugh therefore marshaled his evidence with care. He began by outlining the theory on which they had been working—that an unknown man, for an unknown reason, had murdered Helen Fairlie and had used Edward Latimer's involvement with her as the basis for a skillfully contrived frame-up. He showed, step by step, how it could have been done. He described his discoveries at Mawling Creek and the conclusions he'd drawn from them. He went into details of tides and distances with lucidity and logic, and as he recapitulated them it seemed to him that the Q.E.D. followed as naturally as in a theorem of Euclid. "The point is," he concluded, "that it's all Lombard Street to a China orange that those dinghy marks were made by someone

153

operating from a boat in the Bay—and in fact we now know that there *was* a boat there that could have been used."

Vulliamy had listened to the first part of the recital with close attention, but as it became more technical he grew restive.

"Well, that is certainly a most astounding story," he said as Hugh concluded, "and quite fascinating, in its way. For all your sakes I hope it may be true. But—well, of course, I'm not a yachtsman, and I don't really understand these things. I'm afraid I'm totally unable to help you in this matter. If, as you say, you have traced a boat that might have been used, why don't you find out who the owner is and question him? That seems to me to be the obvious course."

"We *have* found out, Mr. Vulliamy," said Hugh. "That's why we're here. The name of the boat is *Swallow*, and we understand that the owner is your nephew, Guy Vulliamy."

For a second or two Vulliamy stared at Hugh. Then his lean face flushed duskily and he turned to Quentin with a lowering brow. "Do I understand you to be suggesting, sir, that it was my *nephew* who killed this young woman?"

Professional instinct made Quentin recoil at the blunt words, but he said firmly, "As I told you, Mr. Vulliamy, the evidence is incomplete. There are, we know, big gaps in it. But as my brother says, it does seem that the owner of *Swallow* was in a physical position to make these journeys and that nobody else was. I realize that this must be a great shock to you, but we felt that we had to see you and tell you about it."

"But, good heavens . . . !" began Vulliamy, and then broke off, completely at a loss for words. Hugh had expected an immediate explosion of indignation, but Vulliamy seemed in the grip of some more complex emotion. "Have you—have you tried to locate my nephew?"

"We have, yes, but so far without success. In any case, sir —well, quite frankly, it would be difficult to confront him at this stage, and I would be most reluctant to make any direct accusation. We need more information."

"There I certainly agree with you," Vulliamy said warmly. Indignation seemed to be gaining the upper hand at last. "Why, it's—it's monstrous! You come here with a dubious and speculative theory that you can't substantiate in any particular . . . ! I'm surprised at you, sir! Did anyone see my nephew doing any of these things you say he did? Have you a single shred of real evidence against him, except that he happened to be in the vicinity at the time?"

"As far as we know, no one else could have done it," Hugh reminded him.

"I regard that as entirely unproved. I tell you flatly, gentlemen, that in my opinion your allegation is preposterous and— yes, I'll not mince words—in the circumstances, disgraceful! I can understand your desire to help your father, but to make these wild charges against someone else—these totally unsupported charges . . . !" The dark flush rose in his cheeks again and his stringy neck seemed to vibrate in his high white collar. "Why, you can't even show that my nephew knew this woman. Can you? Is there a single thing to connect him with her?"

"Well, yes," said Hugh. "*You* are a connection, Mr. Vulliamy."

"*I* am?" Vulliamy looked more startled than ever.

"Logically, yes. You are his uncle; you were also concerned in a train incident with Helen Fairlie."

Again he expected an explosion, and again it didn't come. Vulliamy subsided into his chair, frowning, cogitating.

"Doesn't it strike you as odd," Hugh persisted, "that you who were connected with Helen Fairlie in that incident, should also be the uncle of the man whose boat was anchored so conveniently in the Broadwater last week and to whom we've been led by a quite independent route?"

"I suppose I had to be somebody's uncle," Vulliamy said irritably. "It's coincidence . . . nothing but coincidence." He seemed to find comfort in repetition.

"That's something we can't believe," said Quentin. "I myself

155

thought for a long time that the train incident had no bearing on the murder except in so far as it gave the murderer his idea, but now I'm not so sure. It seems to me, Mr. Vulliamy, that there's some thread running through this whole affair from the beginning, which links you and Helen Fairlie and your nephew and my father. We have an impression of a deep-laid plot."

"Well, there's certainly no plot as far as I'm concerned," said Vulliamy. "My own part in that train incident was entirely fortuitous, and an experience I would gladly have been spared."

"That's quite understood, of course," said Quentin, "but what of the girl—can we be so sure of her? My father, you know, has always maintained that it was she who deliberately assaulted him, and that what you saw was his attempt to extricate himself."

"I know all about that," said Vulliamy. "I was quite certain, when you rang, that we should get on to this topic, and now I must tell you that I see no object in pursuing it. I am sorry, but I find myself quite unable to accept your father's story. Believe me, I have thought about it a great deal—the whole episode has been most painful to me. But I have to believe the evidence of my own eyes. I can only say again, most emphatically, that I did not receive the impression that the young woman was the aggressor."

"The thing is," said Hugh, "would you have expected to—and isn't that in itself significant? The mere fact that the girl had called for help would naturally have led you to believe that she was being attacked."

"It wouldn't have led me to expect what I saw," Vulliamy said. "Far from expecting it, indeed, I had to adjust my mind to a very considerable shock. When I went into that compartment I quite expected to find some young tough—some drunkard, even—assaulting the girl. The very last thing I expected was to see her struggling with an elderly gentleman who had struck me as having a particularly benevolent expression."

156

Hugh looked at him in surprise. "You mean you'd already seen him?"

"Certainly I'd seen him. I had to go in to retrieve a newspaper I'd left, and your father was sitting in the seat I had vacated." Vulliamy seemed surprised at the expression on Hugh's face. "I must say I can't see anything of great importance in that."

"You can't!" Hugh glanced at Quentin, then turned to Vulliamy again. His voice shook with excitement. "You mean you'd actually changed your compartment?"

"Indeed I had. There was a small boy who kept waving some infernal instrument under my nose, so I moved next door."

"Was Helen Fairlie in the compartment when you left it, or not?"

"No, there was just the boy and his foolish mother."

"Do you hear that, Quent . . . ? Mr. Vulliamy, tell me, do you often travel on that particular train?"

"Why, yes," said Vulliamy slowly. "Every Friday evening."

"Then it's as plain as daylight what happened." Hugh sounded exultant. "The girl got the wrong man! There *was* a plot, Mr. Vulliamy, and it was directed against you, and my guess is that your nephew instigated it."

"This is preposterous," cried Vulliamy.

"You won't think so in a moment, sir. What you don't know is that the day after the assault took place Helen Fairlie saw the police and told them she didn't want to prosecute my father because she herself had been partly responsible for what happened. We couldn't understand her motive at the time, but now it's quite plain. She'd made a mistake over the victim, and there wasn't any point in her going on with the affair."

Vulliamy looked at Quentin almost beseechingly.

"It's quite true," Quentin said.

"But it's fantastic," Vulliamy muttered, "completely fantastic!"

Quentin pressed home their advantage. "That's a matter about which you are obviously the best judge, Mr. Vulliamy. In our father's case it seemed fantastic because as far as we could discover he had no enemies and it seemed unbelievable that anyone would deliberately seek to ruin him by bringing a charge of this sort. Only you can know what your relations were with your nephew."

Vulliamy's face had taken on a gray look. "I find the whole thing unbelievable . . . it's altogether too monstrous to be possible." He glared at Hugh. "This is another of your wild theories. I don't accept it. Apart from anything else, I can't believe a girl would be so wicked. . . ." Sweat stood out on his forehead.

"We know one or two things about the girl," said Hugh. "Nothing conclusive, it's true, but enough to suggest that she might have been pretty unscrupulous if there were enough money at stake. And with all respect to you, Mr. Vulliamy, what we've learned about your nephew suggests that he isn't frightfully scrupulous either."

Vulliamy let that pass without comment. "I tell you it's beyond all belief—you're letting your imagination get the better of you. The difficulties of organizing such a plot would be insuperable."

"On the contrary," said Hugh, "I think it must have been fairly easy to work out. Your nephew would naturally know your movements and habits. Perhaps, from a safe distance, he watched your arrival at the station that day. He saw you get into your compartment and take your seat—I'm just thinking aloud now—and he went back along the platform and told the girl which compartment you were in. And—yes, of course —probably he gave her a rough description of you—a bald, elderly man, say, with horn-rimmed glasses—something like that. She went along to the compartment, from which you had by now moved—saw my father, a bald, elderly man with horn-rimmed glasses, sitting there in the right seat, and

158

naturally assumed he was the right person. The plot went wrong—but it shouldn't have done."

"I agree with my brother," said Quentin. "I think there's no doubt, Mr. Vulliamy, that if it hadn't been for that unforeseeable last-minute move of yours, your social destruction would now be as complete as my father's is. I think you can congratulate yourself on a very lucky escape."

Vulliamy looked from one to the other as though seeking some way out. "I still find it quite improbable. So many things could have gone wrong. For one thing, how could the girl have relied on our being left alone together in the compartment?"

"It's always more than likely beyond the junction," said Hugh. "You must know that yourself. In any case, there were other Fridays. If they'd failed once they could have tried again."

"How could she be sure she'd have witnesses?"

"In a whole coach there's usually somebody to respond to a call for help—it was a fairly safe bet. For that matter, would it have made so much difference if there *hadn't* been any witnesses? A reputation is easily destroyed."

Vulliamy shook his head. "You're very glib with your answers, young man. You forget that the signalman is even more certain than I am that it was the girl who was assaulted. That makes nonsense of your theory."

"I can only say that on that score both of you *must* have been mistaken. The girl naturally put on a convincing act, and you were understandably deceived."

"A girl can't make a man put his hand on her throat and force her head back, however good an actress she is, and that's what the signalman saw."

"That's what he thinks he saw," said Hugh. He hated to admit it to himself, but the fact remained that when they came to Saberton they always seemed to reach deadlock.

"I think, Mr. Vulliamy," put in Quentin gently, "that it would help a great deal if you could clear up this matter of

159

your relations with your nephew. If you were on good terms with him, then I can understand how difficult it must be for you to accept this theory. If, on the other hand, he bore some grudge against you, then that would seem to clinch the matter."

Vulliamy groaned. For a while he sat in silence, his face contorted with the effort to reach a decision. At last he got rather unsteadily to his feet.

"This conversation has gone far enough," he said. "Too far. I cannot believe that I should be justified in discussing my nephew with you on the basis of these—these wild surmises. Gracious heavens, Mr. Latimer, do you expect me to co-operate with you in trying to hang my brother's son? Would *you* do such a thing in my place? You shouldn't have come—you shouldn't have put me in this position. . . ."

"We have to think first of all of our father," said Quentin. "I can understand your feelings, Mr. Vulliamy, but please try to understand ours. He has lost almost everything in the world that he values. His life was a good life, and it's been utterly blasted. He's waiting now in prison, waiting to be tried for a crime he never committed. Unless we can produce the evidence we need, he'll almost certainly be condemned. If someone is to hang, surely to God it shouldn't be the innocent. Mr. Vulliamy, I appeal to you. You have a grave responsibility, and time is very short."

Vulliamy passed a hand over his clammy brow. "Please go," he said. "Go at once. I must think."

17 "So THERE it is—no wonder Helen Fairlie was short-tempered with her customers that week!" Hugh and Quentin were back at Lavender Cottage and Hugh had just finished telling Cynthia and Trudie of the fascinating twist in the case. "Imagine how she must have felt when she found she'd botched the job."

"Imagine how Guy Vulliamy must have felt, too," said Cynthia. "He'd have been furious after all the trouble he'd taken—I should think it was *that* that made her short-tempered, not just the mistake."

Hugh nodded. "Perhaps that was the start of the row between them."

"What row?" asked Quentin.

"Well, he didn't kill her out of gratitude, Quent."

"Oh, I see. Still, he'd hardly have murdered her because she made a blunder."

"I'm not so sure—it seems to me that a pretty sticky situation might have developed. Of course, again, it's only speculation . . ."

"Go ahead," said Quentin, "you haven't done badly so far."

"Well, if we're going to get at the motive it seems to me that we've got to consider the relationship between them from the beginning. As I see it, Guy Vulliamy wanted to ruin his uncle and he thought up this train idea sometime when he was traveling up and down. To carry it out he needed an unscrupulous, avaricious young woman—and I dare say he had an eye for the type. But she also had to be outwardly respectable and prepossessing, so she was going to take some looking for. Anyway, he kept his eyes open—this plan may have been

161

germinating for months, don't forget, perhaps years—and a few weeks ago he met Helen Fairlie. We don't know the circumstances, but he could have been that chap in the shop who was buying undies for his other girlfriend."

"It does sound rather like him," Cynthia agreed.

"Anyhow, he tries her out—makes a date with her and takes her off in his car and gets to know something about her. He splashes his money around in an easy-come, easy-go way, and she decides he's the answer to a gold digger's prayer. He's even attractive and good-looking as well, if we're to believe Figgis, so she's really in luck. She seems to him a woman who'll do pretty well anything if the incentive's great enough. They delve cautiously into each other's murky minds and find common ground. Then he comes out with his proposition."

"He must have offered something very substantial," said Quentin.

"Considering the risk and the unpleasantness, I should certainly think so. Anyway, she finds the inducement sufficient and agrees to undertake the job. The day comes, and she carries it all off brilliantly except that she gets the wrong man. Vulliamy's furious. His carefully thought out plan is ruined—there can't possibly be another attempt after all the publicity. He meets the girl, and they have a hell of a row."

Quentin gave a little nod of assent. "That's all right so far, but we're still a long way from murder."

"Well, are we?—considering what we know about the two of them? Suppose Vulliamy refuses to pay up—as he may very well have done in the circumstances. Helen Fairlie's not going to take that lying down—she's as tough as he is, perhaps tougher than he thinks. She turns nasty. He tells her to go to hell. She knows she's on to a good thing with Vulliamy and she's going to make all she can out of him. Perhaps she threatens him—not that she's in much of a position to, but she may easily have talked wildly. He decides that she's not safe to have around and that the best thing is to get rid of her. Isn't that a reasonable theory?"

"It needn't even have been money they quarreled about," said Cynthia. "The girl might conceivably have fallen for him —and if he'd regarded the relationship as a purely business one, that might have been even more annoying. He'd have been able to handle threats and that sort of thing, but if he suddenly found himself stuck with an emotional woman when all he wanted was to see the last of her, he might have killed her out of sheer exasperation."

"Or, of course," said Hugh, "there is the possibility that right from the beginning he intended to kill her when he'd made use of her, just to be absolutely certain that his own part in the conspiracy would never come out. After all, he'd have got a hell of a sentence if the facts ever *had* been discovered."

Quentin was silent for a while, considering the various suggestions. "Well, they're all useful ideas," he conceded at last, "and they help to fill out our case, but I don't know that we can carry the matter any further just now . . ." He began to make a move.

"There's just one other thing," said Cynthia. "While Hugh was talking about the train incident I had an idea. I believe I see now how the houseboat comes into it all."

"You do, darling?"

"Yes, and it isn't anything to do with smuggling. Don't you see, if Helen Fairlie knew beforehand that she was going to accuse Walter Vulliamy of assaulting her, she must have realized that she'd have to go to court to give evidence and that she'd be asked a lot of questions and that one of the questions would certainly be what she was doing on the train. Well, she had to have a convincing explanation because otherwise it would have been clear that she was making the journey simply to frame Vulliamy and she couldn't say she was going to Alfordbury for a pleasant weekend on her own because it wouldn't have sounded likely, and if she doesn't know anybody there she couldn't say she was visiting. But she *could* say she was going to look at a houseboat, and with Jasmine

Blake's story to back her up and old Tucker to say she'd actually been, that would have been completely satisfying."

"Yes, you could be right at that," said Hugh. "And Vulliamy could have put her up to it. Knowing the district would give him the idea, and he'd be quite likely to see the advertisement in the local paper." He frowned. "What about all the earlier houseboat journeys she was supposed to have made, though?— I'd have thought one would be enough."

"I suppose she was piling up corroborative evidence—showing a long-standing interest, in case anyone should get suspicious. Though for that matter we don't know for certain that she actually made the earlier journeys. She told Jasmine Blake she did, but perhaps she invented them."

Hugh seemed doubtful. "That would have been a danger, not a safeguard. No, I think she must have made them—and as you say, she was just being specially careful. After all, that's exactly what those two have been over everything—meticulously careful—they've taken no real chances. Look how they were never seen about together anywhere—I dare say they only met in his car. In fact that's probably the reason why he's been so confident all through—perhaps he *knows* that a connection can't be proved between himself and the girl."

Momentarily, Quentin's face clouded. "I sincerely hope he's making a mistake, then—from our point of view it's still about the most important thing in the case. Ah, well, we'll see what turns up in the morning."

18 WHAT turned up in the morning, almost before they had finished breakfast, was a telephone call from Walter Vulliamy asking Quentin and Hugh to go and see him straight away.

Hugh was full of excitement. "If you ask me, this is where we get the low-down. If only we knew where Guy Vulliamy was!"

"Should I ring some of those people again?" asked Cynthia.

"Darling, I wish you would. I know it's a bore, but I do honestly think it's worth while. If he's still in home waters he'll have to show up pretty soon for supplies."

They left her hard at it. Half an hour later they were again being shown into the Vulliamy drawing room, this time by Mrs. Vulliamy. She was a thin, desiccated woman who disappeared discreetly as soon as her husband came in.

Vulliamy looked like a man who had been struggling all night with demons. A grayish pallor seemed to have settled permanently on his face and there was a dark bagginess about his eyes.

"Sit down, gentlemen," he said. "I must apologize for asking you to come up here—I should have driven over to you, but to be frank I feel far from well. . . ."

Quentin murmured his regrets.

"We can none of us expect to be free from trials and anxieties in this world," said Vulliamy. "You and your brother have certainly had your share. . . ." He sank into a chair, and there was a pause. "Mr. Latimer," he said at last, addressing Quentin, "after you left last night I thought over what you said about your father and my responsibility in the matter. I

165

searched my conscience—I prayed for guidance. Today it seems to me that there are things I must tell you. . . ."

Quentin nodded and waited.

"I would have been happier," Vulliamy went on, "if I could first have discussed the position with my nephew—it is distasteful to me to be talking about him in his absence without having given him a hearing. I may say that I made several attempts last night to get in touch with him but I had no more success than you. I imagine he is still on that boat of his, and —well, I have to consider the possibility that he may not wish to be found. I'm very mindful of what you said about the need for speed."

"Thank you," said Quentin.

"But before I say anything, I want to make my position absolutely clear. I am not associating myself with the more serious of your charges. I am reserving judgment on the question of Helen Fairlie's death. All I am doing is to tell you some facts about my nephew which you may consider relevant. I am doing it from a sense of duty and with a very heavy heart."

Hugh was growing a trifle restive. He could understand the old man's discomfort, but excitement had made him impatient.

"Very well," said Vulliamy. His manner became more businesslike. "You asked me yesterday, Mr. Latimer, whether it was possible that my nephew bore a grudge against me. The answer, I am afraid, is that he does, and I must now tell you the circumstances in which it arose. Guy is the only son, the only child, of my elder brother Arthur, who died some ten years ago. Arthur and I, with my younger brother John on whom I still lean, were always very close to each other. Indeed, I think it must be a rare thing for three brothers to have quite so much in common as we had. We shared the important things—we had the same principles, the same ideals, the same faith. Arthur was an exceptionally fine man, a man of great integrity and a true Christian. Unfortunately his son has turned out to be his opposite in every respect." Vulliamy paused and glanced at Quentin. "I gather from what one of you said yesterday that you know a little about his record?"

"We've heard some gossip, that's all," said Quentin. "There was a suggestion that he was engaged in smuggling, and another suggestion of—financial unreliability."

"Yes, yes," said Vulliamy with a sigh. "Well, that's certainly very little. How shall I describe him to you?" His eye ran over a shelf of tracts, as though seeking inspiration. "It would convey entirely the wrong impression if I were to call him simply a black sheep. He has not simply 'gone to the Devil' in the colloquial sense, through weakness of character or a lack of moral fiber. I would say rather that he is a man of strong character who has deliberately sought out and embraced the Devil. He is a man—this has long been my conclusion—who has consciously chosen Evil in preference to Good."

For a moment Vulliamy's thoughts seemed to be bogged down in the depths of his nephew's iniquity. Then he said: "I think perhaps it was a great misfortune for him that he was endowed with considerable gifts—gifts which he has consistently used to harm others. He is exceptionally clever, but he has used his brains only for the purpose of swindling and cheating with impunity. He is exceptionally attractive in appearance, but he has used his attraction to seduce and betray. His—his sexual life has been abominable." For the first time a trace of color appeared in Vulliamy's cheeks. "He has shown himself utterly callous toward the unfortunate women he has deceived and abandoned. You won't expect me, I think, to go into details. If I were required to describe him in a phrase, I should call him an unprincipled and dissolute scoundrel. How such a man could have emerged from a God-fearing and Christian home, from surroundings of piety and firm restraint, is beyond my understanding. But there it is."

Hugh's eyes were fixed upon the carpet. He had no reason to doubt that the description of Guy Vulliamy was authentic, but the uncle's solemn righteousness was hard to take.

"I'm telling you all this advisedly," Vulliamy went on, "and

167

after consultation with my brother John, because it explains how difficulties arose between my nephew and ourselves. When Guy's father died, my brother and I considered ourselves *in loco parentis*. We did our best to set his feet on a worthier path. Repeatedly we remonstrated with him, appealed to him. It was all in vain. He treated us with contempt and derision. He seemed to glory in his evil-doing and mocked our way of life. Finally, my brother and I had to take the step which resulted in a complete break.

"Now I must go back a little. Guy's behavior as a lad undoubtedly killed his mother and I think it probably hastened my brother's death. Instead of being a blessing to them, he was the tragedy of their lives. At the various schools he attended he was constantly in trouble; his adolescence was a disgraceful debauch. The appalling thing was that he never showed any sign of sincere penitence. Nevertheless, Arthur never entirely lost hope that one day his son would see the light. He remembered the great conversions and believed the time might come when Guy too would see the evil of his ways. He was quite a well-to-do man, my brother, and when he learned that he hadn't long to live he was greatly troubled about his duty to the boy. He felt that if he disowned his son as his heir, the total severance might plunge Guy more deeply into a life of crime. He hoped that the prospect of a substantial inheritance on conditions might prove an incentive to reform. He therefore made an unusual will. He left the bulk of his fortune in trust for his son, with myself and my brother John as the trustees. Guy was to inherit at the age of thirty, but only if in our opinion he had by that time shown himself a fit and proper person to make use of a large sum of money. The decision was at our sole discretion. In the event of disagreement between us, which was never likely, he was to inherit; in the event of the death of one of us, the other was to decide."

"An onerous trusteeship," murmured Quentin.

"It was indeed, but John and I felt obliged to undertake it out of affection for our brother. Guy, of course, had been

168

acquainted with the terms of the will, and for a short time it seemed to have the effect on him that his father had hoped for. He spent more time with us at our respective homes and he gave the impression of wanting to settle down and live a respectable life. He became interested in what appeared to be a reputable boat-building business. Unhappily, it was all a façade—the will had merely had the result of driving his unpleasant propensities underground. From time to time we caused inquiries to be made and were concerned to find that with his flat and his car and his boat he was living a life of extravagance and luxury which could not possibly have been financed by his small allowance and the sort of work in which he appeared to be engaged. Then, as you know, he became involved in this smuggling charge, and although the jury gave him the benefit of the doubt my brother and I felt that we had had our answer.

"The time came when we had to make our decision. We took counsel together, long and earnestly. We had to ask ourselves what, at that point, Arthur would have wished us to do, and there seemed no room for doubt. In an interview with Guy which I shall remember to the end of my days, I told him that he was to be disinherited and I explained the reasons."

"That must have been most unpleasant," said Quentin.

A reminiscent flush rose in Vulliamy's face. "It was horrible. He abused us in vulgar and disgusting language. He was insulting and impudent and defiant. His conduct on that day would have sufficed by itself to justify our decision. Well, that was last November—and neither of us has seen him or heard from him since. He left us, I fear, with hatred and spite and malice in his heart. It has been a heavy sorrow to us both."

Vulliamy sat back, dabbing his glistening forehead with a silk handkerchief. He seemed to have come to the end of his story.

Quentin said: "He didn't attempt to dispute your decision in the courts?"

"No. He must have known it would be useless."

"Are we permitted to ask what happened to the money?"

"There were alternative arrangements under the will, Mr. Latimer. It has gone, in part, to help in propagating the Gospel in foreign fields, and in part to the furtherance of the temperance cause—a cause which Arthur, and we ourselves, have always had very close to our hearts."

Hugh studied his fingernails. After a moment Quentin said: "You told us at the beginning, Mr. Vulliamy, that you were reserving judgment over the question of your nephew's responsibility for the death of Helen Fairlie. But I gather from what you have said that you *do* think it possible he may have wished to ruin you, and that in fact you now believe he may have tried?"

Vulliamy nodded his head slowly once or twice. "In the light of all the evidence, and of my knowledge of my nephew's character, I have to admit the possibility—or I wouldn't have spoken at all. I think he is a man who would take great pleasure in revenge, as others would take pleasure in doing a kindness. I think he would enjoy planning the details of it, and on reflection I think that this particular revenge is exactly the sort that would most delight him. It was over his relations with women that we had to speak most frankly to him and I'm sure he would have taken a shameful delight in reducing me publicly to his moral level. There is a certain—how shall I put it?—a certain gloating subtlety about this plot, if plot it was, in which I seem to see the hand of my nephew at work."

He ran a hand wearily over his face. "Well, gentlemen, as I say I have done what I conceive to be my duty in this matter. . . ."

His final speech was interrupted by the ringing of a telephone, and a moment later his wife entered. "It's for Mr. Hugh Latimer, dear."

With a murmured apology, Hugh went out to take the call. He was back almost at once, his eyes on his brother.

"Cynthia has found *Swallow*, Quent, and Guy Vulliamy is

aboard her. Apparently the boat came into the river Pye this morning and she's lying there now."

"Oh!" For a moment Quentin hesitated. Then he got to his feet. "In that case, Mr. Vulliamy, perhaps you'll excuse us?"

"What are you going to do?" asked Vulliamy.

"I suppose, sir, in view of what you've told us, the time has come for us to see your nephew. Would you care to be present?"

"I think not. It would be unbearably painful, and as I told you I am not at all myself today. . . . I will see you to the door."

As they emerged into the garden, Quentin turned. "We do appreciate your action, Mr. Vulliamy, in being so frank with us. I realize how unpleasant it must have been for you."

"Thank you," said Vulliamy. "Good-by." He walked slowly indoors with bowed head.

"All the same," said Hugh, as they got into the car, "I'm quite glad I haven't got to go to Uncle Walter for a testimonial."

19 By the time they got back to Lavender Cottage Quentin's habitual caution was reasserting itself and he was having second thoughts about the wisdom of an immediate visit to *Swallow*. This time, however, Hugh was insistent.

"We may never get more evidence than we've got now, Quent. We need something to clinch the case and shock tactics are the best hope."

"I'm not convinced of that. He's hardly likely to confess."

"No, but we'll scare him with what we know and then he may do something rash and give himself away."

Still doubtful, Quentin went to telephone Braddock. When he emerged from the conversation, he seemed satisfied. "All right, Hugh—he thinks it's worth a gamble. We'll drive over now."

"You'll be careful, won't you?" said Cynthia anxiously. She was longing to go with them, but knew that on this trip she would only be in the way. "Don't forget he may be desperate."

"So are we," said Hugh grimly. He looked as though he were spoiling for a fight.

"I'll keep my fingers crossed, anyway. Good luck." She stood at the gate with Trudie, watching the car until it disappeared round the bend at the end of the lane.

It was thirty miles to Brigham, the little village whose yards and moorings served the yachtsmen of the Pye, but though the road was winding and narrow they covered the distance in less than fifty minutes. Hugh stopped the car at a point where a low hill gave a view over the estuary and anchorage and got out his binoculars. Most of the yachts were bunched opposite Brigham, but some were at scattered moorings and a few were on the move.

"There she is!" he cried after a moment, pointing to a solitary white boat anchored just off the main channel near the river mouth. "The end of the trail, Quent!"

Quentin took the glasses. He had a little difficulty in focusing them, but presently he nodded. "Yes, I can read the name. What do we do now, Hugh? This is your party."

"We'll have to hire a dinghy and row out to her. I expect we can get one at Anderson's yard—that's where Cynthia heard that Vulliamy was in."

They had no difficulty in persuading Mr. Anderson to let them have a boat, and what he told them about *Swallow* increased their eagerness to get started. Apparently she had called in that morning to refuel and lay in stores, so she might be off again at any time. In a very few minutes Hugh was pulling out into the river with short, jabbing strokes. The water was almost up to saltings level but it had already begun to ebb.

Quentin sat very upright in the stern sheets, an incongruous figure in the black-and-striped clothes which he had been in too much of a hurry to change. He looked far from comfortable as they drew out into the channel, for though the sun was shining brightly an on-shore breeze was kicking up a slight sea against the tide and the little dinghy was lively. His constitutional dislike of water strengthened with every stroke of the oars.

The current carried them rapidly downstream and in about ten minutes they were abreast of *Swallow*. With its low streamlined hull and sloping glass windows it was almost as enclosed as a car and there was no outward sign of life, but the dinghy straining at the stern showed that the owner was aboard. Hugh, who had been looking forward to examining this dinghy for a long while, edged closer in. Suddenly his jaw dropped and he gave an exclamation of disgust.

"What's the trouble, Hugh?"

"It's the same sort as my own, Quent—exactly the same. And there are scores of them about, so even if it does fit the marks in Mawling Creek it won't prove anything. We're out of luck."

"I suppose that's why he was so careless about the marks," Quentin said. "Anyway, let's get this interview over." The motion of the rocking boat was troubling him.

Hugh pulled in to *Swallow* with a few vigorous strokes and grasped her counter. "Ahoy, there!" he shouted. "Vulliamy!"

A white door opened and Guy Vulliamy emerged. As Figgis had said, he was a big man, dark and curly-haired and good-looking. What neither of the brothers was prepared for was his expression of candor and his engaging smile. Far from there being anything obviously vicious about him, he looked a thoroughly decent fellow.

"'Morning!" he said cheerily, glancing down at the visiting dinghy. He was very much at ease in a pair of old flannels and a gray pullover. "Want me?"

Hugh's knuckles were white, and not just from the strain of holding on. "We want to talk to you, Vulliamy."

"Fine—come aboard. Always glad to have company." Vulliamy took the dinghy's painter and made it fast beside his own. Then he looked inquiringly at his visitors. "You seem to know my name," he said, "but I'm afraid I don't know yours."

"Latimer," said Hugh, very distinctly. "Both of us."

"Well, come on in. The breeze is a bit fresh this morning—you'll find it cozier below." He ushered them into a small but expensively fitted cabin. "Care for a glass of sherry?"

"No thanks!" Hugh sat down on the corner of one of the berths and surveyed him across the little mahogany table with undisguised hostility. "This is quite an act you're putting on, Vulliamy, but it won't do you any good. The game's up—we know all about you."

Vulliamy stared at him. "What on earth are you talking about?"

"The murder of Helen Fairlie," said Hugh, watching him.

174

Vulliamy looked more astonished than ever. "Who's she?"

"As though you don't know! The girl whose body was found on the saltings at Cowfleet the other day."

His brows drew together. "Oh, yes—I read something about it in the Sunday newspapers. Helen Fairlie, that's right. And the blighter who did it was . . ." He broke off suddenly. "I say, you're not related to *that* Latimer, are you?"

"Edward Latimer is our father," said Quentin.

"Oh, Lord, really? I'm sorry—I didn't intend to be offensive. Pretty bad show for you. But—" his glance shuttled between them—"I don't understand. Why come to me?"

"You killed her," said Hugh.

Vulliamy gave him a look of blank incredulity. "My dear chap, you're out of your mind. I don't even know her."

His self-possession was complete. Hugh half rose from the settee, his hands clenched. "You know her all right, you damned murdering swine . . . !"

"Easy, Hugh!" said Quentin, restraining him. His misgivings about the whole trip were rapidly growing. They should have known that Vulliamy wouldn't be the type to give himself away.

Vulliamy had remained quietly in his seat, his hands in his pockets. "Well, I must say this is a bit thick," he remarked plaintively. "You come here uninvited, I ask you aboard in a civilized way, and before you've been here a couple of minutes you start abusing me. Look, suppose you tell me a bit more—I'm completely at a loss. By the way, my name's *Guy* Vulliamy. You're sure I'm the man you want to see?"

"Quite sure," said Hugh. "You're the man who was anchored at the mouth of the Broadwater a couple of weeks ago, aren't you?"

"I was there, certainly."

"Then you're the man who murdered Helen Fairlie. Would you like to hear the case against yourself?"

"This is fantastic," Vulliamy said. "You can't be serious."

"We're so serious," said Hugh, "that we intend to see you hanged for it."

Vulliamy gave a little shrug of resignation, as though Hugh were some lunatic whom he had to placate. "Well, this is quite the most extraordinary thing that's ever happened to me—an accusation of murder straight out of the blue. I'd ask you to leave, but I'm too intrigued. Do tell me what I'm supposed to have done."

"It's a long story," said Hugh. "It starts with your uncle."

"My uncle? You mean Uncle Walter?"

"That's right."

"Well, really! I know the old boy thinks I'm about the lowest thing on God's earth, but I'd have thought he'd have drawn the line at accusing me of *murder*."

"He didn't accuse you of murder—the facts do that. We know a great deal about you, Vulliamy, as you'll hear."

Once again, Hugh settled down to recall the long sequence of events which by now had become so familiar to him, from the birth of the plot against Walter Vulliamy to the "framing" of Edward Latimer on the saltings. As before, it seemed to him that the logical chain was complete.

Vulliamy's face was a study as Hugh took him step by step through the conspiracy. Once or twice a faintly quizzical smile hovered round his lips, but for the most part his expression was one of bewildered interest.

"Well, that's a most remarkable story," he said, as Hugh concluded, "but as far as I'm concerned, of course, it's just a flight of fancy. After all, I'm not the only person on the coast to have a dinghy and a car."

"You're the only person whose car tires will correspond with the photographs we've had taken, when the police get around to comparing them. Doesn't that worry you at all?"

"Not in the least, my dear fellow, for as I haven't been any-where near Mawling Creek for years the marks obviously *won't* correspond with my tires. You're welcome to check if you want to—the car's at the Apex garage at Ramsford, and

176

the garage man will tell you the tires haven't been changed."

"We'll certainly check," said Hugh. "And now that we've got your exact description it'll be interesting to see if any of the assistants recognize you in the shop where Helen Fairlie worked."

"Would that prove I murdered her? You know, Latimer, if you'll forgive my saying so I think you're being just a bit too smart. Of course, I can see what you're trying to do—you want to get your father off, and by God I'd do the same in your place. I'm making a lot of allowances. But you're completely up the pole if you think *I* had anything to do with it. You don't have to believe me now—you'll find it out for yourself. That's an impressive reconstruction of yours and some of the incidents may have happened as you say—I don't know—but you've picked the wrong man. And if you're not very careful you're going to get yourselves into trouble, I warn you."

"You're bluffing," said Hugh. "This boat was the only place from which all those operations *could* have been carried out and you're the only man with a motive for doing it all. It's not a bit of use trying to pretend you're not concerned."

"Now look here," said Vulliamy quietly, "this has gone far enough. I can see perfectly well what's put all this nonsense into your head—you discovered that *Swallow* had been in the Broadwater and then you got on to my uncle Walter and he filled you up with poison. Isn't that so? Now let me tell you something. My father was a very fine chap, and though he was a bit old-fashioned and strait-laced by modern standards I'll say nothing against him. At least he had a sense of humor. But his brothers—my uncles—are fanatics. They're intolerant, bigoted chapelgoers—Bible-punching, Sabbatarian, repressed, and absolutely wrapped up in something they call Temperance. I'm no worse than the next man but I'm not a plaster saint and just because I don't conform to their idiotic standards they've always taken a poor view of me. They've spent the last ten years busily totting up my little peccadilloes because they were determined from the beginning that the

177

money my father left should go to what they call "the cause" and not to me. That's the truth. And now of course they've got to justify their action. If you've been talking to Uncle Walter you naturally think I'm a complete blackguard, but he's hardly impartial."

"It isn't only Uncle Walter," said Hugh. "Wasn't there a smuggling charge?"

"There was," said Vulliamy, "but I was acquitted. If the jury believed me, why shouldn't you? I got involved in something I didn't understand and had a pretty close shave. That's all."

"Commander Figgis, the boatbuilder on the Creech, doesn't take that view."

Vulliamy's face flushed. "How would you like it if I went around picking up ill-natured gossip about *you?* Have you ever heard that there are two sides to every question? Figgis is a rascally old naval type who sold me a dud boat and overcharged me for repairs at a time when I was new to the business. He's a mean snob—kowtows to the big chaps and bullies the little ones. If I'd had enough money behind me to risk taking him to court I'd have done so, but at that time I hadn't. So he got away with it."

"You seem to have acquired quite a bit of money since," said Hugh. "Where did it come from?"

"Now there," said Vulliamy, "I detect an echo of my dear uncle again. I'll tell you where it came from, Latimer. I came out of the Army with a gratuity, like a lot of other fellows, and I bought an interest in a boat-building and brokerage business and did a lot of damned hard work. There was a bit of a boom just after the war, and—well, I suppose I've got a way with customers. Business runs in the family, don't forget—chapelgoers can be pretty hardheaded! Anyway, we bought and sold boats and we had a big turnover. I made a lot of money, but every bit of it was honestly earned, if business ever is honest. And I can tell you this—I never expected to see a penny of that money my father left, and though I think my God-fearing uncles have worked a pretty dirty racket between them I don't even mind any more. I certainly wouldn't have touched it on their conditions—I had a stab at being a good boy and it turned my stomach. God knows what all this has to do with you—if you want my frank opinion you've been meddling in my affairs in a way that amounts to bloody impudence. But I'm damned if I'm going to let Uncle Walter get away with that sort of story."

"You're very glib," said Hugh. "We'd been warned to expect that."

"I'm telling the truth," cried Vulliamy in a tone of exasperation. "If it sounds glib I can't help it. As for this story of yours —well, it's just too preposterous for words. Do you honestly think I'd have gone to those prodigious lengths just to put Uncle Walter in a spot? Life's too short. Anyway, the whole thing's absurd. Until I read that piece in the paper the other day I'd never heard of Miss Fawley—Fairlie—whatever her name is. I never met her, I never knew her. I can't defend myself because there's nothing to defend myself against. I can tell you one thing—if I hear one squeak of this story outside these cabin walls I'll start libel proceedings against you on the instant—and that's no idle threat. The whole thing's a damned outrage."

Hugh felt that the time had come to play his ace. "If you're so innocent, Vulliamy, perhaps you'd care to tell us where you were during those few days when this boat was lying in the Broadwater? And where was your dinghy?"

"If it'll help to scotch this ridiculous accusation of yours I'll tell you gladly. The dinghy was in a mud berth in the saltings opposite the boat, tucked away so that it wouldn't be pinched. This is what happened. On the Tuesday, I think it was, I took *Swallow* round to the Broadwater from the Creech. There was nothing sinister about the trip—I spend most of my time in the summer going from estuary to estuary, picking up tips about boats that may be coming into the market. Today, if I don't miss my tide through all this talk, I'm going up to the Orwell. . . . . Anyway, where was I?—oh, yes, I'd reached the Broadwater. Well, I'd planned to stay there a few days, but I also had a date in town on the Wednesday night. So I rowed across to the saltings, parked the dinghy, walked along the sea wall to Steepleford, and caught a train to London. I was up there all Thursday and most of Friday, came down Friday evening, walked back to the dinghy, and left on Saturday morning."

"Why did you leave," asked Hugh, "if as you say you'd planned to spend several days in the Broadwater?"

"Because I'd passed the time elsewhere and I had an appointment in the Creech for Sunday morning."

Quentin said: "No doubt you can prove you were in London all that time?"

"I don't have to, but I can. As a matter of fact I was with an old flame who'd come over from Paris on a visit. . . . Oh, you needn't alarm yourselves, she's still in London, so she'll be able to bear me out. I also went to two or three pubs, at least three restaurants, a night club, and a theater, and they'll all remember me. I'm sorry, but you're simply barking up the wrong tree."

"If you had already made this date in town," said Hugh, "how could you have intended to spend a few days on the Broadwater?"

"My God, aren't you persistent? The date, Latimer, was for one evening, Wednesday evening, but—well, as a matter of fact the occasion proved to be even pleasanter than I'd expected, so I stayed on."

"Where did you stay on," asked Quentin, "and who was the lady?"

Vulliamy smiled. "If you make it necessary," he said, "I'll be happy to tell the police; in fact I think I'd better do so anyway and get the thing cleared up. But I'm damned if I'm going to trust my private affairs to your discretion."

There was a thwarted silence. Vulliamy took a silver cigarette case from his pocket, proffered it politely, shrugged at their refusal, and lit a cigarette himself.

Hugh suddenly pounced, grasping his wrist. "What's the matter with your hand, Vulliamy?"

Vulliamy glanced nonchalantly at a broad red weal across the back of his right hand. "That? I burned it on the exhaust pipe of the engine. Why?"

"What were you doing—getting rid of scratches?—nail marks? Vulliamy, you smooth-tongued, cunning devil, you strangled Helen Fairlie!"

"You try to prove it, that's all," said Vulliamy contemptuously. For a second, the mask of candor seemed to drop.

Hugh released his wrist—the fellow had an answer to everything.

"Well, gentlemen," said Vulliamy, "do I catch my tide or do I have to invite you to lunch?"

Quentin motioned to Hugh. "We might as well go—there's nothing more we can do here just now."

Hugh's hands were clenched. "You're lying, Vulliamy—your whole story's a pack of lies from start to finish. By God, I'd like to beat the truth out of you."

"Come, Hugh," called Quentin in an urgent tone. "That won't get us anywhere."

Reluctantly, Hugh turned and followed him into the dinghy.

The appearance of the river had undergone a striking change during their long session. The ebb was now well advanced and great stretches of soft mud were beginning to uncover. The wind had freshened and the crests of tiny wavelets kept slopping aboard the dinghy, wetting both its occupants. As he rowed, Hugh kept turning to make sure he was well in the channel, for he had no mind to be blown ashore on to that treacherous-looking ooze. He had to pull hard against the tide, heaving on the oars with short, vicious strokes that matched his mood. It had been a frustrating encounter.

Quentin looked pretty glum, too. "I hope we haven't been letting our imaginations run away with us," he said, as they slowly drew away from *Swallow*. "That was a frightfully plausible story he told."

"It was a false one," said Hugh. "It's *got* to be false. If not, there's no order or logic in the world."

"Well, I hope you're right."

"There were flaws, Quent. Did you notice he said he went to the Broadwater from the *Creech,* and that he went back to the *Creech* afterward to keep some appointment? Yet Figgis said he gives that river a wide berth these days."

"It's a thing Figgis can hardly be sure about. Still, we'll make inquiries." Quentin sat in gloomy silence for a while. "What worries me, Hugh, is that Vulliamy told us so much and in such a nonchalant way. Would he really throw out his explanations so casually if he were guilty, and appear to care so little about the inquiries we're bound to make? Look at that tire business, for instance—it obviously wasn't bothering him at all."

"I've been thinking about that," said Hugh. "The marks were rather faint, you know—they may not be identifiable. It was a bit of bluff on my part, and he called it. He may know we can't prove it was his car."

Quentin grunted. "He was very forthcoming about a lot of other things."

"He gave that impression," Hugh agreed, "but when you come to examine what he told us it doesn't really amount to much. That business about sticking his dinghy in the saltings and walking along the sea wall to Steepleford and getting a train to town—he must know it'll be damned hard for us to disprove it. And as for the alibi, it sounded convincing enough but he was careful not to tell us anything we could check up on."

"That's true," said Quentin, "but at least we've nailed him down to a story and he must realize we shan't leave him alone now until it's either established or disproved. . . . What troubles me, Hugh, is that *if* he's guilty I simply can't see the

182

point of all that stuff he told us today. It's not going to get him anywhere—not in the long run."

A gust of wind caught the boat and one of Hugh's oars touched bottom. For a few moments his whole attention was occupied in getting out of the shallows.

Then the roar of a powerful marine engine came reverberating over the water from the direction of the white cruiser.

"He's not wasting much time," said Quentin.

Hugh was watching the active gray figure on *Swallow's* deck. "He must be pretty certain of the channel to go out at half-ebb—it's more than I'd like to do. . . ." Suddenly he stopped rowing. "Do you know what I think, Quent? There isn't going to be any 'long run'! I think he's skipping."

Quentin looked startled. "What do you mean?"

"Why, don't you see, all he was really interested in was getting us off his boat as quickly as possible. I bet you anything you like he's heading for the Continent and not the Orwell. He's got stores and fuel aboard—what's to stop him?"

"There was nothing to stop him before, but he didn't go."

"He didn't know then what a case we'd got against him. Now he does. Our story is *right*, and he knows he hasn't a chance. He hasn't any alibi—he just reeled off the first thing that came into his head and he doesn't care whether we check or not because he won't be here. Quent, we're a couple of mugs if we let him go. If we can hold him and explode his alibi, we've got him cold. If he disappears, we're sunk."

"What's the good of talking like that, Hugh—there's nothing we can do. Not even the police could detain him without making inquiries first."

Hugh was unconvinced. He began to row again, but so half-heartedly that he barely held his own against the tide. He knew that a climactic moment had been reached. If he turned the dinghy's head, they could be back at *Swallow* in a couple of minutes. They could board her and hold Vulliamy—tie him up if necessary. One of them could stay with him while the other put the facts before the police. It would be a gamble, of course—if they were wrong, if his alibi were confirmed, it would mean prosecution and imprisonment for both of them. But the situation called for risks. They couldn't let the fellow slip through their fingers now.

"Look, Quent," he began, resting on his oars, "we've got to take a chance. . . ."

Then he saw that it was too late, anyway. Vulliamy had gone forward and was hauling up his anchor. A moment later he was back in his cockpit and from *Swallow*'s mechanical siren came four or five short blasts, as though in derisive farewell.

"Swine!" muttered Hugh.

The gap between the two boats began to widen rapidly as *Swallow* turned in the channel and shot off toward the open sea. She was in a hurry, all right—both her engines were roaring and she was throwing up a fine bow wave.

"Well, that's that," said Hugh. "Let's hope I'm wrong—but I'm damned sure I'm not." He gazed after the receding white hull with a look almost of despair.

For the moment Quentin was thinking of other things. The motion of the bobbing boat was worrying him again.

"We're losing all the ground we've made, Hugh. Come on, let's call it a day."

Hugh rowed a dozen more strokes. Then he stopped again, with a sharp exclamation. "That's funny, she doesn't seem to be moving any more."

Quentin turned his head to look. Something was obviously happening aboard *Swallow*. Vulliamy had left the wheel and was rushing about on deck in a frantic way. As the dinghy drifted down on her they saw him fling himself into the cockpit again and a moment later both engines roared at full power. Foam churned up around the screws—not white, but brown and muddy.

"By God," cried Hugh excitedly, "she's run aground."

20 IN ANY other circumstances Hugh would have rowed to the scene at top speed and offered his help, but now he was only too ready to let the dinghy drift and watch Vulliamy's efforts from a distance.

"You all right, Quent?" he asked, noticing the greenish color of his brother's face.

"I shall survive."

"I'd put you ashore, but the mud's not safe here."

"Don't worry. What's he trying to do?" Vulliamy had got into his own dinghy with an anchor and a warp and was rowing furiously away from *Swallow*.

"He's putting out a kedge. He'll drop the anchor well away from the boat, take the warp back aboard, and try to get her off the bank by hauling or winching on the rope."

"Will he manage it?"

"I very much doubt it—he's left it too late. The tide goes down about three inches every five minutes, you know, and you have to move damn fast. Besides, the wind's putting him on harder every second. *And* his angle's all wrong."

"Is he in any danger?—he's rowing as though his life depends on it."

"Perhaps it does!" said Hugh grimly.

The distance between their dinghy and the cruiser was rapidly narrowing and every action of Vulliamy's was now clearly visible. He had let the anchor go in the deep channel and was rowing back to *Swallow* with the same desperate urgency. They watched him clamber aboard and make the warp fast to the winch drum. A moment later it tautened and took the strain.

"I believe she's moving," cried Quentin, as the rope seemed to slacken again. He had almost forgotten his queasiness in the interest of the proceedings.

Hugh shook his head. "It's not the boat that's moving, it's the anchor."

He was right. The kedge had been dropped too close to *Swallow* to do its work and it was being slowly drawn in through the mud. By the time the Latimers' dinghy had once more come abreast of the cruiser, Vulliamy was hauling the anchor back aboard. He looked crestfallen and anxious.

Hugh swung the little boat into the tide and came alongside with a final flick of his oar. Even Quentin could see now that there was no possibility of refloating *Swallow* until the next tide. In these few moments she had taken a slight but perceptible list toward the channel.

Vulliamy wiped his face, which was crimson from exertion, and glared down at them. "What the hell have you come back for?"

"You appeared to be in difficulties," said Hugh.

"I stayed too long talking to you, blast you. Clear off, I don't need you."

"What about coming ashore with us for an hour or two, Vulliamy? We could run over the details of that alibi of yours —with the police. We've decided we don't believe a word of it."

"Go to hell! I've said all I've got to say."

"Where were you going to in such a tearing hurry—France, Belgium?"

"I was going to the Orwell—I told you. And I still am."

"Not for some hours, you're not," said Hugh, as, with a creak of timbers, *Swallow* took another list toward him. "Six or seven, at least. You'll be more comfortable ashore, you know —she'll soon be on her ear." He took an oar and thrust it into the water beside the dinghy to see what the ground was like. Instantly his expression became tense.

"I say, Vulliamy, you haven't chosen a very good spot. There's no bottom here."

With a look of apprehension, Vulliamy grabbed a sounding lead and dropped it overboard beside the dinghy. The line registered seven feet.

"You must be on the edge of a steep-to bank," said Hugh. "You're going to feel quite dizzy up there, Vulliamy, when the tide's dropped another six or seven feet. In fact, I wouldn't be surprised if your boat turned turtle and filled. I've known it to happen. Better keep your dinghy handy."

Vulliamy gave Hugh a glance of pure hate. "You keep your bloody advice to yourself. She'll probably slide off." He began trying to rock the cruiser, but she was firmly held.

"I doubt it," said Hugh.

Vulliamy gazed around the ship with mounting alarm. Hugh could guess what he was thinking. If he *did* lose the vessel, he'd never get to the Continent. He'd have to stay and face the music, and it wasn't going to be sweet music.

The prospect spurred him to new action. Turning his back on Hugh he clambered up the sloping deck with the free end of the kedge anchor warp in his hand and made it fast round the foot of the short mast. Then he lowered the kedge into the uncovered mud on the landward side of *Swallow*. He gave a quick glance around, as though wondering how best to descend himself, but a sudden lurch of the boat warned him that he had no time to lose. A moment later he had taken a flying leap over the deck rail and disappeared from sight behind the white hull.

"What on earth's he up to now?" asked Quentin, startled by the acrobatics.

"God knows," said Hugh, frowning. "He's crazy if he thinks he can hold a boat this size with a warp and an anchor—she's too far over already. Anyway, he'll never be able to carry it through that mud. . . ."

Suddenly, from the other side of *Swallow*, there came a sharp and urgent cry.

187

"He's in trouble," exclaimed Hugh. "God, I wonder if he fell on the anchor!" In an instant he had made the dinghy's painter fast and was scrambling up the cruiser's deck. As he peered over the side at the point where Vulliamy had jumped, a dreadful sight met his eyes.

Vulliamy was waist-deep in mud—soft, almost liquid mud. He was struggling wildly, trying to heave himself up and out on to his stomach. His hands were making futile grabs at the dark slime. With every convulsive movement he sank a little lower. The treacherous, bottomless ooze of the Pye banks had got him.

"Quent!" yelled Hugh. "Quick!—lend a hand!" With trembling fingers he unfastened the rope that Vulliamy had tied round the mast and pulled in some of the slack. Then he lowered the free end over the side. "Get a grip, Vulliamy. Don't struggle, you fool! Here, Quent, catch hold! Right, now —heave!"

Both men put their weight on the rope. Hugh could see Vulliamy's wrist muscles knotting, his forearms straining. The greedy mud gave out horrible gurgling noises, yielding its prey grudgingly. But it *was* yielding. Vulliamy had a good grip and was hanging on. Inch by inch his body emerged.

"He's coming!" cried Hugh.

Suddenly *Swallow* gave another lurch. Quentin, caught unawares, lost his footing on the slippery deck, let go of the rope, and rolled with a fearful crash against the lower rail, almost shooting overboard. For a moment he lay there half-stunned while Hugh clung grimly on. Then he got up and shook himself and came staggering back to take the rope again. But Vulliamy had again begun to struggle, and in those few seconds the mud had regained all that it had lost, and more.

As Hugh gazed down at the half-submerged, helpless figure and felt Quentin's weakened pull upon the rope he realized with a pang of horror that they weren't going to succeed—not that way. The thought was hardly bearable. He had quite forgotten that it was a murderer they were trying to haul out—

it was a man, that was all he knew, a man on the brink of an unspeakable death.

"Can you get the rope round you, Vulliamy?" he shouted. "If you can, I'll try to winch you out."

Vulliamy struggled to pass the rope behind him but he was almost up to his armpits and no longer had the free use of his hands. His face was ashen, except where the mud had smeared it. "I can't!" he cried. "Pull again, for God's sake. Quick!"

Once more the two men grasped the rope and heaved. This time they were prepared for the lurch of the settling boat and when it came they kept their balance and held on. They were gaining a little—an inch or two. Then Vulliamy's fingers began to slip and slide on the muddy rope. His strength was going. Despair was written on his face. Suddenly he let go and the two men fell in a heap together. When, bruised and shaken, they crawled back to the railing, Vulliamy's shoulders were almost covered. He looked like some hideous gargoyle on a plinth. He was gasping, as though he couldn't breathe properly.

Hugh gazed wildly around. "God in heaven, there must be something we can do." He plunged below, and a moment later came up with a long rubber settee cushion. He flung it down onto the mud beside Vulliamy's head, refastened the rope round the mast, and began to tie some of the slack round his waist.

"You're not going down there," Quentin shouted. "Hugh, don't be a fool!"

"I'll be all right—p'raps I can get a rope under his arms. Quent, we've got to do something—we can't just let him suffocate."

Quentin grabbed his brother's arm. "I won't let you, do you hear? If you got stuck, I couldn't pull you up." For a moment they struggled wildly. Then Hugh broke loose and rushed to the edge.

He gave one gasp of horror and covered his face. "It's too late, Quent. Oh, God!"

There was nothing visible down there now but a white up-turned face with staring hopeless eyes and a pair of outthrust hands supported by the mud. Suddenly the pale lips parted and the doomed man gave a single long-drawn shriek. Then the mud trickled over his face, into his open mouth, into his anguished eyes. The head was swallowed up. The two hands stuck out for a while like the masts of a foundering ship; then they, too, were gone.

21   QUENTIN dropped into the high-backed arm-chair which had been Edward's favorite and felt for his pipe. He looked terribly tired. "Well," he said, "the long and the short of it is that we still can't prove our story."

A week had passed since the Pye mud had swallowed up Guy Vulliamy, and the Latimer family were once again gathered at Lavender Cottage, this time to hear Quentin's report on the final state of the defense preparations.

It had been a grueling week. Both brothers had been badly shaken by Vulliamy's ghastly end, and the necessity of going over all the details at the inquest had kept the horror alive in their minds. Quentin had feared that the inquiry might bring out the nature of their business with Vulliamy that day but the coroner had shown no interest in the reasons for their visit to *Swallow* and the secrets of the Latimer defense were still intact. To the public, Vulliamy was a man who had had a fatal accident of a peculiarly unpleasant kind, and that was all.

Swallow had not, after all, tipped over into the mud—after perching precariously on the edge of the bank for a few hours she had been refloated and taken into Anderson's yard. There, after reporting the tragedy, the Latimers had gone over her with meticulous care, hoping they might make some discovery aboard her which would help their case. But they had found nothing except a valid passport, and that, as Quentin said, didn't actually *prove* anything. Since then, every possible effort had been made to fill out and strengthen the defense story. In the view both of Braddock and of John Colfax, Q.C., who was leading for them, it was now about as complete as they could hope to make it.

Nevertheless, they were far from satisfied.

"Vulliamy's death," mourned Quentin, not for the first time, "was a piece of extraordinarily bad luck for us." He had never openly reproached Hugh for the shock tactics that had driven the murderer to desperation, but he had an irritating way of reverting to the subject.

"It's no good worrying about that now, Quent. Anyway, he wouldn't have been much good to us on the Continent."

"And who would ever have expected him to do anything so utterly lunatic as to jump into that glue?" asked Cynthia indignantly. They were all feeling the strain a bit.

"The fact remains," said Quentin, "that we've lost our star witness. If he'd lived, we could have forced him to declare his whereabouts in detail, and then we could have disproved his alibi. As it is, we can't test it at all because we don't know what it was."

"What about the part of the story where he did give some details?" Cynthia asked. "Leaving his dinghy in the saltings and walking to Steepleford along the sea wall and having an appointment in the Creech and all those things?"

Quentin shook his head. "Even if we could show there wasn't any truth in it, which we can't, it wouldn't help. Our account of what he told us wouldn't be accepted as evidence anyway. The best thing we can do in the circumstances is to keep quiet about the whole business."

"Are we any nearer to establishing his contact with the girl, Quent?"

"I'm afraid not. Cynthia's had no luck with her inquiries at Helen Fairlie's end, and we've drawn a complete blank everywhere else, too. We can't offer a single scrap of evidence that he knew her, and that's going to be pretty serious. Braddock's covered an enormous amount of ground—he's had people see Vulliamy's associates at the boatyard, he's visited those two smuggler fellows in prison, he's checked up with every known friend and acquaintance, he's seen all those people in the block of flats where Vulliamy lived, and he's been back at the shop where Helen Fairlie worked, with a photograph. He seems to me to have done everything that's humanly possible—but it hasn't been enough. We've learned a lot more about Vulliamy, and quite a bit about his relations with other women, but there isn't a hint of any contact with Helen Fairlie."

"That merely shows that our earlier view was right," said Hugh obstinately. "Vulliamy met the girl just once in the shop without anyone taking any notice and after that he took good care not to be seen with her. I'd say it was confirmation of the conspiracy."

"To us, yes," Quentin agreed, "but perhaps not to a jury. . . . Well, then, of course, we can't prove any motive. All we can do is to indicate one—a rather sketchy one—which may or may not convince others. We can't prove any financial agreement or any emotional link. We can't prove he took her out in his car and killed her—we've been over the car with a fine comb and there's no evidence there. We can't prove he had anything to do with the faked letters. We can't prove the dinghy marks were his, because as you said there are so many dinghies of that type around. And the tire marks are as inconclusive as you thought they'd be. The experts say it could have been Vulliamy's car that made them, but it could just as well have been somebody else's car. So we're exactly where we were—we have a theory, but we still haven't a single piece of solid evidence to back it up. Not one."

"All the same," said Hugh, "it's a damned impressive theory."

"Well, even as a theory it's not as perfect as we like to think. There's a weakness in the structure. We can't say categorically that the *Swallow* was the only possible place that the murderer's dinghy could have come from—you yourself said earlier that there was a faint possibility—a one-in-a-hundred chance, perhaps, but still a possibility—that it might already have been lying in the saltings. We don't believe that,

193

and we've tended to slur over it as an outside chance, but it is a break in the logical chain leading to Vulliamy—a loophole in our story—and the prosecution are bound to point it out."

"Yes, of course," said Hugh. "Well, there's nothing we can do about that. What about the prosecution's own case? Is Colfax satisfied that we can explain everything they're likely to bring up?"

Quentin looked gloomy. "We've an Achilles heel there, too. The thing that troubles Colfax is Joe Saberton's account of the assault in the train. Saberton still won't admit he was mistaken—he's made a statement which repeats word for word and letter for letter what he's said from the beginning. The only question is whether the prosecution will be able to introduce it, but as it's relevant to motive they probably will."

"Suppose they do," Cynthia said, "how important is it?"

"I'm afraid it may be the key to the whole case, Cynthia. If the prosecution can show that Father assaulted the girl, then our entire story of a train plot falls to the ground and the basis of our case is destroyed. Of course, it works the other way, too. If we could show beyond any possibility of doubt that it was the girl who assaulted Father, then the plot would be proved and the rest of our story would follow logically and reasonably and we'd be certain of the verdict. But we can't prove it—certainly not in the face of Saberton's evidence."

There was silence for a moment or two. Then Hugh said, "So what are the prospects, Quent?"

Quentin sighed. "Well, Colfax was very frank about that. The position is that the prosecution has an immensely strong circumstantial case. We have an alternative theory which answers most of their case. The question is, will the jury believe it? Or rather, will they think it throws sufficient doubt on the prosecution's story to require a verdict of 'Not Guilty.' And nobody can answer that question. The trouble is that the average jury isn't very imaginative. They're bound to be impressed by the prosecution's case because the Attorney General will be able to produce witnesses to the train business, if he can get that admitted, and several bits of concrete evidence—the letter, the hat, the lipsticked handkerchief, and so on. There'll be something they can get their teeth into. By contrast, our story will seem to them to be conjured out of thin air. We'll be accusing someone they've never heard of, someone we can't produce—a dead man. It'll be hard for Colfax to make him seem real to them, skillful though he is. We shan't be able to bring forward a single witness that'll be worth anything, or a fragment of solid evidence. Also, as Colfax points out, much of our story will deal with rather technical matters that a lay jury may easily fail to follow—just as Walter Vulliamy did."

Hugh's face was grave. "In fact, the prognosis isn't hopeful."

"I wouldn't say that. It could be better, but Colfax is pretty confident he'll be able to plant enough misgivings in the mind of the jury to win a verdict."

"Well, that's something, anyway," murmured Trudie, whose face had been growing longer and longer during the discussion.

Hugh pushed back his chair and began pacing about. "It's not enough," he said savagely, "not nearly enough. It sounds a hell of a-risk to me. And it means we've failed, Quent, even if we do scrape through. A technical acquittal isn't everything. What's going to happen to Dad afterward? If he's merely going to get the benefit of the doubt, a sort of English 'not proven' which is the way people will take it—well, to be brutally frank I think he'd be better dead."

"Oh, Hugh!" exclaimed Trudie, the tears welling up in her eyes, "how can you say such a thing?"

"It's true, and we all know it. What do you think he'll feel like living in a world where people point at him and say 'That's Edward Latimer—he was lucky to get off!'? That's not what we've worked for. Quent, he's got to come out of the dock on Monday week with the judge and the jury and the press and the public all knowing and saying that he's been the innocent victim of a monstrous conspiracy, and all anxious to

195

make amends for the bloody time he's had. He's got to be exonerated, reinstated—people have got to be proud to know him again. Otherwise—" Hugh threw out his hands in a gesture of hopelessness— ". . . well, he'll just finish his life a broken, unhappy old man."

"You're right, of course," Quentin said sadly. "But it's no good deceiving ourselves, Hugh—we've done our utmost, and the fact remains that the sort of exoneration you have in mind is more than we can hope for. Father's innocence simply isn't demonstrable in that way. We can show that our theory is rationally possible, we can make people accept it as a possibility, but we can't expect it to produce any blinding flash of revelation in the jury or in anyone else. That's the trouble with the kind of circumstantial evidence we're dealing with—it can't have that sort of impact."

Hugh looked stubborn. "I don't see why not—I seem to remember there've been cases where the jury were swept off their feet simply because circumstantial evidence was put to them in a dramatic way. Cynthia, what was that case we were talking about the other day . . . ?"

"You mean the Brides in the Bath?"

"That's right. You must have read about it, Quent. The prosecution had a theory that the prisoner, Smith, had drowned several women by grabbing hold of their feet when they were in the bath and pulling their legs upward so that their heads went under water. But it was just a theory, of course—no one had seen it happen. So they brought a bath into court and a nurse in a bathing costume and she got into the water and some policeman yanked up her legs and her head went under and she was damned nearly drowned before the eyes of the jury. And that one thing clinched the case."

Quentin nodded. "Yes, I can see that it would—but the prosecution was lucky; they had a point that lent itself to demonstration. We haven't got one. All we've got is a long and complicated theory that covers an enormous territory and an enormous amount of time. What specific thing could we demonstrate?"

Hugh was stumped. "I agree we can hardly invite the jury to spend four or five days and nights rowing about in dinghies on the Broadwater while we reconstruct the crime."

"Even if we could," said Quentin, "it wouldn't be much more convincing than sketches on a blackboard—there'd be nothing to grip their imaginations. But you're absolutely right in principle. What would save us would be a simple, dramatic demonstration that one part of our theory—almost any part, it doesn't matter which—is true. Then the rest would be believed. The trouble is that we can't think of one."

"We've still got a week," said Hugh.

22 CYNTHIA and Hugh returned to town that evening by one of the slowest and dirtiest of the Cuckoo Line trains. Hugh sat hunched in a corner, completely absorbed by his thoughts. Cynthia was reading a local paper which had arrived at Lavender Cottage that afternoon. Under the heading "Yachtsman's Death in Mud" there was a long account of the inquest on Guy Vulliamy and an excellent photograph of him.

Presently she threw the paper down on the seat beside her. "Well, I'll never trust a face again," she said. "There's not a thing about those features that suggests anything even remotely diabolical."

"I know," said Hugh grimly. "A good, clean-living Englishman! I only hope the prospective jurors won't be taken in by his looks—I suppose they'll have to be shown a photograph."

He relapsed into silence. His mind was still running on the problem of how to re-create some incident to make it live. Only once did he raise his eyes—as the train passed Joe Saberton's signal box—and then his face clouded. That was inexplicable.

They continued to dawdle along even when the junction was left behind. Just before the train drew out of Cowfleet station after an unscheduled stop the door of their non-corridor compartment opened and Bill Hopkin, the ticket clipper, swung aboard. He looked a little embarrassed when he saw who the two passengers were. "Hello, Mr. Latimer. Evening, Miss."

Hugh produced the tickets with a wintry smile. "Hello, Bill.

198

You know, it's about time you started paying us to make this journey instead of charging for it."

Bill grinned sheepishly. "The little owd engine's a bit short o' steam tonight." He pocketed his clippers and sat down in one of the empty corners. Presently his eye fell on Cynthia's discarded paper. "That wore a nasty business," he said.

"Horrible," said Hugh. Even now he hated to be reminded of it.

"I reckon they oughter put warnin' boards up in them bad creeks. That Pye's a deathtrap."

"I expect Vulliamy knew and forgot about it."

"Ah!" Bill Hopkin gazed at the photograph. "Nice-lookin' young chap he wore, an' all. Allus so full o' life, too."

Hugh glanced at the ticket collector with sudden interest. "Did you know him, Bill?"

"I seed him plenty o' times—punched his ticket. He wore a good customer."

Hugh tried a long shot. "Did he ever have a girl with him when you saw him?"

"I never seed any girl."

Hugh subsided into his corner again. It was the answer he'd expected. Vulliamy must have done his traveling on this line during the time when he was making up to his uncles, months ago, and long before he had known Helen Fairlie.

Then another thought occurred to him. He remembered Vulliamy's claim to have traveled to London from Steepleford after parking the dinghy. A lie, of course, but . . . For a moment Hugh hesitated, as though unwilling to tempt Fate too far. Then his faith in the defense overcame his fears. "I suppose you haven't seen him lately, Bill, have you?"

"That I have, sir."

Hugh felt a sharp, uncontrollable pang of anxiety, but it was too late to drop the subject now. "When was the last time—do you remember?"

Bill Hopkin seemed surprised at Hugh's interest. "Telly the

truth," he said, "it wore the day your Dad had that trouble on the train with the young lady."

Hugh stared. "Vulliamy was on the train *that* day? Are you sure?"

"I'm sartin sure, Mr. Latimer, an' I'll telly for why—I punched his ticket in the corridor, back in the end coach. . . ."

The train slowed for another station. The ticket collector got up, nodded, and went on his way.

Hugh sat stock still for a moment, frowning. Then, slowly, a look of dawning understanding spread over his face. The last piece of the puzzle was slipping into place. His eyes gleamed with excitement.

"Cynthia," he said, "I believe I can see it all. No wonder Helen Fairlie made all those journeys into Essex. Don't you see—she was *rehearsing!*"

23 SIR ANDREW FERRABY, the Attorney General, tossed his black felt hat on to the rack of the first-class compartment, settled down in a corner away from the corridor, and snapped open his briefcase with the air of a man to whom time was precious.

Ferraby was young to have reached his high position. He was barely fifty, and with his thick black hair, fresh complexion, and alert manner he looked even less. Usually he felt less, despite the heavy responsibilities he carried, but this evening he was a little tired. He had had a busy week in the House, and there was certainly an exacting week ahead of him. A week with the spotlight on him, too—he would need to be at the top of his form. With a slight frown he began to run once more through his brief, stopping from time to time to make a note in the margin.

The truth was that this Latimer case worried him a little. Ferraby was more than an ambitious politician and a brilliant law officer; he was a conscientious and sensitive man, and in spite of the evidence he couldn't quite make himself believe in Edward Latimer's guilt. At least, he couldn't understand how a man like Latimer could have come to commit such a crime. It seemed so entirely out of character.

All the same, he told himself, it was absurd that as prosecutor he should start with a prejudice in favor of the prisoner —for that was all it was, a prejudice. The evidence seemed conclusive enough. There were a few small gaps—a few minor inconsistencies, even, which as prosecuting counsel he would not attempt to gloss over. It was his job to present the case fairly, not to secure a conviction at any price. Apart from those minor points, the sequence of events was clear enough and he hadn't much doubt what the jury would think.

He couldn't imagine what form the defense would take. Foreseeing the defense, at least in broad outline, wasn't usually very difficult, but in this case he hadn't an inkling. Insanity was obviously ruled out in view of the medical reports. No doubt they would say all the usual things about the dangers of circumstantial evidence, but that wouldn't help them much—it was inconceivable that they could have any other explanation of the undoubted facts. Besides, some of the evidence wasn't circumstantial. The hub of the case was Latimer's assault on the girl in the train, from which his motive and the murder itself had sprung, and there were eyewitnesses of that. Latimer would presumably stick to his fantastic story that the girl had assaulted him, but Saberton's evidence would dispose of that nonsense. All the same . . . ! Ferraby still wished he could envisage Latimer as a man of uncontrollable passions and hates.

He glanced out of the window as the guard blew his whistle, and checked his watch by the station clock. At that moment a girl came running up the platform and jerked open the compartment door. The train was just beginning to move and she was carrying a suitcase. Ferraby jumped up to help her with it.

"Thank you so much," she said with a grateful smile, watching him lift it to the rack. She was a little out of breath. "That was a near thing!"

Ferraby returned her smile. A nice-looking girl, he thought —very smart in that navy-and-white rigout. He resumed his seat and picked up his brief again. The girl opened an evening paper.

For half an hour Ferraby was absorbed. Then he put his work aside and sat admiring the tranquil landscape that drifted unhurriedly past the open window. It was a warm, lovely evening, and it would be delightful down in Essex. These summer days made it well worth while to have a house

202

in the country, even if one did only see it at occasional week-ends. He wished the train would go a little faster. He looked at his watch again and saw that they were already ten minutes late.

"Shocking line!" he said, as the girl glanced up and caught his eye.

She nodded, smiled, and bent again over her paper. She was certainly attractive.

Ferraby studied her for a moment, and then closed his eyes and relaxed in his corner. He even dozed a little, for when he next became aware of his surroundings they were running into the junction. Only four more stations, he thought. His wife would meet him with the car, and they would have a glass of sherry on the lawn and a civilized meal. It was a pleasant prospect.

As soon as the train moved out of the junction the girl picked up her handbag and slipped out of the compartment, closing the corridor door behind her and leaving a slight per-fume in her wake. Ferraby continued to gaze out of the win-dow. They were approaching the single line now, slowing almost to a halt. Ferraby noticed the signalman standing on the steps of his buff-and-green box, watching the carriages go by. That must be Joe Saberton. He didn't look much like a star witness at the moment because he had his mouth open and a rather foolish expression on his face, but no doubt he'd be all right in court. He'd make a fine, clear statement.

Presently the corridor door slid back and the girl came in. She put her bag down, glanced up at the rack, and then looked hesitatingly at Ferraby. "I'm sorry to bother you again but would you mind awfully lifting my case down for me?"

"With pleasure," said Ferraby, springing to his feet and dumping the case on the seat. "There you are." It wasn't often, he thought, that one had the chance to earn quite such an en-chanting smile.

"Thank you so much," said the girl. For a moment they were jammed together in the narrow space between the seats. She looked up into his face. Then without any warning she threw her arms tightly round him, raised herself on tiptoe, and kissed him on the mouth. Completely taken aback by what seemed in the circumstances an exaggerated display of gratitude, Ferraby jerked his face away and put his hands remonstratingly on her arms, trying to release himself from her determined grip.

Then she screamed—screamed at the top of her voice. "Let me go, you beast!—oh, ycu *beast*, you're hurting. Help!" The cry went ringing along the corridor. Ferraby stopped being gentlemanly and exerted all his strength to free himself. The girl held on, her hands locked together behind his back, pummeling him with her head and yelling all the time. Still struggling, they fell on to one of the seats. At that moment the corridor door opened with a crash and a muscular hand tightened on Ferraby's collar. "Let her go, sir!" came an indignant voice, "Let her go instantly!"

The wrestling figures fell apart. The girl collapsed into her corner, clutching the neck of her dress which had come open in the struggle, and sobbing. Her rescuer, a gray-haired but sturdy Christian in a dog collar, looked sternly at Ferraby, whose mouth and cheeks were smeared with lipstick. "You'll have to answer for this, sir. What a disgraceful exhibition!"

"He attacked me," moaned the girl, holding her wrists as though they still hurt her.

"That's a damned lie!" shouted Ferraby, his eyes blazing, his customary calm completely shattered. "She assaulted me. By God, this is intolerable!" He turned on the girl. "Why, you little . . . !" Suddenly he broke off, as the incident snapped into focus. Assault in a train!—again! And the same train! He eyed her with wary suspicion. "Who are you, young lady, and what exactly are you up to?"

"It's you, sir, who should do the explaining," snapped the clergyman. "Really, this is outrageous . . ."

By now other passengers were gathering in the corridor, drawn from the length of the train by the disturbance. They all wanted to know what had happened, and the clergyman told them, his voice still vibrating with righteous anger. The girl provided a corroborative background of sniffles. There were sympathetic murmurs, and a woman was heard to remark in a very county tone that people like that ought to be lynched. "Disgusting behavior! I suppose he's been drinking." She shot a barbed glance over the clergyman's shoulder at the disheveled Ferraby, who was silently wiping his face with a pocket handkerchief and making a supreme effort to control himself.

"It may interest you to know," he said icily to the clergyman, "that I'm the Attorney General, Andrew Ferraby."

"I'm Gracie Fields," said an unsympathetic male voice behind the refined lady.

The clergyman stared at Ferraby. "Nonsense—it's not possible." Then something about the features recalled pictures he had seen in the newspapers. "Bless my soul . . . !" he said, and his face turned very red. "Well, sir, all I can say is that you've the more reason to be ashamed of yourself. As far as I'm concerned, you're nothing but a common hooligan."

"I tell you she attacked me . . ."

"My dear sir, I'm not blind. I saw exactly what happened. You had your hands on her arms and she was struggling to free herself from your embrace. Your excuses are wasted on me—I should save them for the police."

For the first time, a flicker of anxiety crossed Ferraby's face. It was quite fantastic, of course, but this might become extremely awkward. He found it difficult to think—there was a babble of noisy, hostile talk all around him, and the guard, who had come belatedly upon the scene, was looking at him as though he were an escaped tiger. He felt relieved when, a few moments later, the train ran into Steepleford station.

As it slowed, the altercation that was still going on drew Tom Leacock, the stationmaster, to the compartment. He opened the door with an angry jerk. "Now what's the trouble here . . . ?" he began.

"This man attacked me," said the girl faintly. "We were alone in the compartment and he tried to kiss me and . . ."

Pandemonium broke out again. Everyone was talking at once—the girl accusing, Ferraby denying, the clergyman confirming, the guard explaining. Tom gave a growl of disgust. "Better all come along to my office. We'll see what the police have to say." He turned and led the way, a worried expression on his face. He couldn't think what the Cuckoo Line was coming to. After thirty years of uneventful stagnation, two assaults so close together had practically deprived him of speech.

Half a dozen people trailed into the office behind him. One of them was Hugh Latimer, looking pale but very determined. He caught Cynthia's eye and smiled encouragingly. She had begun to make a very good recovery.

Tom sat down at a rickety old table and put on a pair of steel-rimmed spectacles. "Well, now, let's have your names and addresses." He began to write with a scratchy pen.

Hugh peered over his shoulder and gave a low whistle. "Sir Andrew Ferraby! I say, that's going to make good headlines."

Ferraby glared at him. "Who the devil are you? What *is* this—a public meeting?"

"My name's Latimer," said Hugh. "I'm sure it's familiar to you."

"Latimer!"

"That's right. My father is Edward Latimer. The lady you assaulted is my fiancée."

"So that's it!" cried Ferraby. "I knew it. The whole thing's a put-up job. Why, you must be off your heads!"

Tom Leacock stopped writing and looked at Hugh in bewilderment.

"I assure you, stationmaster," the clergyman intervened, "that it was no put-up job at all. This—this man was holding the young lady and she was making frantic efforts to release herself. He undoubtedly assaulted her—I saw it with my own eyes." He shot an indignant look at Ferraby. "And I shall feel it my duty to say so in court."

"There you are," said Hugh. "Talk yourself out of that, Sir Andrew."

Ferraby, who had been growing more and more thoughtful, turned his back on Hugh and addressed the clergyman. "I'm not questioning your good faith, sir, but I tell you you're entirely mistaken. It was *I* who was struggling to get away— this girl was deliberately holding me."

"It's extraordinary," murmured Hugh, "how history repeats itself."

There was a sudden clatter outside as somebody threw a bicycle up against the wall. Then Joe Saberton came in. He looked hot and flushed, as though he had ridden hard.

"Hello, Joe," said the stationmaster in a tone of relief. He jerked his head toward Ferraby. "That's him."

Joe looked uncomfortably at Ferraby. He was baffled by this repetition of events, but he had no doubts about what he had seen.

"He was going for the young lady, Tom—no two ways about that. Damn nearly throttling her, by the look of it—he'd got her head right out of the carriage window and was squeezing her throat. . . . You all right, miss?"

"Much better now, thank you," said Cynthia.

Ferraby looked grim. "You know, Saberton, you're completely wrong about that."

"Oh, no, I'm not," said Joe stoutly. "I saw it with my own eyes."

The engine outside gave an impatient toot, and Tom Leacock got up. "We'll have to get that train away. You two people had better wait."

"I hardly think it's necessary for me to stay," said the clergyman. "You have my name and address and the police can call upon me." He looked coldly at Ferraby, nodded to Cynthia, and went off to continue his journey.

"Well, Sir Andrew," said Hugh, "how do you like the weight

207

of evidence against you? Do you think a jury will believe you?"

Ferraby had occupied the stationmaster's seat. He looked quite cool again now, and his eyes had a gleam of more than professional interest. "It's remarkable," he said. "How did you do it, Latimer?"

Hugh smiled. "Are you prepared to admit that you've been the innocent victim of a plot?"

"Admit? It's an odd way to put it. I don't seem to have any option, though, do I?"

"Well, here's the story," said Hugh. "It was an exactly similar plot that involved my father in that incident a week or two ago. The man who afterward killed Helen Fairlie—and we can tell you all about him, Sir Andrew—was on the train with her that day, just as I was with my fiancée tonight. He was by himself, in the rear coach. Just after the train left the junction, Helen Fairlie went out of the compartment where she was sitting with my father, ostensibly to make up her face after getting something in her eye. But she didn't go to the toilet—she went a little way along the corridor and met this man, by prearrangement, in an empty compartment. As the train passed Joe's box, she leaned backward out of the window and let the man grasp her throat and give every appearance of violently assaulting her. The timing's not difficult when you know the line, and they'd rehearsed it. And that's what Joe saw. Immediately afterward she went back to her own compartment and assaulted my father—and Walter Vulliamy drew the wrong conclusions when he rushed in, just as your clergyman friend did about you. Tonight, my fiancée and I re-enacted the whole thing."

"Blimey!" said Joe.

Cynthia looked at Ferraby as though she wasn't sure whether he'd respond to a smile or not. "Will you ever forgive me, Sir Andrew?—it was a dreadful thing to do, I know." She risked the smile. "I *do* withdraw the charge."

"It was an extreme step," he said with a preoccupied air.

"My father is in extreme danger," said Hugh. "It was the only way we had of explaining Joe's evidence . . . . Of course, we're in your hands, Sir Andrew. If there are consequences—well, we're prepared to accept them."

Ferraby seemed hardly to hear. In his fascination over the turn of events he had almost forgotten that he had been the victim of a most embarrassing conspiracy. There were hundreds of questions he wanted to ask, but as he delved in his capacious memory there seemed to be just one thing that cried to be cleared up without delay. He turned to Saberton.

"Was what you saw tonight *exactly* what you saw the other time? Try to picture the two incidents. Was every detail the same?"

"Well," said Joe, "it was a different young lady, of course, but everything else was the same."

Ferraby pressed him. "Surely not? If I remember rightly, the first assault took place in a third-class compartment."

Hugh gave a sharp exclamation. Joe pondered. "Oh, no," he said slowly, "in a first-class. Right in the middle of the coach, just like tonight. Same train, same coach."

Hugh gripped his arm. "Are you *sure* about that, Joe?"

"Quite sure," said Joe. "I can see it now—the girl's head out of the window, pressed back, slap in the middle where all the firsts are. Right above the British Railways thing that's painted on the coach as a matter of fact, and that's bang in the middle."

Hugh gave Ferraby a triumphant smile. "Well, that seems to settle it, Sir Andrew, doesn't it . . . ? Oh, Joe, why didn't you tell us this before?"

"Nobody asked me," said Joe.

The Attorney General got to his feet. "Astonishing—quite astonishing!" He looked at Hugh and Cynthia with something very near a grin. "You know, I think I'd better hear the rest of your story as soon as possible—as far as I can see at the moment, Counsel for the Crown is likely to be called as the chief witness for the Defense! We must try to avoid that!"

24   EDWARD was sitting out on the lawn in a deck chair, surrounded by his family. He was wearing his old alpaca jacket and a brand new panama hat, a present from Cynthia. Outwardly, at least, he was taking his new freedom very placidly. His face had the serene look of a man home again after a long journey.

It had been a hectic weekend. The lawyers in the case, summoned from golf and siestas to a conference with the Attorney General, had turned Sunday into a working day, and their efforts had borne fruit in what Monday evening's papers were describing as "staggering disclosures."

In the brief court session that day, new precedents had been established right and left. Mr. Justice Hanbury, privy to the amazing developments, had presided with an almost avuncular benignity. Sir Andrew Ferraby, instead of opening the case for the prosecution, had stated categorically at the beginning that the wrong man was in the dock and had co-operated with the defense counsel in unfolding a story which, as he said, was "more fantastic than any work of fiction." In due course the Judge had directed the jury to find in favor of the prisoner and had discharged Edward with a little speech of condolence and congratulation. In the subsequent demonstrations outside the court, Edward had appeared to be the only person not touched by hysteria.

Now he had been home for several hours, and the excitement was beginning to die down a little. The stream of people dropping in to shake him by the hand had abated; Trudie was no longer required to spend every second at the telephone.

The London reporters and photographers had been and gone. Lavender Cottage was taking on its old, tranquil air.

Hugh lay back in his chair with a smile of beatitude on his face. "You know," he said, "the problems of adjustment are not going to be easy. Trudie's cooking is going to seem pretty rough after all that good prison fare."

"That's a libel," said Trudie.

"Slander," said Quentin amiably. He gazed around at the happy faces, the peaceful scene. "So it's really over!"

"Thanks to Cynthia," said Hugh.

"Thanks to Cynthia!" Quentin echoed. His law-abiding soul had been shocked to its depths when he had first learned of her assault on the Attorney General, and only the spectacular results had reconciled him to it. It had been like heroic disobedience in battle—success had made it meritorious.

"I must say," remarked Hugh, "I hardly expected the Judge to give us an accolade. I can see that crinkled old face of his now, hovering on the edge of a grin. 'It is not for me to approve the—er—the unorthodox means by which this remarkable case has been elucidated, but as a result of those means it may well be that a most appalling miscarriage of justice has been averted.' "

"I thought he was a pet," said Cynthia. "And so was Ferraby. He took it all frightfully well."

"He had no complaint—I bet he was never kissed by a prettier girl. . . . And that reminds me, Dad—if you're lunching with Ferraby tomorrow, travel up in the guard's van. It's the only way to avoid these harpies."

The telephone rang again and Trudie went in to answer it. Edward, as though to escape any further congratulations, excused himself and sauntered down the garden path with a rake.

As he reached the bushes, a head poked out.

"Hello, Mr. Latimer!"

"Why, hello, Carol Anne. How are you?"

"I'm lovely, thank you." She stood on one foot and regarded him hopefully. "My mummy says I can play."

Edward smiled. "Tomorrow, perhaps. I'm rather busy today."

"My mummy says you've been away. Did you have a nice holiday?"

Edward gave a little chuckle. "It could have been a lot worse," he said.